Sleepwa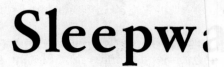

stories

Marion Arnott

Elastic Press

ISBN number: 0-9543747-3-8

Printed by Blitzprint (www.blitzprint.com)

Cover photography: Andrew Hook
Cover Design: Robert Arnott/Elastic Press
Sleepwalker: Phillippa Renn
Snow Angel: Frances Keen
Typeset by Marie O'Regan

Earlier versions of some of these stories have appeared in the following: *Chapman, Crimewave, Hawakaya Mystery Magazine, Northwords, Peninsular, QWF, Roadworks, Year's Best Fantasy & Horror, and West Coast.*
They have been edited for this collection.

Published by:
Elastic Press
85 Gertrude Road
Norwich
UK

ElasticPress@elasticpress.com
www.elasticpress.com

For my three treasures, Vicky, Katy, and Robert, and for
Mum, Dad, and Sis, who are the best.

Also, a salute to Andrew Hook, who believes in short stories
and is dynamic in promoting them.

Table of contents

Prussian Snowdrops

Traudl arrived with the spring, which was sudden that year. Karl was taken unawares by both, startled awake one glittering white night by the sound of the spring thaw: the river cracked like a pistol shot and, in the shivering dark, began to move through sundered ice. Karl's hot water bottles were flabby and chill as fish on a slab and he cursed between chattering teeth: spring nights in Prussia were noisy with crashing ice and gurgling water, howling wolves and the drip-drip of melting icicles. He longed sleeplessly for the soft air of Berlin, gently gilded and scented with hyacinths.

He longed even more once he met Traudl. He was crossing the square to the inn that Sunday, when he saw what looked like a bundle of rags on the stone bench beneath the statue of the Teutonic knight. He peered through fluttering sleet and saw that the bundle was a woman, ugly, lumpen, and scowling ferociously.

"Your pardon, *Gnädige Frau*," he said before he walked on, shaken both by her malevolence and a painful yearning for cheerful girls in stylish hats.

"Who was that, Ernst?" he asked when he joined the little company in the warm corner beside the fireplace.

"Traudl," the schoolmaster said, tamping down his pipe.

The postmaster nodded. "I thought she had given that up. It must only have been the winter kept her away."

"She reminded me of that story," Karl said. "You know – 'What big teeth you have, Grandma!' 'All the better to eat you with, child.' I

1

thought, any minute she's going to spring and tear my throat out. Why is she sitting out there in the cold?"

"Waiting," the teacher said. "And before you ask what for, no one knows. She's from the asylum – quite incoherent. All she'll say is that she's waiting. Every Sunday afternoon she waits until darkness falls. And then she goes home."

The postmaster smirked into his *bierstein*. "I did hear one story. A man gave her a kind word thirty years ago and said he'd be back soon. So she waits in hope."

Karl sniggered. "That face never had a hope and has always known it."

"Well, then," Ernst said. "Hopelessly ugly, therefore no story to tell, therefore not to be written about in 'Tales From A Village'. Now who's for another beer?"

Karl was amused by the attempt to influence his articles; the teacher's status as most educated villager, and the only one who had joined the Party *before* the Führer swept to power, had gone to his head; or rather to his flat cheeks which puffed out like a hamster's whenever he recalled that fact. He insisted that the Tales reflect well on his village, and Karl made sure they did when he whiled away long Prussian nights with schnapps and purple prose. The villagers, he had written, helpless with laughter at the thought of the schoolmaster's coterie of turnip-witted farmers, were purest Aryan stock, a living link with Germany's heroic past; soul brothers of the men who had fought Roman, Turk, and Russian, and poured their blood into the soil, making it theirs forever; of the same Germanic tribe admired by the noble Tacitus for virtuous beautiful women and merciless moral men.

Blood and soil and heroes made the schoolmaster's spectacles mist with emotion; Karl never knew how he kept his face straight while the tedious little man polished them clear. Even funnier, the Führer himself had proclaimed the Tales inspirational, which only confirmed Karl's opinion of the Führer, and since then, the villagers had bombarded Karl with local legends of the Knights of the Teutonic Order, heroic resistance to Jew landlords, and of Aryan bloodlines untainted since the Dark Ages.

Karl put them all in his column. They were his living, and possibly a ticket back to Berlin, hurriedly abandoned after his coverage of the Führer's reception for the world's ambassadors. The sight of booted blackshirts displaying courtly manners and a knowledge of fine art –

the Führer had issued a general order that they should – was hilarious enough, but when they got drunk, groped the French ambassador's wife and dumped her in the fountain along with her protesting husband, he lost all sense of self-preservation and reported it. Half Berlin sniggered, the other half wanted his blood. 'What you must remember,' his editor said, 'is that Nazis have no sense of humour. East Prussian office for you until things cool down.' 'But there's nothing to report there,' Karl protested. 'Find something,' the editor said, 'something not funny.' Karl found Tales From The Village.

Karl sighed. The schoolteacher was telling him of his plans to revive an ancient summer solstice festival: bare-breasted blonde Valkyries holding sheaves of corn, together with bare-chested blonde Titans wielding swords, would re-enact an authentic pagan sacrifice in the water meadows. Ernst elaborated to a distressing degree until the flow of scholarly claptrap was interrupted by the arrival of the beer.

"My round, *meine Herren*," Karl beamed. The answering smiles displayed broken brown teeth and cavernous gaps. The sight plunged Karl into despair: you'd think there'd be dentists, even in East Prussia. He averted his eyes, and through the sleet blooming on the window pane, glimpsed Traudl, solid as a boulder wrapped in a blanket. The prospect of dozens like her displaying their all among the wheat sheaves rendered him speechless, and the schoolmaster, mistaking his silence for interest, began describing an entire calendar of pagan festivals. Karl sighed heavily.

Traudl was under the statue every Sunday. Karl always met her unwavering stare with a polite bow and a 'Good afternoon, *gnädige Frau*.' This was brave of him because her intensity made him nervous, and it provoked the schoolmaster to pontificate on the subject of degeneracy. He would steeple his fingers under his chin and say 'And now if I may move on to matters esoteric' and serve Karl, the only man in the village with sufficient intellect to understand him, a dollop of Nazi science.

The day that Traudl first spoke to Karl, the schoolteacher passed the afternoon blaming the high incidence of imbecility in East Prussia on the proximity of the Polish border. Karl struggled not to laugh as he imagined diseased Slavic wits drifting across the frontier like dandelion seeds to seek out a hapless Aryan womb in which to root. Ernst claimed that Traudl was a mongrel produced by a Polish father

3

and a morally degenerate mother, and that in spite of the best efforts of the Party, that kind of unregulated breeding would continue to degrade Aryan bloodlines until the Führer's programme for purifying racial stock was carried out.

Karl smothered a yawn and the schoolmaster rebuked him mildly. "Sometimes, Karl, I don't think you take eugenics entirely seriously."

"On the contrary," Karl smiled, "I was remembering the last time the Führer spoke on the subject. At Nüremberg. We ended the rally with the *Horst Wessel Lied*. It was most moving. You know, Ernst, we must get you to Berlin so that you can experience it all for yourself."

The teacher, who never cared to be reminded that he had never personally witnessed the Reich's ceremonies, resumed lecturing. He had devised a course on eugenics for his village pupils: responsible breeding, the duty of individuals to the race, sterilisation of the unfit and so on, and he thought perhaps that Karl might care to write a little something about his work.

Karl nodded enthusiastically, stopped listening, and thought about the rally. He and Siggi and Friedrich had been as drunk as lords and bawled out the first verse of the *Horst Wessel Lied* because it was the only one they knew; then gradually they realised that everyone else knew all the verses, every last turgid one, which seemed to them hysterically funny. 'They're word perfect,' Friedrich said. 'No one but a man of genius could have inspired them to it. We have underestimated the Führer.' Siggi said that the Führer would rise in his estimation when they could all sing in tune. As he spoke, the arc lights which blazed a cathedral's vaulted ceiling across the night sky were suddenly extinguished, and they found themselves giggling into a black void, unable to stop.

Karl looked out of the inn window to hide another grin. Traudl was out there as usual, sitting in the shadow of the knight, waiting. She could have been a statue herself, she sat so still, except that sometimes she tilted her head as if she were listening. Karl followed her gaze. She had a view along the river and the road which wound beside it; and in the far distance, the ruined church in the water meadows, its collapsed tower, its roofless walls, its screen of naked trees piercing the pale glassy sky. She was looking at nothing and listening to nothing and waiting for something to come of it all, which, he decided, made her no more feeble-witted than half Germany.

4

It was night when she spoke to him. He was weaving unsteadily back to his lodgings in the thickening darkness, slithering across icy cobbles, when she stepped out of an alley and stood in his path. Her accent was coarse, her voice harsh.

"*Mein Herr*, I have been waiting for you."

She was nervous, but determined. Karl bowed, trying not to notice her troglodyte eyebrows.

"*Gnädige Frau*, it is late and very cold. Some other time – "

"A word. Only a word." Her face in the acid light of the wrought iron street lamp was yellow and surly. "A word can't hurt, can it?"

No, he thought, and a smile wouldn't either. Then, seeing the heavy bony face darken to jaundice, decided that it wouldn't help in the slightest.

"Another time. Next Sunday – "

He made to pass her by, but she seized his arm with surprising strength.

"Not in the village. They wouldn't like that."

"Who wouldn't?"

"The schoolmaster. The postmaster."

Karl hiccoughed and reclaimed his arm. "*Gnädige Frau*, the schoolmaster may like or dislike as he pleases. It is a matter of impreme sudifference to me. Supreme indifference." He giggled and shook his head.

"Are you laughing at me?"

"Not at all. I am drunk, as you see. In no condition for a gossip. *Gnädige Frau*, good evening."

She came after him, her heavy boots thumping dully on stone cobbles.

"I have money. You can have it all."

She snatched at him, but he twisted away, fell, and lay dazed while she fumbled in a woollen stocking cap which she fished out of her pocket. She was breathing heavily and he was suddenly afraid – *what big teeth you have, Grandma* – but it was only money she pulled from the cap, wads of *Reichsmarks* tied up with string. She loomed over him, yellow-fanged and panting, trying to push the notes into his hand.

"All for you," she gasped.

Her excitement alarmed him. He had heard of women possessed by erotic fantasies; there had been a case in Berlin, a bloodied knife –

She hauled him up by the lapel of his coat. "The money," she said.

5

"Take it. You do something for me. An easy thing."

"Please," he said, thrusting the money back at her, "there's nothing I can do for you."

"A letter. Write me a letter. That's all."

He blinked and swayed. "*Gnädige* Frau, what on earth would I write to you about?" He laughed and stepped back.

"From me. You write a letter from me."

"Why?"

"Because I can't write!" Anger flared like lightning in her dull eyes. "You write lots of things. It's not much to ask." Her voice deepened in desperation. "I can pay."

He hardly knew how he came to agree, but he did, partly from pity, partly because she wasn't going to go away unless he did, and partly from a humiliating fear of her flickering urgency. He salvaged his pride by grandly waiving payment, and then was in such a hurry to get away that he forgot to ask what kind of letter she wanted.

Karl wrote to Friedrich about the mystery of Traudl's letter: he imagined pleas to the Lost Lover to return, advertisements for the marriage columns ("I can pay!"), and postcards for display on the noticeboards of dubious nightclubs ("Honestly, I can pay!").

His cousin's reply was prompt and full of Berlin gossip and their friend, Siggi, who was the subject of most of it. Siggi was in 'this-time-you've-gone-too-far-trouble' with the editor. He had drawn the weedier Party leaders – round shouldered under the weight of masses of silver braid and deathshead insignia – demonstrating the etiquette of saluting Nazi style: the full stiff-armed salute, delivered along with a stentorian *'Heil Hitler!'*, was given by inferiors to superiors; the half salute from the elbow, palm up, with a drawling *'Heil Hitler!'* was a sign of very high rank; and a half salute, palm down, was terribly, terribly sweet and greeted with whistles and cries of 'Hello, darling!' from the prettiest boys in town. Respectable citizens were worried about giving the wrong impression, and Doktor Göbbels was incandescent with rage. Siggi could not see what all the fuss was about because he had, after all, shown considerable self-restraint by not drawing Göring in his Chinese silks and green nail polish.

Karl laughed at the cartoon which Friedrich had thoughtfully enclosed with his letter. The Party leaders reminded him of Ernst in his Sunday best SA uniform, self-important nonentities with an awesome talent for talking bilge. Siggi often said that listening to them was the penalty for living in the Age of the Common Man; he doubted that the Reich would last the promised thousand years, but judging by the amount of speechifying that went on, it was going to feel as if it had.

As for the Troglodyte, Friedrich wrote that there was hope for her yet: the Führer had promised every Aryan female a husband and decreed that it was a civic duty to breed for Germany. Siggi was ecstatic about it: all over Berlin, patriotic women were throwing themselves at men, pleading to be impregnated. The SS, flower of Aryan manhood, were the favoured target and Siggi was desperate to join, but didn't think they'd let him in after the saluting business.

Karl's homesickness was particularly acute all that week.

On the following Sunday, Karl waited for Traudl at the appointed place and time: at the back door of his lodgings after his landlady had gone to church. 'No one must see,' Traudl had said. 'No one.'

He led her into the parlour. She was intimidated by *Frau* Haar's brutal cleanliness and would not sit down until the third invitation, and only then after she had stretched her woollen scarf under her boots to protect the linoleum. She hunched silently on the edge of her chair, staring at her big red hands lying loosely in her lap.

"*Gnädige Frau* – "

"I'm not married."

"*Gnädiges Fräulein* – "

Her quick upward glance revealed dull brown eyes lit by a reddish glow. "Are you laughing at me?"

"Your pardon – "

"That's how the Doktor speaks to the rich relatives. Me, I'm just Traudl."

"It was a courtesy, but… Traudl, if you prefer."

She stared him full in the face, making up her mind, and he was absurdly relieved when the light in her eyes faded to the colour of old stone and she resumed the study of her hands.

"You wanted a letter written, Traudl. Shall we begin?"

"I don't know how."

"What do you want to say?" he said, whittling a pencil to a point with a penknife. "And where do you want to send it?"

"I don't know."

It took an hour to make sense of it all: Traudl wished to notify her former employer that her services as a laundress were still available. The difficulty was that he had decamped in the night without leaving a forwarding address, a course of action with which Karl could sympathise if *Herr Doktor* Reichardt had been often exposed to Traudl's efforts at conversation. He told Traudl that without an address, it was impossible to write to the Doktor.

"But he must be somewhere."

"He could be anywhere."

"You're clever. You could find him."

"He could be anywhere. And perhaps he doesn't wish to be found."

She shook her head. "No. He was looking for the patients. To bring them home."

The mystery deepened. First, a mislaid Doktor, then mislaid patients. How careless Traudl had been!

"I think, Traudl, that if the Doktor wishes to employ you again, he will be in touch."

Her heavy brow furrowed with the painfulness of thought. "How? He knows I can't read. And the telephone at the hospital doesn't work any more." Unpaid bills, Karl decided. The good Doktor had fled his creditors.

"Perhaps you should seek some other employment until the Doktor is settled again."

"He left me in charge," she said, shaking her head. "I have to look after his dog."

"Without an address, I can do nothing," he said kindly.

Her protests turned her complexion an ugly brick colour as she repeated over and over, "But he must be somewhere. You could find him."

Her disbelief and his denials collided across *Frau* Haar's hearthrug. Traudl rocked backwards and forwards in her chair, her fists clenched in her lap. "He told me he'd be back soon!" She made a sound somewhere between a growl and a whine. The scene was becoming distasteful. Karl rose and crossed to the door. "I'm sorry, Traudl. Try the police. It is their job to find missing persons."

Her rocking stopped suddenly. "No!" She pounded her fists on her knees. "No! No! The Doktor said not to talk to them. They're bad."

"Then I don't know who can help you." Karl opened the door wider. "You must go now, Traudl. *Frau* Haar will be back shortly."

She lunged out of her chair. He sidestepped quickly, but she only swooped over the pencil shavings and scooped them up.

"She likes things tidy," she said and blundered past him to the kitchen door. He heard the heavy boots thumping across the vegetable patch, then the creak of the back gate. When he looked, she was gone.

The morning wasn't entirely wasted; it gave Karl the opportunity to tease the schoolmaster. The little man drew Karl aside as soon as he arrived at the inn.

"Karl," he said heartily. "You look well today. You have colour in your cheeks. The spring air?"

Karl nodded. "Delightful, isn't it? I didn't have to break the ice in the wash basin this morning and the electricity supply reappeared in the night. Suddenly life is full of promise."

"Karl – " The schoolmaster removed his spectacles and polished them, then folded his handkerchief neatly into his breast pocket. "The strangest story has come to my ears. Rumour has it that you were consorting with Traudl this morning."

"Consorting? What a quaint expression, Ernst."

"Of course, I said I found that hard to believe."

"That was thoughtful of you."

"An unlikely tale, isn't it?"

"If you say so."

"You're fencing with me, Karl," the schoolmaster said with a tight smile. "Is there any truth in it?"

"I don't know, Ernst. It depends what you mean by consorting."

"Then she did visit you this morning?"

"Yes, she did. I'm relying on you to keep that quiet, Ernst."

"Too late for that. People are wondering what you could possibly want with her."

"My business, surely?"

"Nevertheless, people are talking."

"There isn't much else to do on a Sunday afternoon." He took the schoolmaster by the arm and drew him over to the fire. "Except to sit in the warm and have a beer and some good conversation."

The schoolmaster returned to Traudl's visit several times, but Karl refused to be drawn and Ernst was reduced to a series of irritated harrumphs.

Karl wrote to Friedrich that night. 'My learned friend was so cross that he didn't mention his beloved Valkyries and pagans once. With any luck, he's going to ban me from attending his festivals. He did give some fatherly advice about keeping bad company. And a little lesson in eugenics. Because of her Polish blood, Traudl can be violent; because of her mother's depravity, she can be promiscuous. I'm not sure whether Ernst fears most for my virtue or my life.'

He had to end the letter there. The light flickered twice and went out and he couldn't find the matches to light the oil lamp. The drumming of the river filled the room; it seemed louder in the pitch dark. So did the wolves.

His next meeting with Traudl came after he heard from Friedrich again. 'Tell the Troglodyte,' Friedrich wrote, 'that her Doktor is dead. He committed suicide in the foyer of the Ministry of Health at Tiergarten No.4. Before he pulled the trigger, he said, 'I can't live with the guilt.' No one knows what he meant and, interestingly enough, no one wants to know. He was a respected psychiatrist and his death didn't even make the Stop Press. Siggi says the importance of a story can be measured by the silence it engenders; this silence is riccochetting round Berlin and everyone's running for cover. Even Siggi's friends, who are always in the know even when they aren't, declare to a man that they haven't heard about the very public suicide of *Herr Direktor* Reichardt or his guilt complex. They've never heard of Tiergarten 4 either. Since most of them pass it on the tram home, Siggi has concluded regretfully that they are all lying in their teeth. He is now in pursuit of what he is sure is a very nasty scandal.

He has found a charwoman who saw Reichardt hanging around the foyer for days before he died. Every official was too busy to see him. That didn't surprise the char. She didn't approve of his unshaven appearance or his stale shirt or the way he paced up and down the foyer pushing his fingers through his hair. More than once she had to ask him to move so that she could mop the floor; he won her good opinion when he apologised charmingly for being in her way, but the poor gentleman didn't half make a mess of the marble tiles when he blew his brains out.

Siggi wants you to quizz Traudl. He feels suicide is a massive overreaction to an unpaid telephone bill. You're to find out how he lost his patients and what was worrying him. If necessary, you're to sacrifice your virtue.'

10

Karl knew Siggi was like a hound after truffles when it came to scandal and that he would have no peace until he found out something, anything. Accordingly, he left the inn early the following Sunday afternoon and waited in the alley, intending to startle Traudl for a change.

"Traudl!" he hissed and leapt out into the lamplight. He felt foolish when she only hesitated for a moment before walking on. He fell into step beside her. "Traudl. We must talk."

She plodded onward with a sulky bovine tread which made her chins tremble. Only East Prussia could produce such a creature, he thought; perhaps there was something to the schoolmaster's theories after all.

"Traudl, are you angry?"

"No."

"Yes, you are. No time for chat tonight."

"Nothing to say."

"You had lots to say last week."

"You didn't."

"I have now."

He could not see her expression. They had moved out of the circle of light under the lamp and the shadows had erased her features. She turned off the main street and took the narrow path down to the river.

"Where are you going, Traudl?"

"Home."

"May I come with you part of the way?"

They trudged along in silence. There were no lights beyond the village and Karl soon lost sight of her in the icy dark. The path sloped sharply downwards and was slippery with deep sucking mud. He clung to bushes and skeletal branches to steady himself.

"Traudl! Slow down!"

Her heavy tread never faltered, but her voice floated back to him in the darkness. "Go back! I don't want to talk to you!"

"But it's about the Doktor!" The wind threw his words back at him – Doktor! Doktor! – and startled him. His foot caught on a root and he plunged headfirst down the slope into a cold slime of rotten leaves. He lifted his head and smelled the airy cleanness of open water nearby. There was a rustling movement in the inky darkness, and then Traudl was standing over him. She stooped and dragged him upright.

"Did you find him?"

"Let me catch my breath."

"Did you?" She tugged at his arm and swung him back and forth like a rag doll. He remembered big square laundress's hands which could wring blankets dry as easily as twisting a kiss curl. He could not tell her that the Doktor was dead, not out here in the lonely dark. There was no telling how she would react.

"I have news," he said. "Come to *Frau* Haar's and I will tell you."

"No, now."

" *Frau* Haar – "

"No. Not her house. Here."

"But – "

"Where is he?" she shrieked, shaking him harder.

"Berlin. He's in Berlin."

"Is it far?"

He laid a hand on hers and patted it tentatively. "Oh, yes, Traudl. Very far. And you don't know the way." He could feel her thinking and he grew cunning, remembering Siggi's hopes of a spectacular scandal. "The Doktor's in trouble, Traudl. He needs your help before he can come home."

"The patients. Are they with him?"

"No, they're still lost."

"He said they'd be back. Like last time."

"Last time?"

"Yes. They all came back."

"But they haven't come back this time, have they?" Karl improvised wildly. "And everyone says it's the Doktor's fault." He detached himself carefully from Traudl's grasp. She stood immobile, gazing up at a black sky flecked with sparks of steel, and tilted her head as if she were listening. "Don't you want to help the Doktor, Traudl?" he asked softly.

She wrung her hands and shuffled from foot to foot. "I'm not to tell. The Doktor could get into trouble. Me too. I helped."

Karl moved closer to her. "But he's already in trouble, *liebling*."

She cracked her knuckles in her agitation. "Do the police know what we did?"

Karl felt one of his headaches coming on and wished he knew what they were talking about. "They've locked him up," he said desperately. "He must have done something bad to the patients."

"Not him. Never."

"Well, then, tell me about it. I'll write in the newspapers that he never did a bad thing, ever, and the police will let him out."

She whirled suddenly and stumped along the path. "No, I promised not to tell." She barged down the path, arguing with herself.

"Traudl! You must help me help the Doktor!"

She halted abruptly when she reached the river bank. "Is it help if I tell about the last time? The time they all came back? That's not a secret. Everyone knows. They only say they don't."

"I think it might help, yes."

Traudl decided quickly. She flopped down on to one of the large rocks which littered the river bank. "All right," she said and chewed at the cuff of her mitten. "All right. He didn't do bad things. The hospital was a good place after he came. He wasn't angry like the one before. No hitting with wet towels. No electric wires on us."

"Oh, that was kind," Karl said, taken aback. "Now, what was the 'last time' you were talking about, the time when they all came back?"

"That was later. He let me work and gave me money for it. I learned to be tidy and wash things. Nobody made the sheets as white as me." She halted on a note of coy pride until Karl murmured admiringly. "I ironed the little cloths for his breakfast tray. I never forgot. That was the first year he came – "

"What trouble are you and the Doktor in, Traudl?"

" – he said I was his best laundress. And a good talker too. I never talked before he came but he helped me. I don't talk to everyone. Just him and some of the patients. And you."

Karl silently cursed the good Doktor. Traudl was going to talk mountains of trivia – he knew the signs. And Siggi would kill him if he didn't listen. He gathered his coat around him and perched on the rock beside hers. She began talking and continued all through the night. He struggled to keep the story orderly in his mind, but names, events, happy-days and phone calls, Traudl's matter-of-fact recital and the shrieking wind made a whirling kaleidoscope in his head.

On his way home, he saw that dawn had turned the horizon ice pink on the far side of the river. Birch trees, black lace against the skyline, speared the new morning. What had she said? Little Heinrich was afraid of the birch trees and she always had to hold his hand to calm him down.

Frau Haar kept a respectable house and preferred that he keep respectable hours. Karl slipped into the house by the back door. In the hall, he put out a hand and touched the silver framed photograph of *Frau* Haar's grandchildren on the dresser. This was the frame Traudl had described, silver, etched with a pattern of feathers. It was the first proof of the veracity of her story. It had been Elvi's frame, and Elvi had searched everywhere for it, crying for her mother's photograph. *Frau* Haar had been housekeeper at the hospital and she was angry with Elvi for losing the picture the way she lost everything, the careless stupid half-wit, it was no wonder her father had had her locked up. Traudl knew all the time that *Frau* Haar had taken the frame – she liked pretty things – but she didn't say anything, because *Frau* Haar had a bunch of heavy keys and she often hit Traudl for staring too hard, or Elvi for crying and getting on her nerves.

Karl considered *Frau* Haar's love of pretty things. He tip-toed quietly to his room so as not to disturb his landlady. He didn't think that he could stomach her smiling grandmotherly reproof this morning.

He spent most of the day writing it all down for Siggi and Friedrich. Traudl's story had been like a country ramble down winding lanes and through thickets of detail, but he summarised it ruthlessly: in the summer of 1933, men came to the asylum. They were uniformed and had long boots and guns. The Doktor had argued with them for a long time in the hall, but they showed him papers. The Doktor telephoned to Berlin while the patients were being brought out; he shouted a lot until the man with the papers pulled the telephone wires out of the wall and asked which patients could work: he didn't want any dangerous or very feeble-minded ones.

The Doktor wouldn't tell, but *Frau* Haar took the men into the office where the files were kept. One of them stood in the doorway and called out names written on white cards: Elvi and Maria and Detlef and lots of others. He called Traudl's name too, but the Doktor said she was an employee, not a patient, and the man burst out laughing. "Oh, I do apologise, *Gnädige Frau*."

All the patients in the locked ward were left behind, but the rest were taken away. The men shouted and shoved them to make them go faster. Elvi cried and cried and one of the men said she was a pretty little silly who should play it smart and not make herself red-eyed and ugly. Then the Major came out in his old uniform jacket with the Iron Cross on a ribbon. The man looked at his card. 'What's wrong with him?' he asked. The Doktor told him the Major had shell-shock and that he was a war hero. The man with the white card saluted and told the Major to stay in the hospital because he had already done enough for Germany. All the soldiers smiled, but the Major was upset. His bad dreams came back and he screamed all night long. The Doktor said it was because of the guns.

One other thing happened that night. *Frau* Haar said the patients wouldn't be spoiled where they were going. The Doktor slapped her face hard and told her to get out. She stood there with her hand on her cheek and her mouth flapping open. She never came back again and the Doktor let Traudl be housekeeper, but there wasn't much work. There were hardly any patients left –'

Karl put his pen down and leaned back in his chair. Apart from a hiss of excitement at the telling of the slapping of Haar's face, Traudl might as well have been reciting a railway timetable. He had asked for details, but her memory was a repository for irrelevance: she didn't know the name of the man with the cards, the surnames of the patients, the date of the visit, or the name of any of the Berlin personnel that Reichardt had contacted. But Friedrich and Siggi would find out. This was going to be the Tale From the Village to end all Tales. Ernst was going to be furious! Karl picked up his pen again.

'And that's when she first started waiting,' he wrote. 'The Doktor got the phone fixed and phoned Berlin. He was promised his patients back when the road building season was over. He told Traudl they would come home soon, and all that summer on her afternoon off, she sat in the village square, watching the road for them. Little Heinrich had taken his flute with him and she listened for him piping the others home along the riverbank. All summer she watched and listened and waited.

They returned one frosty night in autumn in a big lorry. The Doktor came downstairs in his plaid dressing gown and opened the big front door. He had to sign bundles of papers. The patients came in quietly and stood in the corner, looking down at the floor. None of them said hello. The man with the papers said they had been good little soldiers once he'd knocked the nonsense out of them. The Doktor told him to leave and he went out laughing.

The Doktor didn't laugh. He walked up and down the line of

patients in the corner and didn't say a word. Elvi began to cry and the others shouted at her to stop before they all got into trouble. She stuffed a rag into her mouth and cried without noise. 'Good little soldiers,' the Doktor said, and then he sat on the stairs and cried. Then they all did.'

Karl stopped writing again. Traudl had almost criticised her Doktor then. What was the use of crying? Heinrich was blue with cold without his shirt and Detlef had a broken arm and Elvi was walking on the carpets with dirty bare feet. Traudl had to see to everything all by herself because the Doktor only cried and pulled his hair. 'I can't believe that this has happened,' he kept saying.

But Traudl believed. She knew the things that happened in the world. She was the first to know that Elvi and Maria were pregnant. She knew about Maria because she was sick every morning. She knew about Elvi because she sat rocking on the floor all day, saying her alphabet over and over. She thought her mother might come for her if she could prove she wasn't stupid. Traudl guessed from the rocking that she would have a baby soon, because she had rocked too when a bad thing had happened to her. She had rocked and rocked but she didn't know her letters and so she had sung a little song. That was when they put her in the hospital. The three men didn't get put anywhere, though. She had seen Karl drinking with them at the inn. No, she wouldn't say their names because they'd get her locked up again. And what did it matter? These things happened all the time. She didn't understand why a clever man like the Doktor didn't know that.

Karl chewed his pen, thinking of Traudl and her three men. She had hummed her song for him, tilting her head and tunelessly crooning a cracked counterpoint to the shrieking wind which drove the clouds away from the moon and whipped at her scarves and wrappings. He decided to censor that little tale from his letter. No one would ever believe that the Troglodyte could attract three men. He thought of the farmers he drank with in the inn – no, not even in East Prussia could any man be that desperate. This was clearly the erotic fantasy of a madwoman, and would cast doubt on her truthfulness if it were known. But the fantasy didn't mean that she had lied about everything else. The tale of Reichardt had the ring of truth, was even touching in its way. And his suicide was a verifiable fact. But for the life of him, Karl couldn't think what the Doktor had to reproach himself with.

16

'And,' he wrote to Friedrich, 'we may never know, because Traudl refuses absolutely to discuss the second time the patients went away.'

It was a week before he heard from Friedrich. 'Traudl must spill the beans,' his cousin wrote, 'for Siggi's sake. He has been afflicted with moral outrage. We all thought it was some new joke at first, but now we fear the case is genuine and irrecoverable. Siggi is earnest and never amusing and no one can stand his company for long. He darts like a firefly all over Berlin, enquiring about forced labour and vanished lunatics; he pins T4 clerks to walls and bribes them to bring him the contents of their superiors' waste paper baskets.

So far he has gleaned that the Ministry at Tiergarten 4 researches eugenics, fertility, and insanity. They distribute grotesque photographs of the insane to demonstrate the effects of degeneracy on racial health. Siggi produces these gross pictures without the slightest provocation, even at the dinner table. He rages that his zanies have been rounded up and put into labour camps along with politcos and other undesirables. He considers it a harrowing fate to have to dig roads and be lectured at by the politically committed.

Certainly, some sort of forced labour programme was in operation last year, and yours is not the only report of non-return from labour duties. All enquiries are met with referrals to other departments and officials – there are dozens of them. The Führer breeds them like rabbits and they are all alike: they know nothing and they write down in triplicate the names of people who want to know. Siggi makes them spell his name aloud three times in case they get it wrong.

He is full of high purpose. The editor refused to print his latest cartoon (he's still apologising for the saluting business), but Siggi persuaded him. You should have heard him: 'Of course it will embarrass the government! Why else are we here?' 'Someone has to worry about the poor lunatics digging roads while being preached at by socialists and trade unionists. Why else are we here?' 'The cartoon is NOT mocking the Party. It isn't the slightest bit funny – '

And it wasn't, Karl had to agree when he looked at it; it was chilling. It showed the Pied Piper of Hamelin with a deathshead face and a flute at his mouth, dancing a ragged file of grotesques up a wooded mountainside. One by one, they disappeared into a narrow cleft in the rocks while the deathshead grinned and fluted. 'Where are they now?' the caption underneath read.

It was a grim flight of fancy, but Karl chuckled. Moral outrage! Not Siggi! More likely he was suffering from a prolonged hangover and plain old-fashioned guilt. He had a sister confined in an institution. He had mentioned her once at the end of an evening of inventive depravity when he was reviewing his life through the bottom of a glass: 'SShhh!' he said. 'Today is someone's birthday, but I must not say her name. My father forbids it. She brought shame on us by being peculiar, you see, and so forfeits her place in the family and the world. All day long she hears the voices of angels and devils, all kinds of voices, but never ours. Her photographs have been removed from the mantelpiece and the lock of her baby hair from my mother's jewel box. No one remembers her. Except me.' He grinned slyly and drew letters in the beer slops on the table. 'You see? Her name.' He rubbed it away with his cuff before Karl could read it. 'SShhh!' he whispered. 'Her name must never be spoken; her absence must never be noticed. Have you any idea how much effort it takes not to notice someone who isn't there? But I keep her here.' He had knuckled his forehead so hard that Karl pulled his hand down and pinned it to the table.

Karl frowned. Siggi was odd sometimes. Perhaps there was a family weakness.

The schoolmaster had regained his good humour by the following Sunday. "I brought you my lesson plans, " he said, basking in the rosy firelight beside Karl. "Eugenics. Perhaps your readers would be interested. Berlin should know that we are not all backswoodsmen out here."

"Very thoughtful of you, Ernst. The electricity, plumbing, and church gargoyles may be mediaeval, but the village is in the vanguard of the new science. Your influence, of course."

The schoolmaster flushed with pleasure. "I try. One likes to pass the torch of enlightenment to the next generation."

"Your lesson plans may well be of interest, Ernst. There is a Ministry in the Tiergarten entirely devoted to – "

"Oh, yes, I know. I send for all their public information pamphlets. But I believe I have refined the theories to a consistency suitable for children to digest. I have devised a programme – "

And he was off. Karl waited patiently for a break in transmission. When the schoolmaster paused for a swallow of beer, he said suddenly, "And did you ever have contact with the asylum here, Ernst?

To increase your understanding of the problem?"

"Goodness, no. It's seven miles outside the village and you know these places – closed doors and no outsiders, please." He placed his empty *stein* carefully on the table. "What makes you ask?"

"I wondered if the patients were the inspiration for your studies."

"No, not really. We occasionally met the better behaved ones in the village, exchanged a good morning and so on. They were not inspiring."

"I understand the hospital is empty now."

"Yes. The *Direktor* abandoned the place once the inmates had gone."

"They're not coming back then? The patients? I believe they left once before and returned."

"Oh, they didn't exactly leave that time. They were temporarily seconded to a labour-therapy squad. The programme was successful, I believe."

"But that's not why they left the second time?"

The schoolmaster's spectacles misted over. "They didn't exactly leave then either, Karl. There was an outbreak of typhus. Most of them died, the rest went home, and the *Direktor* abandoned the place."

"The *Direktor* shot himself."

The schoolmaster blinked rapidly. "Really? How sad that is. But, you know, the man was as unstable as his patients. Ask anyone in the village."

"He had something on his mind. He said he couldn't live with the guilt."

"Perhaps he neglected the hospital drains." The schoolmaster emptied his glass. "The interesting question is, does psychiatric work attract the unbalanced, or do they become like that through contact with the insane?" He signalled to the barmaid. "Did I tell you that I am planning a trip for the children? To *Nürnberg* for the autumn rally? We are all so excited."

Frau Haar was even less communicative than Ernst. She said nothing about life in the asylum except that she had been like a mother to those poor souls. As for Reichardt's suicide and the fate of the patients, she knew nothing at all about what happened there after she retired. But she would pray for the good *Doktor*.

Like Siggi, Karl concluded regretfully that they were both lying in their teeth.

Wednesday's weather was milder, if not quite springlike. Karl wrapped up warmly, and with Siggi's cartoon in his pocket, set out for his tryst with Traudl. He had persuaded her to show him the snowdrops at the place where the patients had their happy-days, and the birch trees which had frightened Heinrich. He put it to her that it was the least she could do if she wouldn't tell him her story.

The air was crisp and the sky a glassy blue. Karl enjoyed the brisk walk past gardens sparkling with frost until he turned down the path which wound beside the river. It was like entering a dank tunnel. The path was overhung with branches, bushes and trailing grasses, which rotted mournfully in the mud. He took his mind off his discomfort by planning how to make her talk.

He was wet and filthy by the time he reached the little white style where Traudl awaited him, swathed in shawls and scarves. "The snowdrops are this way," she said, and without another word led the way across the water meadows. They waded knee-high through grass crunchy with frost, and only halted when they reached the birch trees which pallisaded the edge of the meadow.

She waved her mittened hand. "The birches," she announced. "The ones Heinrich was afraid of." She clearly expected a reaction. He struggled to find one. "Ah, yes," he said at last, "where Heinrich lost the race."

She nodded. "Every summer. Heinrich kept up with Detlef when they ran across the meadows, but Detlef always won because Heinrich stopped at the trees. They frightened him. He wouldn't go in the woods unless I came and took his hand." Traudl gazed dreamily into the leafless thicket.

"Is this where Heinrich played his flute, Traudl?" He had to ask her twice.

"Not here," she said at last. "He didn't like the trees whispering to him. Or Detlef running off through the woods. He could hear Detti's sandals getting further and further away – " She clapped her mittened hands together in a light rapid rhythm. "Like that. Slap. Slap. Slap." She clapped again and added helpfully, "The path is hard like biscuit in summer. Slap. Slap. Further and further away until Heinrich couldn't see him any more. 'Oh, Traudl!' he shouted every time. 'Where's Detti? Where's he gone?'"

Karl was amused to find that just for a moment, he felt Heinrich's dread of the silent forest closing in over the sound of invisible running feet. Traudl was still speaking. "But," she said, "he was all right when I carried him."

"Carried him?"

"He's small for his age."

"How old – ?"

"Ten. But small."

"Ten? In an asylum?"

"Since always." Traudl grinned wolfishly, pushed her eyelids into a slant, and sank her chin into her shoulders. "He's funny looking. The snowdrops are this way."

The clearing was a long way into the forest. He arrived panting and overheated. Traudl was well ahead of him. "This is where the happy-days were," she said with a sigh. A tiny ruined chapel stood to one side. Birches crowded spikily upwards from inside its roofless walls. The clearing was studded with flat table tombs, each carved with a great crusader's cross, symbol of the Teutonic knights, the flower of the Aryans. Karl sat on a tomb and lit a cigarette. His feet were buried to the ankles in a carpet of snowdrops which trembled thick and white in the breeze.

Traudl tramped round the perimeter of the clearing, slapping her arms to keep warm. "Is it pretty? Do you like it?" she called to him.

He nodded. "Very pretty. And peaceful."

"The Doktor said the snowdrops were a sign that winter was nearly over. We all – "

Karl flicked his cigarette into the snowdrops and heard it sizzle. "I have something to show you, Traudl." He held out Siggi's cartoon. "Look. My friend drew this. It's in the newspapers."

She began circling the clearing again. "Heinrich didn't like it here."

"Traudl, come and see."

Her speed increased to a lumbering trot.

"Traudl!"

She turned and ran in the opposite direction.

"Why didn't he like it here, Traudl?" He patted the space beside him. "Come and tell me all about it."

She stood still. "I told you. He didn't like the trees. Or those." She pointed at the tombs. "There's dead people in there. See? Pictures of their bones."

Karl glanced at the table tomb; it was carved with skulls and scythe-bearing skeletons, their bony fingers pointing at a Latin inscription – *Memento Mori*. Traudl came closer. "Heinrich heard claws scratching to get out from under there."

Karl grinned. "Heinrich had a vivid imagination."

Traudl pouted sulkily. "He heard them scratching like rats." Her whisper was like the rustle of dead leaves. "He thought the trees grew out of their bones." She pointed skywards. "See their fingers? And their arms?"

The birches, naked and slick with ice, soared dizzyingly above their heads. Twigs were like fingers flexed in frozen anguish, branches like arms uplifted to Heaven, and the wet silver bark which covered them looked like rotten dead flesh. Or so a little boy might think, Karl thought with a shudder.

"Woo! Woo!" Traudl screamed suddenly. "WooHoo!" She leapt at him and he tumbled backwards off the tomb. She slapped her thighs and laughed. "The *Doktor* fell off too. Every time. Good joke, isn't it?"

"Yes," he said, brushing wet debris off his trousers. "I can see why you call them happy-days."

"Yes. Heinrich laughed and laughed and then he wasn't frightened. He asked questions. Why do trees grow upwards? Why do snowdrops grow in circles? I didn't know, but the *Doktor* did. Do you know why?"

Karl seated himself and lit another cigarette. "I don't think I do, Traudl," he said patiently. "What did the Doktor say?"

She recited carefully. "Trees and snowdrops are just like people – each grows according to its nature." She pursed her lips. "That's clever talk, isn't it?"

"Yes, it is, Traudl. Wouldn't it be wonderful to have the *Doktor* back?" She nodded and dropped her eyes. "I think I know how. Will you look at my picture now?" She sidled nearer. "See, Traudl? The patients are being led away. It says, 'Where are they now?' My friend is worried about them. He would bring them back if he knew where they were."

"I don't know where."

"Did they go with the soldiers like before?"

She kicked idly at snowdrops. The smell of smashed stalks rose green in the air. "The picture's wrong," she said. "Heinrich had the flute, not the soldiers. And they didn't walk. They went in a big lorry."

"So the soldiers did come again? You know, *liebling,* if we tell

22

about the soldiers, then the *Doktor* will be let out. And we'll make the soldiers tell where the patients are. But if we don't tell, then maybe you'll never see any of them again."

Snowdrop stalks snapped and squeaked under her boots. "I could get into trouble. I don't want to be locked up."

There was real terror in her eyes. Karl patted her arm. "Traudl, tell me about it. If it will get you locked up, then I'll keep it a secret. If it won't, then I'll put it in the papers and find the *Doktor*. Is it a deal?"

He was frozen to the marrow of his bones by the time she agreed, and even then the ordeal was not over – she insisted he accompany her to the hospital because she had to give Fritzi his dinner.

"I thought all the patients had gone away," he said.

"Fritzi's the *Doktor's* dog," she said.

"Oh. Sorry."

She grew confidential. "Fritzi gets his dinner early or he makes a pest of himself when the patients are having theirs."

"But there are no patients."

"It's still Fritzi's dinner time."

There was no arguing with that.

It was about four miles through the woods to the hospital. Karl stumbled after Traudl while she barked amusing anecdotes about Fritzi over her shoulder. The animal was, apparently, every bit as remarkable as the *Doktor*. He gasped admiration whenever he could summon the breath and swore inwardly that Siggi was going to pay for this.

The hospital was a gracious old hunting lodge with carved wooden gables and a solid square frontage half-hidden in red creeper. He might have admired its prettiness if he hadn't been exhausted. They entered by a side door. Traudl stood by the oak coat-stand in the little hallway. "Overshoes," she chanted. "Coat. No drips, please. I polish the floors on Wednesdays."

He divested himself of wet garments while she removed layers of shawls and scarves and an old military greatcoat. Her hair, he saw, was iron grey and cut short with a side parting scraped back in an enormous diamante clasp. The effect was oddly childlike. She smiled her wolf's fang grin and touched her clasp. "Pretty, isn't it? The *Doktor* won it in the Christmas lucky dip. He said he would give it to his best girl. That's me. I'll feed Fritzi now. You can watch if you want."

The kitchen was warm and bright and the little daschund frantic with joy. Karl restrained him while Traudl filled his bowl with meat.

He pulled a chair close to the stove. "Tell me about when the soldiers came."

She said it was like the first time: the soldiers, the papers, the shouting, the lorry. Elvi was hit with a gun to shut up her screaming. And they pushed the *Doktor* to the floor when he tried to help her. The soldiers walked right over him. 'My God,' he kept saying, 'what have I done?' But Traudl didn't tell.

Karl was bewildered. He studied the coffee pot in front of him. "But what could you have told, Traudl? The Doktor hadn't done anything. None of this was his fault." She was suddenly busy, mopping up a coffee splash, muttering under her breath. He waited patiently.

"They took the Major with them this time."

"They didn't before. Why did they this time?"

She polished furiously at the bass taps shining over the sink. "Because of what the *Doktor* did. And me."

She left Karl in Reichardt's office while she took Fritzi for his walk. Slowly he began to make sense of what she had told him. The phone, black and gleaming on Reichardt's desk, had rung two days before the soldiers came. A voice warned Reichardt he was about to be visited again. He shut himself in his office all that day.

Traudl knocked at the door after everyone had gone to bed and brought him sandwiches. What a mess the room was in! The drawers in the filing cabinet were open and there were little white record cards all over the desk and the floor. He was typing and Traudl asked if she should send for *Fräulein* Harkus, because typing was her job, but he said he couldn't trust her and gobbled down his sandwiches.

'But I can trust my best girl, can't I, Traudl? Not clever Harkus or my loyal nurses. Only you. You must never say anything about this, Traudl. It could mean big trouble for us both. You can keep your mouth shut, can't you?'

Karl stood in front of the desk where Traudl must have stood that night. The desk was wide and covered with green leather. There was a green shaded lamp to one side. He imagined Reichardt, pale and unshaven, in a splash of light among the shadows, peck-typing and wolfing down sandwiches. His eyes would have been bright and feverish when he told Traudl his plan. 'It's a paper game,' he told her. 'Paper gives them power over us. We shall fight paper with paper.'

Traudl hadn't understood, but she'd fetched the garden refuse sacks, and while he typed, obediently shredded all the little white cards he pointed at, then filled the sacks with them.

He had a pile of new cards beside his typewriter. 'What shall I say about the Major, Traudl? And Elvi – we can't let them take her, not after last time.'

Traudl couldn't remember what he said about the Major and the others, but she had allowed Karl to look through the filing cabinet. Maria Barbel, Elvi Polk, Heinrich Reinke, Major Beck – according to the records, they were all suffering from multi-syllabic psychiatric illnesses, presenting as hallucinations, delusions, violent outbursts, and a total incapacity to follow a disciplined regime. In short, unfit for work.

Karl understood. The soldiers hadn't wanted the severely disordered the first time and so Reichardt had transformed his patients, working throughout the night to produce records showing false diagnoses and hopeless prognoses. Traudl kept him going with coffee and burned the old records to wisps of ash in the boiler room furnace.

Karl stood entranced, seeing it all happen by the light of a green shaded lamp, hearing the quiet flip of a card across the table, the rip as Traudl tore it to pieces, the tap-tap of the typewriter. He saw Reichardt yawning and filing his new records so that everything was in order, proper and correct.

When the soldiers came, Traudl hid in the cupboard in the hall. They were smiling and polite this time. So was the Doktor as he regretted that he had no patients fit for work. The soldiers were delighted to hear it. It was the unfit they had come for this time. 'What for?' Reichardt demanded. 'What use are they to you?'

'None at all,' the soldiers said. 'They are being relocated.'

The *Doktor* turned chalkwhite then. He said they couldn't do that, but they showed him papers and said he should be pleased to be rid of the troublesome ones. They were going to a special hospital for people like them. Reichardt fetched his coat and said he was coming too, but the soldiers locked him in his office and told him there were enough *doktors* where they were going.

From her hiding place, Traudl saw a scene from Hell. The patients were screaming, running everywhere, trying to get away from the rifle butts. Elvi hugged her baby and cried. One soldier was kind and stroked her hair. 'Do you think we are monsters, *liebling*? Would we

25

hurt our little Elvi?'

Reichardt hammered on the door of his office, shouting that he was going to report this, but the soldiers only laughed. Traudl let him out after they'd gone and he spent the next two days on the telephone. But it was no use. 'No one can say where they are, Traudl,' he said. Due to staff shortages, the paperwork has been held up. We will be informed in due course.' He laughed till he trembled. 'They've been lost like parcels in the post. I must go to Berlin and see these people face to face. I shall make them give our people back.'

When Traudl returned with Fritzi, Karl told her firmly that her story must be told. There would be no trouble. The newspapers would protect her. Once people knew what was going on, the soldiers would be in trouble and Doktor Reichardt and the others would be brought back home. He would be proud of his best girl and know he had been right to trust her.

"I shall send the story to Berlin, Traudl. I'll show it to you first, of course."

She shrugged. "I can't read." She fiddled, frowning, with her diamante clasp.

"I'll read it to you. Would you like that?"

"I don't have much free time," she said almost coquettishly.

"You can polish the floors while you're listening," he laughed.

"Will the Doktor read about me too?"

"Definitely."

He was halfway home and tramping through the snowdrop clearing before he remembered that Reichardt was dead. With a stab of pity he pictured again the pale unshaven man in the green lamplight. Karl rested on a tomb for a few minutes, thinking and smoking. Snowdrops glimmered ghostly white around his feet in the fading light; they were everywhere. His eye travelled along jagged lines of them into the long grass under the trees while he planned his exposé, and his future. There was no telling where this would end. Governments had fallen for less and the credit would be his. Reichardt had done his best and he would mention that – but for the life of him, he still couldn't understand why the man had shot himself.

There was a letter awaiting him at *Frau* Haar's. Karl sat stunned on the edge of his bed when he'd read it. Siggi was in hospital after a drunken brawl with some blackshirts. The details were sickening. Siggi had been identified by his press card, which had been the only recognisable thing about him. His friends had prayed that he would live, but now they prayed he would die, so severe was the damage to his brain, which was slopping around in his skull like mashed pumpkin.

Karl hugged his knees to his chest, sick to the pit of his stomach. Friedrich said that Siggi had been delighted by the response to his Pied Piper cartoon. At first, furious relatives of patients denied that the patients were missing – they had died of typhus and they had the medical certificates to prove it. The trouble was, there were hundreds of them, all dying of the same disease, in the same span of time in places scattered all over Germany. Now the relatives were asking hard questions about the conditions the patients were being held in. The editor had been summoned to T4 and been harangued by an official about the distress that Siggi's cartoon had caused the recently bereaved, and about Siggi's relentless badgering of T4 staff. The official was moved to question the role of the Free Press in a civilised society. The editor had apologised profusely, swore that it would never happen again, returned to the office and told Friedrich that Siggi had been right all along and they were going to prove it. Friedrich advised Karl to break the story before someone else did; for Siggi's sake, he'd added, or he'll come back and haunt you.

Karl spent the rest of the day planning how to introduce the patients to the public. He would have to make them interesting. The hard facts about their removal from care and subsequent ill-treatment would send shockwaves round the Reich. In tribute to Siggi, he would head the story 'Where Are They Now?' Everyone had heard rumours about the conditions in labour camps. The Party had as good as deliberately infected the patients with typhus by sending them there. He would lead the crusade to bring the survivors home and make his reputation forever.

He laid out his typewriter, carbons and paper and began. Words had never flowed so easily before. Reichardt must have felt like this the night he changed the patients' records: no fatigue or hesitations, no stumbling after the right phrase. He worked on through the night, sealed his scoop in a large brown envelope and took it to the postbox

27

at the end of the street.

Dawn broke as he turned back home. The river rushed noisily through crystalline light and made him think of Traudl. He considered the unexpectedness of things that happened in the world: who would have thought that a dismal night spent on a riverbank with a Troglodyte would lead to all this? He shook his head in disbelief and when he reached his lodgings, plunged straight into a deep sleep.

He woke suddenly with the crack of a pistol shot echoing in his ear. "But they don't!" he cried out. He sat bolt upright and snapped on the light, but the room was empty and quiet: no pistol shots, no sandals slapping across earth baked hard as biscuit, no flute piping off-key. Shivering, he pulled his blankets round his shoulders. Such a strange dream: bright sunshine and screams, a blue and golden summer day, and thousands of snowdrops, splashes of out-of-season frost, zigzagging through the grass towards the trees. And above the screams and shots, a child's voice, clear and sad like a flute's: 'Why do snowdrops grow in circles?'

"But they don't," he said aloud.

And they didn't. He was back in the clearing by midmorning. On one side, snowdrops formed circles like ever-widening ripples round the trees and tombs; on the other side, the ripples were broken into jagged lines, as if the earth and the bulbs clinging underneath had been disturbed. His eye followed the jagged lines and traced a pattern of grassy rectangles humped side by side among the snowdrop circles.

He lit a cigarette and slumped against a tomb. He saw it all now. The patients had been permanently relocated, and much closer to home than anyone had thought, right under the birches which had terrified little Heinrich. Perhaps he'd had a premonition. Maybe Reichardt had too when he'd turned white at that word 'relocated'. 'What have I done?' he kept asking. Had he sensed he'd signed their death warrants? He couldn't have – such a thing was beyond guessing. But he found out somehow. Then he shot himself.

Suddenly, the rotting dead flesh of the birches nauseated Karl and he crashed through the snowdrops, out of the clearing, and went running home. He had an article to re-write.

The schoolmaster was sipping tea from *Frau* Haar's wedding china when he arrived. "Karl!" he called cheerfully as Karl made to slip upstairs. "I was about to send out a search party! Come and have some tea. You look frozen."

Karl took a seat by the fire; it would be a comfort to feel warm. The schoolmaster looked pointedly at his boots. "You've been walking, I see."

"Yes. I needed the exercise. I've been lazy lately."

The schoolmaster's cup chinked in his saucer. "Lazy, Karl? A little bird told me you were working all night." He stirred his tea, smiling gently. "*Frau* Haar was concerned, especially when you went out so early this morning, and then went out again without breakfast. Some tea?" He turned to Karl's landlady. "*Frau* Haar, when you're in the kitchen, tell the boys I won't be much longer."

Frau Haar left the room, and through the open door, Karl glimpsed three burly brownshirts sitting at the kitchen table. A finger of unease stroked his spine.

"We're on our way to a meeting," the schoolmaster said. "But there was something I wished to discuss with you first."

Frau Haar returned with a cup and saucer. Karl beamed warmly at her and gestured at the tray on the table. "You've been baking, *Frau* Haar," he said," This looks wonderful."

"Then eat," she said coldly as she went out again.

Karl took a piece of *stollen* cake. He had to sit with it in his hand. *Frau* Haar had forgotten to bring him a plate.

"So, Karl. Where did your walk take you?"

"Down by the river."

"Really? Wilhelm says he saw you in the woods."

"Did he? Well, nowhere is very far from the woods around here." Karl bit into his cake, but the icing sugar clogged his tongue like sawdust and he couldn't swallow.

"You look weary, Karl. But if you will burn the midnight oil – the work must have been very important."

Karl shrugged. "The usual, Ernst. A little Tale From The Village."

"You're too modest, Karl. The chief charm of the Tales is their variety. They dot here and there, into the distant past, the recent past, back to the present, and cover all sorts of subjects on the way. There's no telling what you'll come up with next, except that it will be vivid and interesting. That's a great gift. Come. Indulge me. What is the new Tale?"

Karl swallowed hard and looked for somewhere to put his cake, which was growing sticky. He laid it on the embroidered tablecloth. "You'll see when it's published, Ernst."

"This sounds mysterious."

"There's no mystery. It's just that – oh, I can see I'll have no peace until I tell you. But you're spoiling your own surprise."

The schoolmaster's teaspoon clinked cheerfully. "Surprise?"

"Yes. The Tale concerns your calendar of pagan festivals and ancient rites."

The schoolmaster smiled briefly and nudged the leather coat which lay across the arm of his chair. There was an envelope, large and brown and addressed in Karl's handwriting. It should have been well on its way to Berlin by now.

"That was an unworthy lie, Karl." The schoolmaster laid the envelope across his knees. "And a stupid one. The postmaster is a devoted Party member. He helps me keep an eye on things. I have said it before, Karl – you don't take us seriously enough. One cannot put an old head on young shoulders, but someone of your intelligence should have a firm grasp of the realities of life. Your friend, Siggi, is another such, although I fancy he has a firmer grasp now. Don't frown, Karl. We read all your correspondence to and from Berlin." Ernst stared steadily at him through gold-rimmed glasses. "I am glad you found us all so amusing."

There was a short painful pause while the schoolmaster collected himself. He steepled his fingers under his chin and for one hysterical moment, Karl thought he was going to say, 'And now if I may move on to matters esoteric', and if he does, he thought, if he does, I'll giggle and won't be able to stop.

But the schoolmaster was concerned with reality today. "Your friend stirred up a furore. He was warned several times. Did you know that? But he was stubborn and wilful and inflamed by the gossip you sent him. Oh, yes, Karl, you bear some responsibility for what has happened." He blinked rapidly. "I hope you will accept that it would grieve me should a similar unpleasantness enter your life. But there's no reason it should, is there? Your friend let emotion overrule his intellect and his own best interests. I fancy that you are not a man of that stamp."

The pause this time was longer and much more painful for Karl. It only ended when he dropped his eyes. The schoolmaster carried on

30

gently. "A young man of your talents has much to offer the Reich, but you do need guidance, Karl." He tapped the envelope on his lap. "This article is what I would have expected from you – angry, full of appeals to popular sentiment. Well, a young man should have heart and feeling – that is to his credit. One would need a heart of stone not to feel for little Heinrich and pretty Elvi. Do you think I have a heart of stone, that I cannot feel?" A sense of grievance pursed Ernst's lips. "I thought you knew me better. If I had no feeling, would I be talking to you now like a Father? Now, don't lie to me. You went to the clearing yesterday with Traudl. And you went there again today. May I take it that the secret is no longer a secret?"

Karl's heart lurched and he sat very still, uncomfortably aware of the deep rumble of brownshirts' voices in the kitchen. He pictured a brain like mashed pumpkin and felt the colour and warmth drain from his face. The schoolmaster nodded. "I thought as much. And you came racing home to write about it, full of outrage and popular sentiment." He steepled his fingers again. "Why, Karl, do you think a quiet schoolmaster like me, with some pretensions to culture, is involved in this unsavoury business? You see? I am trusting you. I admit I played my part in it. Do you understand why? These unfortunate creatures are a threat to us all, a virulent bacteria in the bloodstream of the race. Just as a doctor takes drastic action, such as amputating a diseased limb so that the rest of the body may thrive, so we take action against them. Sometimes, Karl, awful things have to be done for the higher good, things that one would shrink from if left to oneself and mere human sentiment." Ernst gazed thoughtfully into the fire. "It takes a brave man and a strong one to recognise that truth, to take action when he bears no malice, to rise above natural inclination and engage with necessity – "

"A merciless moral man?" Karl asked, and thought, my God, he believes all this. He lives according to his nature and calls it philosophy.

"That's what I admire about you, Karl, the apt word, the telling phrase. The Party has need for that talent. You must consider your future. Next week your newspaper is being bought over. In the time you have been writing the Tales, you have touched a chord in thousands of hearts and the Führer himself admires your work. People identify with the noble simplicity of your stories. A thousand texts by our philosophers and scientists could not win us the converts you

31

have."

Something shrivelled in Karl as he listened: he knew he was complicit; knew he could never be a Siggi or a Reichardt; knew he was already considering his future. He loathed the schoolmaster for understanding these things about him.

"It is only because of your potential contribution to the Reich's success that I make time for you now," the schoolmaster said. He held up Karl's envelope and tore it in half. "Look. As a gesture of goodwill, I will destroy this." He tossed the halves on to the fire. "See? All gone. Some things are better left unsaid, unwritten and unread. Now it is your turn to show goodwill. You could write that piece you spoke of – my calendar of festivals and their importance in the Aryan tradition. Do it well enough, and you will make both of our reputations in Berlin."

Karl nodded. The schoolmaster rose and put on his coat. "Good. I shall collect the piece on the way home and post it myself." He turned in the doorway. "By the way, does Traudl know about – ?"

Karl shook his head.

"All the same, she remembers more than she should. We must arrange her silence. Don't look so stricken, Karl. Nothing dreadful is going to happen. We shall organise another institution for her, one where no one will listen to her ravings."

Karl decided the wisest course was to believe him. He wrote the article and pulled out all the stops. Ernst's spectacles must be made to mist with emotion.

Traudl waylaid him in the alley the following Sunday night.

"You didn't bring my story."

Karl stared. There appeared to be two Traudls. He had drunk too much again. "*Gnädiges Fräulein,* how nice to see you again."

"Did you put it in the papers?"

"Oh, yes, *liebling*, that's what I do. Put things in the papers."

"You didn't read it for me." She was electric with excitement.

"No, I've been busy. But I have it here."

He produced a Party pamphlet Ernst had given him. The front page was devoted to the virtues of euthanasia and its alter ego, mercy. And it listed all the categories of people who would be better off out of their misery.

They were standing under the light which burned at the end of the alley. It was the last lamp before the path turned down to the river and the smothering dark. Karl felt as if he were standing at the edge of the world. Traudl was in her listening pose: head tilted sideways, gaze fixed on the stars above. Her woolly scarf slipped back to show her diamante clasp dazzling in the lamplight. It wouldn't do any good to warn her, he thought, because where could she go?

"The story is on the front page, Traudl." He improvised wildly. "'The mystery of the disappearance of thousands of mental patients was solved today thanks to the courage and kindness and honesty of a woman named Traudl – '"

Traudl was radiant. He had never seen her smile before; this must be a happy-day for her. He gave her his most deathless prose. It would be cruel to short change her.

Fortune's Favourite

Nowicki threw in his hand with a shrug and a smile and left the table. He was pleased to have lost so heavily: it was a good omen because, as the old saying had it, a man who was unlucky at cards was sure to be lucky in a certain other direction. Nowicki refused to name that other direction, even in the deepest recesses of his heart, because there were other old sayings about counting chickens and crossing bridges too soon which he took very seriously. All the same, that other direction hovered nameless and thrillingly warm at the edge of his consciousness and suffused his pale face with a glowing radiance. For several days now he had lived one breath behind a crazy urge to laugh or sing for joy, an urge he could only control by reminding himself every ten minutes that Lady Luck was inscrutable and fickle and best not taken for granted.

He made his way to the dining car at the front of the train, stepping aside for ladies with a courtly bow, for gentlemen with a polite nod. It was surely another good portent that his civilities were so well received: he sensed respect in the smiles which answered his – some of them from people who only a week before would have passed him by on the street without even a glance – and revelled in the status accorded him as the only volunteer on board the train. His smiles became ever more gracious as he progressed along the corridor; his small plain face was transformed by a rare sweetness.

Rosa, he saw as he approached her, had noticed a change in him. He watched her deep blue eyes lighten and brighten with relief at his coming. In spite of his wariness of counting on anything, he was buoyed up by a sudden optimism and for a moment he allowed himself to feel what it was like to be enrolled in the ranks of the chosen ones, the favourites of fortune.

The air of resignation which hung about him as shabbily as his old black suit fell away from him; he straightened his tie, tugged at his waistcoat, and slid confidently into the seat beside her. He was struck dumb with pleasure by the sight of her face bathed in the pink glow from the table lamp; its tiny crystal pendants trembled with the motion of the train and their light rippled across her face like rosy water.

"Max, you've been gone a long time. I could not think what had become of you."

He heard the quaver of strain in her voice. "Rosa, I am sorry. You know how it is when men get together over cards – always just one more hand. And everything else, no matter how important, is forgotten."

He was pleased with his bluff and hearty man of the world air; Rosa had always liked it when van Borselen spoke like that. 'Oh, you!' she used to say, half laughing, half chiding, 'You are impossible, van Borselen.'

"Max, did no one speak of what is to become of us, of what lies ahead?" The quaver in her voice had become a vibration.

"No, my dear. We were more concerned with van Ess's Royal Flush. Do you know what the odds are against one of those? Goldblatt was apopleptic with rage – the man has no style. One should win or lose with the same composure or not play at all."

He hoped that he sounded cosmopolitan. Rosa was impressed by men who said such things, men with shrewd eyes, expensive dinner jackets and big cigars. Their confidence made her feel safe. Nowicki tugged the travelling rug snugly round her knees and promised silently that he would become whatever she needed him to be.

"Max, I should be much happier if they would only tell us where we are going – "

"Rosa, you must stop worrying. It's such a waste of time. We're going where we are going and that is all there is to it. You remember the rumours that we were to be shipped out in cattle trucks or shot on the outskirts of the city? You were terrified." He tapped the crystal pendants swaying from the lamps until they shivered with tiny laughter. "Well, here we are. No one murdered us, and if it is a little

36

crowded in here, it is hardly a cattle truck, is it? All that worry for nothing."

"But surely they could tell us our destination! Why won't they?"

"Because it is an eastern backwater which even they have never heard of and probably can't pronounce. You must concentrate on what they did tell us. First, it is a safe place far from air raids and rationing." He gazed steadily at her until the worry lines disappeared from between her eyes. "Secondly, there will be hard work and plain food. I imagine the place will be boring and provincial, but I shall be there to look after you." He steadied the pendants again. "Really, Rosa, I have lived through worse times in worse places. When I was a boy in Russia…well, you don't want to hear that dreary old stuff. But I did learn that the trick to getting by is not to mind too much where you are and to remember that it can't last forever. I have much experience of this kind of thing." He laughed more ruefully than he intended, but she squeezed his arm and seemed comforted. "Now, Rosa, you must take some rest and be thankful that it is not the Cossacks we have to deal with. You have hardly closed your eyes in three days. Everything looks bleak when one is tired."

She leaned against him with her head on his shoulder. The little feathers in her hat tickled his cheek. He could smell her violet-scented face powder. It brought to mind the cafes and restaurants of the city and Rosa at the glittering centre of it all, far above him, beloved, unattainable to a man such as he with nothing to offer.

He blew gently at her feathers, amused by their insouciance. How like Rosa they were! After two years in an occupied city, after the mad whirl of the evacuation and three days of hunger and thirst on a packed train, still she kept up her appearance. He was touched by this feminine gallantry, so different from a man's which depended on the transformation of the inner self, not the outer. Sometimes he was awed by the success of his own metamorphosis from Nowicki the dreamer to Nowicki the man of action.

Rosa stirred sleepily beside him. "Max, it was a lucky day for me when you walked into my shop." Nowicki blushed scarlet to the roots of his hair and was glad of the concealment of failing daylight. "You know", she murmured, "van Borselen wanted me to turn you away."

Nowicki stiffened at the mention of that man's name, then smiled above Rosa's head. After all, van Borselen was hundreds of miles behind them, pining for Rosa, with only his wealth, charm, and his brilliantined wavy hair to console him, while Nowicki had the privilege of sharing Rosa's future.

It was unlike van Borselen to miss an opportunity, but he had calculated the odds and let this one pass him by. Nowicki edged closer to Rosa and considered his own policy of keeping fingers crossed and trusting to luck, if it could be called a policy when mostly he had never had any choice. Van Borselen maintained that there was no such thing as luck, only calculated risk, but Nowicki knew this idea to be both cynical and naïve, and somehow the measure of van Borselen's soul. Nowicki knew that there was no such thing as a calculated risk because Life was entirely unpredictable. If he knew anything at all, he knew that. No plan could prosper without a sprinkling of luck. How could it be otherwise when risk calculation involved taking all factors into account and it was impossible to know them all? There were always unknown quantities. Even the great Emperor Napoleon had acknowledged that fact. "But is he lucky?" he asked of every general, no matter how victorious and martially minded. Napoleon's own luck had run out in Russia, as all the world knew, and he had been lost. Nowicki himself knew what it was like to run out of luck so spectacularly. That was something he had in common with emperors and kings and dukes – his greatest enterprise had been lost by the vagaries of chance.

After a lifetime's persecution and fleeing from country to country, he had at last understood that the greatest obstacle to universal brotherhood was a superfluity of languages. He, the most pacific and harmless of men, had discovered that wherever he went, he was the object of fear, loathing and contempt. Irrational. Quite irrational. Often, so often, he had wished that he could say, 'It is only I, Max Nowicki, a nobody-in-particular, so what's to hate?', but he had never been able to because the hatred was expressed in a babble of European languages, most of which he could not speak. He had come to believe that the world spun on an axis of horrible misunderstanding. He had met with very little real wickedness on his travels, but a good deal of ignorance and fear. It was the potential of Esperanto to wipe out all misunderstanding which had inspired him to action. He planned to produce Esperanto Books at low cost to promote universal communication.

He dreamed of Esperanto for the Housewife, for the Traveller, for the Military, for the Statesman. For two years he had attended night school to learn the language; he had invested five years' savings with a publisher; and for eight months he had trudged the streets of the city lugging suitcases full of his phrasebooks. His only reward had been the amusement of booksellers and a letter of congratulation from a fellow visionary living in exile in Spain.

There had been nothing amiss with his Grand Plan, of that he was certain, but Luck had dealt him a wild card, a completely unforeseeable wild card, in the shape of an outbreak of nationalism. Suddenly, everywhere, the fashion was for patriotic rhetoric. People sang rousing folk songs and searched for national heroes in the distant past. Blood, soil and national enemies were all the rage. His Esperanto phrase books had been no match for the feverish distraction of territorial dispute, invasion and war. Who could have predicted that insanity? Anyone would think that every government in Europe had been taken over by Cossacks!

He still burned at the memory of van Borselen's great booming laugh at this explanation for his failure. 'Yes, yes, Max. When this is all over, a great many people are going to agree that it was all a horrible misunderstanding. Poor Max. The world isn't quite ready for you yet. Perhaps next year.'

The one consolation for the whole miserable debacle had been Rosa, living proof that there is always some meat in the thinnest of soups. She had taken pity on his hoarse cough and knife-blade bones and employed him in her bookshop. Her kindness, that rarest and most undervalued of qualities, had overwhelmed him. And how it had irritated van Borselen! 'He is a leech, Rosa, a parasite. He takes advantage of you,' he said often, always just loud enough for Nowicki to hear. But Rosa never wavered. 'Nonsense, Paul. To assist the gentle and the helpless is not to be taken advantage of.'

Nowicki suspected that van Borselen was jealous of him, which was a matter of some pride to him. Oh, Rosa might flirt with the wealthy jeweller, she might dine and dance with him, and consult him about her business affairs, but her kindness was reserved for Nowicki. It was for Nowicki that she had made hot chicken soup that first savage winter of knowing her; it was Nowicki whom she reminded to change his collars and trim his hair; she had been a mother and a sister and a best friend to him. And if his feelings for her were a little stronger, he had kept that fact to himself. Even a visionary must recognise reality sometimes.

Then Fate had intervened again when war camped out in the city. The early days had been van Borselen's triumph: van Borselen the black marketer, the fixer, the man with the most surprising connections in high places. He had shed confidence like sunlight and persuaded all those around him that he could stand between them and the creeping despair which wreathed the city like a fog. Even Nowicki had been grateful to him: he had kept Rosa from hunger and want, and when the evacuations began, he had bribed, cajoled, and called in favours to keep her from being sent on ahead of her friends.

But even van Borselen could not always arrange the universe to suit himself. When Rosa's name appeared on someone's list for the second time, he had felt unable to intervene. Procedures, he said, had been tightened; there was too much risk. Nowicki had been outraged, seared to the core of his being by Rosa's paralysed terror and her efforts not to show it. Who but a van Borselen would stop to calculate the odds in the face of her gut-wrenching courage?

Nowicki had had nothing to offer her but his company into exile, but he well understood that the worst terror was having to endure alone, and he was more than willing to spare her that. And as it turned out, his hard won certainty that the worst times could be lived through had been riches to Rosa. He was the living proof that one could descend to the bottom of the pit and crawl back out again. Nowicki sighed as he remembered how with tears in her eyes she had tried to talk him out of his offer by reminding him of the dangers. He had answered her every argument with a defiant nonchalance which still thrilled him.

'Everywhere is dangerous these days. Why there more than here?'

'So what if there are soldiers? All my life there have been soldiers: soldiers in navy uniforms, green, khaki, black. Personally, I find the current fashion for field grey rather elegant.'

'So what if we are sent to a foreign place? The world is full of them. I myself have been swept westward across five – no, six – frontiers in my lifetime and have lived to tell the tale. Going east will make a nice change.'

'So what if we are to live among strangers? Everyone is a stranger until you know them. And we will have each other.'

Nowicki sighed again. That had been his finest hour. A man would have to live many lifetimes to have such an opportunity again. Even van Borselen had been impressed. He never again referred to the flotsam and jetsam of Europe in Nowicki's presence; even he did not have the nerve for that, not after he had seen Nowicki and Rosa clutching each other and weeping. Nowicki treasured the memory of van Borselen dewy-eyed and shame-faced. He would treasure it forever.

It was from that moment on that the current of luck began to run in Nowicki's favour. Fortune favours the brave and She could be generous. All the arrangements for Nowicki's evacuation had been made without difficulty: the forged identity cards, the travel warrants, the ration cards, his name on the right list for a small fee. He had felt himself carried along on a swelling tide of outrageously good luck. There hadn't been even the tiniest hitch. And it had been like that ever since.

Nowicki kissed the top of the sleeping Rosa's head and sat back as the train raced into the dawn. The darkness outside was vast. Pine forests and picturesque hamlets and a million hard little stars flashed by. Nowicki was lulled by the rhythmic click of the wheels and lay drowsing.

Sunrise was slow and chill and it stained the snow with deep purple shadows. Nowicki yawned and looked forward to Rosa's awakening. When she had adjusted her hat and stretched the stiffness out of her limbs, they would share their daily joke. He would offer her a cup of ice chipped from the window frame and she would say, 'Why, Max, the coffee is a little cool today.' Long married couples had little rituals like that. The thought made him wriggle with pleasure.

The train slowed and came to a shuddering halt. Nowicki was instantly alert. Was this journey's end? With his fist he rubbed a clear circle on the frosty window glass. He peered out, but there was nothing to be seen but a picture postcard railway station half buried in snow and indifferent to their arrival. He could see directly into the stationmaster's office. There was a light showing and a feeble fire. Surely someone up and about at this hour meant someone brewing tea, even coffee? How wonderful it would be to see Rosa's face when he handed her real coffee instead of ice! He glanced at her. Her face was pinched with cold; a hot drink would hearten her. He raked through his pockets for money, but he had gambled it all away. All he had left to barter with was his grandfather's battered silver cigarette case. So be it then; he had no cigarettes to put in it anyway.

He slid out of his seat and stepped carefully over evacuees sleeping in the aisle. He reached the corridor without disturbing anyone, not even the guard asleep at his post. He gasped for breath in the cold air and almost cried out when he sank to his knees in snow as he stepped down to the platform. He shoved his hands into his pockets and trudged to the station master's office through a crystalline silence.

His tentative knock was answered by two round-faced peasants in railway tunics undone at the neck. They were startled by his presence and he pointed towards the train, which seemed to startle them more. Nowicki smiled reassuringly and wondered where they thought he had come from. His request for coffee was met by an exchange of puzzled glances between the two men. Nowicki gestured towards the stove and the pot of coffee bubbling deliciously on top. He held out his cigarette case and the bargain was struck.

Two cups of coffee were poured. There was even a little milk and sugar. The two peasants murmured at one another; one laughed and the other shrugged. Nowicki sensed some heavy meaning. It was at times like this that his faith in Esperanto was restored. As it was, he could only guess at what the two peasants were muttering about. There appeared to be some kind of disagreement between the two, but Nowicki could make no sense of one pair of eyes which would not meet his and another which stared at him much too hard.

The coffee was cooling. Nowicki pulled himself together and, careful to keep his two cups of coffee level, bowed and smiled his thanks. The smile settled something in the mind of the man with the cigarette case. He tugged at Nowicki's arm, pointed to the train, and shook his head vehemently. The other man grinned unpleasantly, and still staring much too hard, shook his head also. Nowicki, filled with sudden dread, backed away, but the men advanced on him, chattering at great speed and more and more loudly, as if he were deaf. One waved towards the thick black forest of pine behind the station, while the other, grinning still, mimed a choke hold on his own throat.

The man with the cigarette case lost patience and lunged at Nowicki, seizing him by the arm and trying to drag him into the trees. Nowicki panicked. They must think that he had more valuables! He had heard tales of the horrors inflicted on unsuspecting travellers in these godforsaken areas. Just about anything was possible! Fear spasmed in his stomach and he jerked himself free. His coffee splashed into the snow with a hiss, then he heard a louder hiss and the clanking of wheels. He turned in time to see his train pulling slowly

42

out of the station, gathering speed with every yard.

He began to run. He fell heavily into deep snow and as he scrambled to his feet, wild despair clawed its way out of his throat in a howl of protest. Rosa! His luck could not desert him now, not when everything was going so well! He ran slipping and slithering towards the train, calling on Luck and Providence and God, promising that he would never ask for anything again as long as he lived if only he could get back on the train. He pictured Rosa, alone and afraid, believing that she had been abandoned, and he screamed, "Mein Herr! Mein Herr!" to attract the attention of the guard.

He ran and ran until his heart was bursting and his throat scorched by freezing air. The sound of clanking wheels carrying his future away from him spurred him on. He leapt for the observation platform and hung from the rail by his fingertips, kicking furiously and choking on thick black smoke studded with cinders which billowed back from the engine. He was only saved from falling by a strong arm clad in field grey which gripped him by the scruff of the neck and hauled him aboard the train.

"Herein, Jude!"

"Oh, that was lucky," spluttered Nowicki gratefully.

The guard looked blankly at him.

Nowicki used the international sign language of the bow and the smile to demonstrate his appreciation. Unaccountably, the guard was convulsed with laughter. Nowicki bore the man's amusement with perfect dignity. Anyone would think the buffoon had never seen a man running for a train before.

A Small Miracle

The bench was slick with melted snow. Matthew sat down and sucked in cold air until his lungs burned. Hope had come to him in the same way as bad news had, kicking his heart out of its familiar rhythms; he was dizzy with its wild beating and the roaring of blood in his ears. He peered through the darkness at the nursing home looming black against the wide, snow-lit sky. It was still draped in its Christmas lights, which twinkled feebly in the gloom and failed utterly to look festive. The place always made him uneasy: too much divine mystery and not enough of the human touch for his taste. But the nuns were assiduous in their duties. Kate was well cared for.

He knew he should rise and go up there, knew he should be inside this very moment, celebrating his miracle. He blamed Sister Theresa for his reluctance to face it. She had broken the good news to him suddenly, making no effort to prepare him for it, unlike the last time she had made a midnight telephone call. That time she had tip-toed round the news so delicately and for so long that it had been almost a relief to hear the worst. This time the phone had shrilled him out of sleep and she had begun babbling at once. 'A miracle! There's been a miracle! Katherine is talking again.'

Matthew huddled in the cold, still trying to take it all in, but he could not think past the heavy pounding of his heart, or the need to hold back the tide of hope which was threatening to engulf him; for a long time, his only strength and refuge had been stoic resignation and without it, he would be defenceless.

It had taken him months to become accustomed to the frantic muttering which Kate thought was speech; even longer to be able to bear her silent tears when no one understood her; longest of all to accept that she no longer recognised him. He had persisted in believing that she was aware of him because he was the only one who could soothe her when frustration drove her wild. He would sit and brush her beautiful white hair and murmur that the nuns never did it the way she liked it. 'There, there, Katy, that's more like your old self.' She always became calm then, all the proof he needed that she knew that he was there. He had survived on that belief until he saw that it said more about his own need than reality. Finally he had understood that it would take a miracle to bring Kate back from wherever she was and he hadn't believed in those for years.

But now Sister Theresa had proclaimed that miracle, and all he could do was hide in the dark, feeling old and confused. It was as well that Kate could not see him now. He tried to imagine the kind of thing she would say to get him up, but heard only the night silence and the slither and drip of snow melting off trees. He was an old fool to be sitting here with icy water dripping down his neck, thinking about his wife who was only fifty yards up the drive in a nice warm room, probably wondering why he wasn't there. The thought of her waiting was enough to make him rise to his feet.

Sister Theresa opened the great front doors to him. He knew better than to expect a show of pleasure from the good sister: Sister Theresa held the joys and sorrows of this world to be of no account. They greeted one another with their customary silence; they had hardly exchanged two words since the night of Kate's second devastating stroke. He followed her inside and was deposited among the soft shadows of the hall while she turned back to the doors to lock up. He heard the muted clinking of keys and the drawing of long brass bolts. She was careful, this keeper of the keys and his Kate; and how was it possible for the woman to take so long over locking a couple of doors?

Matthew shifted restlessly. Hope hurt like feeling rushing back into a numbed limb and jabbed pins and needles at his self-possession. He looked round for a distraction, but there was nothing here to steady him. In fact, the statue of Our Lady only made him feel more uncomfortable. Her prim half-smile reminded him overmuch of Sister Theresa and her smug certainties; and on Kate's behalf, he resented the plastic flowers twined round Her feet. 'Tacky,' Kate would say.

'Terrible tacky stuff.' That's what Kate would say. If she could speak.

Unexpectedly her voice, warm and vibrant, rang round inside his head. 'Tacky, Matt. Isn't that just awful?' The realness of it pierced him through and through with longing. He heard the exact tone of the convent girl devoutly raised and rebelliously lapsed, embarrassed by past fervours and still afraid of her own daring. She had never quite stepped out of the shadow of superstitious awe, something which he understood very well because he was the same way himself. They had often laughed together about this: two Catholic agnostics, passionate socialists both, finished with the Church but never able to shake off entirely the old fears learned at the priest's knee. He had lived to see the decline of religion and the rise of New Labour, and by the time he reached his eightieth birthday, it occurred to him that of all the things he had ever believed in, the only thing he had been right to trust was Kate's great heart. She alone had never failed. But by the time he knew that, she was already lost to him and he hadn't been able to tell her.

Her first stroke hadn't been all that serious, a warning the doctor called it. Kate had remained in good spirits, and being admitted to a Catholic nursing home had amused her. 'Right back where I started,' she said, 'and feeling like a naughty little girl already. I keep saying sorry. I feel I ought to be saying sorry for everything I ever did, thought, or said. Once a Catholic...'

It was Sister Theresa made her feel like that, Matthew felt. She had an odour of disapproval about her, drifting from the folds of her habit like dust. Kate had thought the same thing. 'Isn't that Sister Theresa the grim one, Matt? She says she never wanted to be a nurse. Her mind was set on the contemplative life, but she does her duty for the love of Christ and the mortification of her flesh.' They had exchanged glances and stifled their laughter for fear the nun might hear. 'That put me in my place, I can tell you, Matt. What a thing to have lived so long and ended up as someone's penance. I mortify her as often as I can, just to be obliging, but all she ever says is that suffering has a beauty all its own. I never know whether she means mine or hers.'

And mortify the good sister Katy did. They were forever debating things: the meaning of life; the necessity of faith; the need for suffering in the world. 'I can't help getting heated, Matt. She thinks the horrors of the world are no more and no less than we all deserve. Why I let her get to me, I don't know. I shouldn't expect anything else

47

from a woman whose best friends are suffering saints and tortured martyrs.'

Matthew remembered the last debate clearly. There had been a documentary on TV, flies on a dying baby's eyes, a woman with empty breasts who had long given up weeping. Sister Theresa had smoothed the snowy sheets on Kate's bed and squared the corners precisely. 'It is God's will,' she said. 'We must all accept it.' 'God's will, Sister? God's will? That's man's work and no excuses, thanks very much. Any God who would will that is a devil.'

Matthew, waiting in the shadows for the nun to return from locking up, shivered as he relived Kate's indignation. It was not the first time Kate had challenged the nun, but Sister had been particularly upset that day. And that very night, Kate had been struck down by her second devastating stroke. Sister had sent for him and the first thing she said to him when he arrived was, 'God is not mocked.' Then she crossed herself. Once Matt would have laughed that off, but he could not this time. He hadn't even felt any anger at the nun's crassness until she informed him solemnly that she would pray for forgiveness for Kate. For Kate who had never harmed a living soul in all her life!

The memory of that moment chilled Matthew more than the dripping snow had outside. Then he heard Kate's laugh, so close to his ear that he actually turned, expecting to see her; but it was only Katy-in-his-mind again, talking the way she used to. 'That woman, Matt, has the mind of a mediaeval peasant. Didn't we always say that too much religion could spoil an imperfectly good human being?' Matt smiled tremulously. Hope had him by the throat again and he wanted his miracle; he wanted to talk to Kate again.

He stepped further back into the shadows to dry his eyes and was presentable when the nun returned at last. Stiff with starch and duty, she swept him along dim corridors filled with the ragged mutterings of old sick people sleeping fitfully. At Kate's door, she turned to face him. 'Our prayers are answered and God has restored her to us. But Katherine is very tired and must not be encouraged to talk for long. A few minutes only.' Incredibly, she leaned forward and patted his arm. 'You have travelled far for such a short visit, but I knew that you would want to know as soon as it happened. You've waited a long time for this day.'

He thought he glimpsed a small half smile, but before he could be sure, she had moved off along the corridor leaving him bemused and oddly touched to go into Kate. She was propped upright on a mound of pillows. Her head lolled a little to one side. He stepped forward and straightened her. She hated to wake with a crick in her neck. Then, suddenly shy of her, he retreated to the foot of the bed. 'Hello, Katy.'

She was asleep. He studied the dignified peaceful features. The deep lines around her mouth and eyes looked ready to spring upwards into laughter at any moment. Matthew's heart swelled until it was too big for his chest – he could feel it hammering against his ribs. He could not take his eyes off her. She was back. He knew it. She would wake soon and turn to him and they would talk. He wouldn't ask for more, would not expect total recovery or to have her home again. But to talk – just to talk with her again. That would be enough.

'Kate? Did you catch that thought? About what I'd ask for? Once a Catholic! Just give me this one thing, God, and I'll never ask for anything else again. Just one miracle, that's all.'

He pulled up a chair beside her bed and noticed her hands. Gently, he removed the rosary which someone had looped round her fingers, and slipped into her bedside locker. 'You'd have something to say if you woke up and found that there, wouldn't you? That was taking advantage of you when you were down and out and not looking.'

He recalled Sister Theresa reaching out to him at the door and relented. 'Ah, I expect she meant well, Kate. We all live by our own lights.' He realised that he was talking aloud. Was it going to be that easy to fall into the old routine? But why shouldn't it be? It was a night for miracles and hard things made easy. Suddenly, he could not wait for her to wake and words came spilling out, tumbling over one another in his excitement.

'Wait till you hear about Theresa, Kate. She smiled. Really she did. I saw it. Two miracles in one day. I felt like thumbing my nose and saying, 'See, Tess? God, if he exists, doesn't hate my Kate after all.' He lifted the sleeping woman's hands and stroked the fingers which were curved and twisted out of shape. 'The thing is, Kate, although I knew she was trying to be kind, I couldn't smile back. I've never forgiven her for the night she crossed herself. God is not mocked, she said. I'd have struck her if she'd been gloating, but she wasn't. She was terrified out of her wits.'

His mind brimmed with memories of Kate and one obliged his need to hear her. He thought he heard her giggle. 'Matt, you were terrified too! Admit, it. For one moment, she had you believing in the wrath of

49

God.'

With some embarrassment, Matt remembered a shudder of fear. He said nothing, but Katy-in-his-head knew everything and chuckled with delight. 'I knew it! Your face was as white as your shirt.'

Matt laughed quietly. 'Give me some credit, Katy. I managed not to cross myself at least. Though it was a close thing when she went on and on about God's anger. You were lying there not able to speak, after saying God must be a devil – ' He tailed off. Another echo of Kate sounded in his head. 'Didn't my mother always say that my big mouth would get me into trouble one of these days? But who would have thought that exonerating God from blame would have brought a thunderbolt down on my head.'

Matthew was so engrossed that he almost missed Kate stirring in the bed.

'Katy?'

Her eyelids fluttered open and her head turned on the pillow; she was smiling and looking straight at him.

'Katy! Hello, stranger.'

Stupidly, he could think of nothing else to say. He rubbed her hands which were still clasped between his. 'How are you, Katy?'

'Is it time for Mass yet? Have I slept in?'

The voice was childish and afraid and he didn't recognise it. She tugged feebly to free her hands and he let them drop. She began to grope around the bed. Her panicky search frightened Matthew.

'What is it, Kate? What have you lost?'

With some relief, he saw that she understood him.

'My beads! I can't find my beads!'

Like a sleepwalker, he took the rosary from the locker and pressed it into her hands. She smiled gratefully, then bent her head and kissed the crucifix.

'In the name of the Father – '

Matthew winced at her intensity. 'Katy!'

'The Lord is with Thee – '

She didn't know that he was there with her! 'Kate!'

She stared past him, quietly and ecstatically absorbed. Her face was radiant. It reminded him of when he was young: there had been bright Sunday mornings and the cleansing of the Mass, certainties, and a quiet stillness within. She had gone back there and left him alone again. He heard her pray in words as clear and precise as a child's.

'Blessed art Thou amongst women – '

Matthew rose and stumbled from the room.

Sister Theresa, outside in the corridor, was flushed with excitement. 'Did you hear her for yourself?' she cried. 'Isn't she beautiful? She has found her voice and returned to us.' Tears glittered diamond hard in the nun's eyes. Then with a fluttering gesture of the hand, she went into Kate.

Matthew slumped against the wall. God is not mocked, but He mocks, He mocks. What kind of mind finds joy in that? He sensed that he was being watched. He looked along the corridor. The sad-eyed Christ on the Cross at the end of the hall was looking directly at him. The eyes pitied and spoke to him. You see? the eyes said sorrowing, God is not mocked. Fear stroked Matthew with icy fingers. He closed his eyes, consumed with the need for those compassionate outstretched arms and the terror of their comfort.

The shadows were thick with night whisperings. Matthew listened to the voices in the dark and the clamour of dreams being shaped into words.

The old man in the room opposite called sharply for his mother.

The woman in the next room sang 'Twinkle, twinkle, little star.'

Fragments of dreams came at him from all directions, and above them all, sweet and clear, Matthew heard Kate praying.

Dollface

There's wide starless night and there's wide black water and the rowboat moves smoothly between. Charlie rows and keeps his eye on the small hooded figure hunched in the stern. His father is brooding and silent in the thick darkness. Somehow Charlie knows that he must find a safe shore soon. He rows and peers ahead, but wherever he looks, at sky or wide water, there's only impenetrable inkiness. He listens out for water being sucked on to land, but hears only the tiny splash of oars.

He rows steadily. Cool air soothes him until the boat begins to rock; on a tideless, windless lake, the boat rocks violently from side to side. Charlie flattens the oars, but the boat leaps forward like a thing with a life of its own and skims across the surface of the water; then, with a stun of disbelief, he sees the hooded figure in the prow tip soundlessly over the side.

He drops the oars and leans out of the boat. There's no sound of a struggle, no cry for help. He gropes blindly in the murk for an arm, a leg, a head, but comes up with nothing but fistfuls of black satiny water. 'Dad! Dad!' he yells, but his cries are stifled by the dark. For an agonised age, he gropes and scoops, and then a movement catches his eye: it's the hood, bubbled sodden on the surface of the water. Panting with relief, he hauls it into the boat, but it sags weightless over his arm. 'Dad! Dad!' he sobs, and ferrets about in its folds until he's sure it's really empty. He buries his face in it, but it wriggles out of his numbed hands and plasters itself across his face. For a moment,

53

he's blinded. Then it wriggles again and moulds round his mouth and nose and it isn't empty: it's lined with a sludge which slithers into his mouth and nostrils. He claws at his face, desperate for air, but he's choking on rank liquid earth and there's no Dad, no safe shore, only a piercing sense of loss and the great terror which always comes with it. He's suffocating on a dark stinking sludge which floods thickly down his windpipe; he's stifling on foul blackness and there's a voice in his head, a quiet chant of 'eternity'...

Everything began with the dream, and that began when Dad was dying. Dollface began then too, but the dream came first, ending each time on a chant of 'eternity' in a cultured voice like Christopher Lee's. Always, as I opened my eyes, I realised groggily that it wasn't really Christopher Lee, that it was only Dad impersonating; and always, as I eased upright in the armchair, I thought I was a little boy again, giggling round one of Dad's building sites – I swear that, for a moment, I could hear the excavators gouging out earth by the ton, and saw myself running about challenging mummies, vampires and ghouls to come out, come out, wherever they were, while Dad talked like Hammer House of Horror.

Always, about then, my vision cleared and I saw the bottle of Lucozade on the table, the white bed, the pallor of the dying man in it, and I knew I was in Dad's house, and that it was now, not then. In this room, the important past and impossible present met and mixed like whisky and soda. I used to wake and see the hospital cleanliness of Dad's bedroom, but my nose was still full of the smell which followed the breaking in of the ground: dank earth and crushed mountain, old cold stone and stagnant water, all rancid with the stench of the living things the earth had swallowed and held until they rotted. Building sites smell like that, even on sparkling sunny days, and when I was little, the cold stench made me solemn with unease. Dad used to make me right again by grabbing me round the waist and talking like Christopher Lee – *'And now you know how the grave smells, Charlie. This is the smell of all eternity...'* – until I squealed with terrified delight. There was tickling then and a change of voice to Peter Cushing's prim precision –

'So gather ye rosebuds while ye may,
 Old Time is still a-flying
 And this same flower which blooms today
 Tomorrow will be dying'

Big burly Dad used to fold to the ground like a lily in a heatwave and sigh wistfully when he got to 'dying', a protracted polysyllabic dying and sighing, which made me scream with laughter.

But when Tomorrow came, and his long dying began in earnest, there was nothing funny about it. Dad lay tidy between the sheets, flat as an envelope ready for posting, and it was hard to believe that he wasn't really there, that everything that made Dad who he was had been sent on ahead somewhere: the rough and tumble games, the frowns, the half-shamed tendernesses, the rueful grin he faced the world with when things got bad, then worse and worse.

I talked to him a lot. The doctors had agreed that it was possible that he could hear me, or at least that it wasn't impossible. 'Wasn't impossible' was good enough for me. I told him about my week, which didn't take long because the focus of my life was Saturdays and Sundays in that room with him. The rest of the time I ate and slept, and travelled fretting round the building sites – he'd never have forgiven me if I'd let the business slide – but stayed in the site office mostly, not liking the nightmare smell of the ground being dug up.

Dad never took to Dollface. We met her about six months before he sank into the morphine stupor. I came into his bedroom and found him sitting at his computer, cosy in his plaid dressing gown and blue cotton pyjamas. He tried to hide the screen, but I saw he was in a Lonely Hearts chat room. An Adult Lonely Hearts Chatroom.

"Jesus, Dad! Betty Boobs? Hot4U? Foxon Heat?"

Dad looked at me, half-shamed, half-mischievous, an elderly wrinkled toddler about to be sent to bed. "I might be old and ill, son, but there's life in this old boy still." A comic downturn of the mouth, a sly wink. "And nobody in my life."

I looked over his shoulder, incredulous. "Dad, you're not Young Stud, are you?"

"Well, I was once, son." A rueful shrug; an explosion of laughter which I had to share, a laughter which became helpless as Dad explained to Foxon Heat how he'd acquired his nickname, and she replied in kind. Dad giggled till he coughed and spluttered. "It's just a bit of kiddology, Charlie. There's no way of knowing who's at the other end of these messages. We can be whoever we like."

And Dad wanted to be anybody but an elderly man who had begun dying.

It occurred to me over the next few weeks that Dad had never in his life had such fun relationships with women. He laughed and joked and talked dirty, they did the same, and all parties were satisfied. There were none of the usual disappointing revelations, recriminations, slammed doors and leaving forevers. Just good, honest, dirty fun. He even inveigled me into competing for the attentions of Hot4U and Foxon Heat, but they beat me hands down when it came to sleazy snigger and soon returned to Young Stud. Then one Sunday afternoon, Dollface arrived. '*Hello, roomies,*' she said. '*Hi, Dollface,*' I typed. That was the start.

That first day, Dad shook his head at her chat: coarse sniggers were not her thing. She misunderstood or else she fell into an embarrassed silence. By silence, I mean of course that she didn't type a message for ages. How did I know she was embarrassed? I just did.

That first day she tried to change the subject – some chance – with a question about everybody's favourite films. She was answered with a royal flush of cinema's great erotic moments. '*Oh,*' she said. '*I haven't seen any of those.*' Young Stud told her she ought to get out more, but Foxon Heat flashed the snigger Smiley and told him there might be something interesting keeping her at home. Speculation about that kept them entertained for the rest of the afternoon.

Dollface didn't deign to reply, although she stayed in the room, and she was there every Sunday afternoon thereafter, not joining in and irritating Dad out of all proportion. He thought she was being superior, a big no-no in his book, and week after week, he teased her.

Come on, Doll, SHARE your dreams. We're all dying to know what rings your bells.

Dollface, we've showed you ours. Time for you to show us yours.

Hey, Dollface, you getting off on our fantasies? Are we helping?

Dollface, come on out and PLAY 'stead of sitting there taking notes.

She never responded. In the end, Dad gave up, and she and I lurked quietly together in dignified disapproval on the sidelines. After a while, occasionally and then more often, she threw in questions for me: films, books, hobbies – all that.

Now and again she made me smile. That Valentine's Day, she got on to the subject of romance and started spouting the Nation's Favourite Love Poetry. It was surreal, because simultaneously, some sad bastard calling himself BitOfRough was looking for a lady to volunteer for a *9½ Weeks* scenario. *'I want to use a woman. I need to use a woman,'* he typed over and over, while the adult ladies waxed creative over leather masks and dog leashes. BitOfRough swore he was willing to travel anywhere in the country and keep it confidential; Dollface quoted the love poetry of Keats, Shelley and Burns, which she'd thrilled over at school.

Does anyone feel like that any more? she asked. *So important to feel it, even once. Have you ever, Charlie?* I was spared the necessity of answering because Young Stud got in before me:

That's Fantasy, Dollface.

So's your stuff, Stud.

Don't see anyone else quoting Romance, Dollface.

Don't see anyone volunteering for a dog leash either.

More exciting than love, Doll.

In your world, not mine.

I don't live in Cloud Cuckoo Land.

She signed out then – I could *feel* her affront. And that annoyed me. She didn't have to come in the room; she didn't have to chat. The whole scene pissed me off anyway, both the roomies' relentless verbal masturbation and Dollface's resolute saccharine. You pays your money and you takes your choice, but I wouldn't have given you a bent franc for either. All kiddology, see? All of it. I've always known that.

The following week, she was back as usual, asking after my favourite books and films. That provoked Dad too. "Jeez, son, that snooty bitch's got her eye on you. She'll be wanting to know your astrological sign next – compatibility, all that. Waste of time, that one. Nice lady. The kind that gets on your nerves after a while, but."

She certainly got on his, which made me smile. Even at 80, he liked to be the centre of attraction, and her delicate-getting-to-know-you questions were reserved entirely for me. I talked to her sometimes, just to wind Dad up a bit.

I didn't have that excuse by the time summer came. Dad slipped into his long deep sleep and I had a man in a white bed to talk to. I pm'd Dollface for the first time – she compelled politeness somehow – and told her my father was dying and that I wouldn't be around much now.

That's terrible, but. If you need a friend to talk to, I'm always here, Charlie. Three o'clock, Sundays.

Thanks, Dollface. CYA.

I had no intention, though. The chatroom was Dad's idea of fun, not mine. And my next few weekends were taken up with pretending he was still there. I talked to him, and when I ran out of things to say, I read aloud the weekend papers (plus supplements) from cover to cover. I fussed over him: straightened his quilt, tucked him in, combed the silvery thickness of hair which flopped boyishly over his forehead. I chatted cheerfully – after all, he might be able to hear – and every now and then I'd say, "Still with us, Dad?"

There was no answer but the stupefied struggle for breath which forced his ribcage up and down. I couldn't stop listening to that. *Slowly up. Painfully up.* The breath took forever to reach the top. *Slowly. Slowly. Up. Up. Up.* I found myself filling my own lungs with air and holding it until I was dizzy, willing Dad to overtake me, dreading the silence which meant he'd broken down somewhere on the road. But Dad's breathing always reached the peak and was soon shuddering all the way back down.

And when listening exhausted me, and you would be amazed at how exhausting it was, I sat in the silence and watched over him. The silence in a sick room, the silence which attends your father's dying, is like a heavy weight, like boulders piled on your rib cage, crushing the life out of you; it's like a winter night, when you inhale needles of frost and they line your insides and you can't get warm; it's an empty place too, the shadow of tomorrow, that freezingly empty time which is no place to be alone; it is unbearable.

I'm always here, Charlie...OK, she was a stranger, but who better than a stranger to tell how you really feel? Who else *can* you tell? *Always here*...if she was, she would be the first woman who meant it, but then again, Dollface was definitely different, and the monitor was right there in the corner beside the window, staring blankly over at Dad and me, ready to spring to life at the touch of a button – maybe there was someone at the other end, someone who would dissolve the frozen silence of the dying room. I booted up, knowing she wouldn't be there, but

Charlie! You're here.

Hi, Dollface.

How are you?

Fine.

I've been so worried about you...

I remember wondering if she was for real, and then deciding that it didn't matter. The web is the home of charades and fantasy where you can make what you like of what you see. And that day I was glad to believe that someone was thinking of me. All that summer I was glad.

Dollface never told me much about herself, not that I asked at first. Too full of my own troubles, I came to talk, not listen: Dad, morphine deadness, loneliness, nightmares, loss – I spewed it all out, week after week.

Dollface, I keep having this nightmare.

Nightmare?

It's strange. I'm in the nightmare, but I'm looking on too.

I know that feeling.

It took an age to peck a full account on to the screen, but Dollface, as always, was endlessly patient.

That dream makes me shudder, Charlie. Really frightening.

Sunday wouldn't be Sunday without it.

Oh, don't joke. It's not funny.

I'm all right.

It's a fear of loss dream.

There's a surprise.

You must be very close to your father.

Yes. Morecambe and Wise. Laurel and Hardy. Lone Ranger and Tonto. All that.

Loss is a terrible thing.

Tell me about it.

But Charlie, you never really lose people...not so long as you remember them. No one is really dead until they are forgotten.

He feels dead already.

I read once somewhere that death is no more than a stepping into the next room. You'll meet again. I believe that's true. It's a comfort.

What do you know about it, Dollface? You can't have been there if you can get comfort from that slop.

She exited the room, stage left, and I didn't care. Homilies of the Hallmark Greetings variety were a habit of hers and I usually smiled at them, but that day she got to me. The slick sugary placebo she offered angered me. Death is *enormous*, has *enormity*, has *finality*; it's all the unhappy endings ever written rolled into a bullet aimed right at your head. I wanted to scream that agony at her, but at the same time, a terrible longing fluttered like a bird in my chest, a longing to believe something, anything, that would make living easier. It would have been good to surrender to that feeling, but deadly too, because hope failed is worse than no hope in the first place.

It was Dad saved me. I heard his great gust of laughter – just in my head, you understand, I'm not saying he was *really* laughing – and his voice sure and clear, saying the kind of thing I'd heard him say a hundred times: *'Another Thought For The Day, Charlie boy? She should be on Songs of Praise.'* And then his chuckle rolled round the room. *'When you're dead, you're dead. Finito. Endgame. None of this Heaven and Hell, Pulse in the Eternal Mind malarkey. That was all invented to keep us behaving and fearing. Truth is, when you're gone, you're gone, and there's no coming back.'*

You're gone. Or maybe you're only waiting in the next room. Two contradictory ideas. Dad, the toughest man I ever knew, faced the world with a scornful defiance I could only envy; Dollface believed in any kind of ludicrousness that made living bearable. I envied her too.

As the summer wore on, I began to wonder about her: who she was, what she was like. In a way, we had become close. She knew a lot about me, although I knew next to nothing about her. Not being used to confiding, I felt exposed somehow. After our quarrel over what happened when you died, I decided to keep off that subject, maybe get her talking about herself for a change. I felt guilty about snapping at her – after all she meant well – and the thought occurred that since the beginning, I had been hogging the show with all my troubles. That thought made me feel even more guilty. Why had she needed the comfort of 'the next room'? I hadn't even asked. Maybe she had things she wanted to talk about, maybe she was as lonely and full of pain as

61

me. Why else would she come into a chatroom, for Christ's sake? I decided to give her the opportunity to open up a bit.

Hi, Dollface. How are you this week?

Fine, thanks. What about you and your father?

The same. Both of us. Let's talk about something else. You must get fed up with me and my miseries.

Not at all, Charlie.

You never say anything about you, Dollface. Tell me something.

Nothing to tell.

Come on! Must be something!

What do you want to know?

Anything – a/s/l?

Younger than you/female/somewhere and nowhere.

How do you know you're younger than me?

Women are always younger than the men they know.

I'm nearly fifty, Doll.

And I will never be fifty.

Very funny, Dollface. You a sweet little mystery, Dollface?

Definately, Charlie.

Behind me, Dad started muttering, which he did now and then, so I signed out with apologies. I was peeved at Dollface, anyway. OK, it's dangerous for women to reveal too much about themselves in chatrooms, but she and I had been talking for weeks. She *knew* me. I felt rejected. Why didn't she share her woes? Her life? Fair exchange, all that.

I sat with Dad, quietly fuming. He had fallen silent again. I'd missed whatever it was he might have been trying to say. "You were right about her, Dad," I said. "Nice lady. Gets on your nerves, but." I sat grumbling for a while, then dozed off and plunged straight into the nightmare.

Charlie's heart is racing. Dad, hunched in the stern of the boat, turns his head slowly towards him. Charlie can't see the eyes in the dark, under that hood, but he feels them bright with fear, fixed on him. He knows the eyes are pleading. He knows. Dad's afraid! Charlie wants to touch his hand and tell him, 'All right, Dad' although he knows it isn't. But words stick in his throat and he can't let go of the oars. He tries to wrench his hands off them, but they're stuck fast together. Charlie, frantic because he knows what happens next, struggles and splashes black evil smelling water all over himself, while Dad tips over the side. He slips into the water, twisting slowly round as he falls. He's trying to get one last look at Charlie. He slides silently under black water and leaves his blind pleading gaze behind, burning cold as starlight on Charlie's face...

I woke up tasting filthy sludge again. I took a mouthful of Lucozade and swilled the dry sweet bubbles round my mouth. And maybe because I had got into the habit of Sunday afternoon revelation, I told Dad all about it.

"Hey, Dad," I said to the white bed after I'd described the choking sludge. "That was a real cracker, wasn't it, but? You'd have loved it."

The old childhood formula relaxed me. I heard Dad's gruff Hammer House of Horror chuckle once more, making everything all right, the way it did when I was little and we'd been watching our favourite Hammers on a Friday night. I loved them: *Dracula, Prince of Darkness; Frankenstein; Witchfinder General*; all the gory others. Scary fun with the lights out: Price, Lee, popcorn and Cushing, and me in my dressing gown snuggled up to Dad, covering my eyes when it got too much, but peering through my fingers because I didn't want to miss a minute. Then the blood red credits and the eerie music at the end and Dad chuckling because I was all a-tremble. "Hey, Charlie," he'd laugh, "that was a real cracker, wasn't it, but?" And everything was all right again.

It was that day too because his chuckle flew straight as an arrow from the past into the present. "A real cracker, but", I thought, and found myself laughing in the old way. Who needed Dollface's soothing when I had Dad to laugh it off with?

I realised something else too: nobody but Dad ever said 'wasn't it, but?' It was one of his Scottish-isms. He stuck 'but' at the ends of sentences all the time. It doesn't mean anything except that the speaker hails from Glasgow. Dad's gravelly Scots accent had been refined over the years we'd lived in England, but he still said 'wasn't it, but?' and 'DEFF-in-ATE-ly' instead of 'yes'. Nobody in the whole city of Glasgow, he told me once, could spell 'definitely' because in that part of the world they pronounced it with an 'a'. Dad did too, out of habit, or national pride.

And so did Sweet Little Mystery Dollface. *'Definately, Charlie'*. And *'terrible, but.'* She'd used the Glasgow 'but' a few times, now that I came to think of it. What with hearing Dad's Friday Hammer chuckle, and guessing where Dollface came from, I suddenly felt better, as though I'd stolen a march on her.

Hi, Dollface. How's things in the far north?

No idea, Charlie.

But you're from those parts, aren't you?

Sorry?

Glasgow.

Once. Not now. How did you know?

Where now then?

No place in particular.

You're being mysterious again.

64

No. I move around a lot so I don't come from anywhere really. How did you know?

I couldn't resist a gloat about 'definately'.

Clever, Charlie. So you're from Glasgow too?

Originally.

Whereabouts in Glasgow?

Don't know. We moved away when I was small.

It's a beautiful city. I loved it there. I've never felt at home anywhere else. Do you remember it at all?

No.

That's a shame.

Except there was a park near where I lived.

Glasgow's full of parks – 'the dear green place' – when I was small, I thought it was called that because of all the parks.

It was a green park, big, with a pond and a waterfall. I had a boat with blue sails. A swan attacked it once. I remember screaming.

Swans can be scary. They hiss. Have you ever heard them hissing? Beautiful though. I used to love feeding the swans, especially in winter.

I was always terrified of them.

Who rescued you from the swan? Did you get your boat back?

I don't remember.

But you remember the swan. People always remember the things that frighten them.

What frightened you when you were little, Dollface?

Being lost. Getting separated from my Mum in the shops. Being left alone.

Like me and Dad.

Yes, but when you're little, it's your Mum's loss you fear. She's the centre of your world at that age.

I suppose.

I lost my mother when I was small.

Sorry to hear it.

I thought the world was ending when she died.

I know the feeling.

You never mention your Mum, Charlie. Only your Dad.

Never knew her. Not that I recall, anyway.

What happened to her?

No idea.

She made no response. That was a trick of hers. She'd leave the screen blank so long that it got to feel like a demand, and somehow, before I knew where I was, I was typing in more than I ever intended to say.

You still there, Dollface?

You know me – never far away.

Another long silence and an acre of screen waiting to be filled,

Dollface waiting to be told, me resisting. I don't know why. My mother was old history and I had told Dollface about much more sensitive things.

Charlie, you still there?

Yes.

I thought you were going to say more about your mother.

No. I told you I don't remember her.

That is sad.

Only memories can be sad, Dollface. No memories can't be anything at all.

I suppose not. Terrible not to know your own mother, but.

Might have been even more terrible to know her. The kind of woman who runs away to Wales to find herself –

Find herself?

That's what she told Dad before she left. She had to find herself.

In Wales?

In Wales. Could have understood it if she'd fled to Paris or Shanghai. But Wales? With an insurance assessor? Reminds me of the man who ran away from the circus to become an accountant.

Lol – I see what you mean, Charlie, but it must have been awful for you to be left behind.

Could have been worse. She might have taken me with her. Imagine having to admit you came from Wales. She sent me a couple of postcards with views of the golden daffies. That's all I remember of her.

Still, your mother...

Dollface, Dad is restless. I have to go. CYA next week.

Bye, Charlie...

I signed off quickly. I could tell she was headed for one of her psychological analyses. It would, on past performance, go along the lines that the reason I'd never had good relationships with women was because of this early betrayal by my mother. Inability to trust and so on. And then she'd start in again on the necessity for me to make a life of my own once Dad had gone. Find a partner. Find Love. Start a family. She could never let that subject alone. Her sincere efforts to help drove me crazy sometimes; that day I didn't feel up to them.

I moved the chair over to Dad's bed. "Still don't know anything about her Dad. I found out that she used to live in Glasgow, but then she changed the subject. Swans today. And then Mum and the man from the Pru. Dollface is still a Sweet Little Mystery."

Thinks she's making herself more interesting by being mysterious, Charlie.

That was something we used to laugh about a lot – the daft ideas that the females of the species have about what makes them interesting. There was a girl I brought home from uni, always dressed in black, always pale and soulful about some great unspecified tragedy which she would never get over. *'Tell her the answer's in Wales,'* Dad whispered as she was putting on her coat to go home. *'New South Wales should be far enough.'* Then there was the one who claimed to be psychic and chanted *'Deep waters, black waters,'* over and over while Dad and I sat on cushions on the floor, staring into mirrors which reflected candle flames – I forget why, but my eyes were dazzled by little golden lights for hours after and Dad wound me up by going about the house chanting 'black waters, deep waters' in Christopher Lee mode. There were a couple of intellectual ones too – *'Charlie,'* Dad said in wonderment, *'why do clever females always have flat chests?'* And in twinkly eyed bewilderment at my marine biologist, *'The sex life of sea mice. Dead interesting that. What have I*

68

been missing all these years?' And he laughed and laughed. *'Son, you're like your old man. Not much of a picker.'*

Foxon Heat and Hot4U were what Dad called knowledgeable about what hooked a man's interest. Both of them described themselves as blonde, bouncy and bounteous, green or blue eyed, leggy, mischievous, naughty when the moon was in the right quarter, naughtier when it wasn't – all that. *'Your Dollface,'* Dad said often *'has no idea.'* We speculated often about the reality of our roomies: wrinkled, toothless, decrepit, manless, and desperate, we decided, or else they wouldn't be touting themselves on the Net. Dollface was different though. We could never work her out. We laughed at all three, but especially her. Dad thought she was Mary Whitehouse's shade come to reform us, or Mary Poppins to sort us out, or the Virgin Mary to lead us to the good life – *'funny how all the Marys are virtuous,'* he said, *'except for Mary Magdalene, and she stopped being interesting once she was repentant.'*

I laughed out loud remembering that, and then I had another of those whisky and soda moments, because if I tried, if I really tried, I could hear Dad laughing, not in memory, but right along with me.

Hi, Dollface.

Hello, Charlie. How are things this week?

You've invaded my dreams, Dollface.

Me?

Swans. Big black hissing swans. The nightmare as usual, except that before Dad goes over the side, I hear hissing coming closer and closer out of the darkness, hundreds of hisses closing in on the boat. Then I see tall narrow black shapes writhing against the night sky. Snakes, I think, hundreds of them, standing on their tails in the water, hissing and writhing and churning up the lake. Then the air is filled with the beating of giant wings, and I see they're not snakes, they're swans unfolding their wings, rearing up on the surface of the lake and clapping their big wings so hard, the wind knocks me back on to my bench. Dad puts out his hands to ward them off and he falls right into that hissing mass. I search in the water for him, but the swans loop

69

their necks around my arms and their feathers brush my face and their slimy webbed feet drum against my hands...

Stop! That's terrible. Charlie, I am sorry. I never meant for that to happen.

Sorry for what? It's my nightmare.

I should never have mentioned the swans and the hissing.

Don't be daft.

But you told me the swans made you scream. I should have dropped the subject there and then.

It was only a dream.

Yes, of a childhood fear. You see? I sparked it off by touching on an old fear.

No, it's not a memory. This is my fear of loss dream. Remember?

It's both. That row boat and the black lake mean something. An old loss? An old fear? Your mother? That's how dreams work.

I don't think dreams mean anything very much, Dollface. Dreams are the place where we get to run safely insane.

They come from childhood.

I don't know...brb

There was a stirring from the bed and a low moaning. I was across the room in two strides. Occasionally Dad surfaced for a while, sometimes because his morphine drip needed adjusting, sometimes for no reason. He never recognised me, but there was always the chance. I checked the drip, ready to ring for the nurse to come upstairs if he needed her, but everything was fine.

"OK, Dad?"

A murmur, a low rush of exhaled breath, "Challiechallie…"

Challie. My baby name. My eyes filled and I turned back to the computer.

Dollface, I think Dad's asking for me. Have to run.

He was moving his head feebly, his breath coming through his lips like the rustle of dead leaves. Challiechallie…

"I'm here, Dad."

He neither saw nor heard me. I sat by his bed, disappointed. He was still again, austere and dignified, his face lined and seamed like an Indian statue's. Well, he'd spared me Dollface's dream analysis at least. I didn't need it because I'd worked it all out for myself years before.

My mother shaped the lives of Dad and me. Everything we are, everything that happened or didn't happen, was down to her. The summer she left, I was so afraid that Dad too would go out the door and never come back, that I wouldn't let him out of my sight. In the mornings, I clung to his legs when he was leaving for work, screaming till the street echoed; at night, I kept him awake with my noisy screaming nightmares. In the end, he gave in and took me with him when he went out to the building sites. I spent my time avoiding holes full of creepy crawlies and hating the smell of new turned earth; I built little houses with broken bricks and bits of planking to hide in if the excavators came near. Dad told me often that he could forgive my mother everything except that hellish summer and the state she left me in. *'But I got you through it, son, eh?'* And so he did.

He didn't come out of it so well. Never again in his life did he have a solid relationship with a woman. *Trust's gone*, he used to say and it made him difficult, which he was the first to admit. I lost count of the number of bouquets Interflora delivered on his behalf as an apology for loss of temper, unreasonable jealousy, a sudden slap. But it has to be said, some of them went out of their way to provoke him.

He explained to them all how difficult it was for him to trust –I've seen him cry as he explained – but they didn't listen and carried on in their own sweet way. They went on their girls' nights out and came home drunk and giggling and later than they said they would; they spent his money and lied about it; they practised all kinds of cheap manipulations to keep him sweet; and the consequence was that they forced him into acting in a way that was different from who he really was. There would have been no trouble if they'd just gone along with the ground rules, but it was as if they enjoyed getting him going.

The last one in residence finished him with housemates for good. She took delivery of an 'I'm sorry' bouquet, stuck it in the bin, and had the police supervise the removal of her belongings from the premises. *'As if,'* Dad said after, still pale from the police visit, *'I'd have tried to stop the silly tart leaving.'*

There was never another one after her and I was glad. But one good thing came out of it all: I knew every trick in the female book by the time I was sixteen, and I never fell for a single one as I grew older. The only woman I ever *really* talked to was Dollface.

I needed her, irritating as her preaching could be. The summer Dad was dying, I went through a phase of thinking I was going mad. That time I heard Dad laughing with me – it wasn't the last time. As I remembered at his bedside, I *heard* him chuckle to frighten the ghouls and nightmares away, and I *felt* his rough stubble against my little boy cheek – *Daddy, will my face be scratchy like yours when I'm big?* – as he scooped me up in his arms and hugged me; a split second later, I was older and listening to him in the pub when his latest affair had gone wrong – *I'm a bad picker, son, always have been. Only good thing I ever got from a woman was you* – and I had a big lump in my throat because it never occurred to Dad that it wasn't his picking that was bad; it was just that there wasn't much to pick from.

I chatted to his bed, sometimes aloud, sometimes in my head, saying the things I wished I'd said at the time. The trouble was, he often answered, only in my head, but it felt real, as real as the cane chair I sat upon and the snowy sheets he lay between. I heard him.

Dollface, I think I'm going mad

Why's that, Charlie?

And I told her all about the silence in the white room and how it pressed on me and squeezed the past out of my brain like toothpaste, and how I was never sure what and if and when I was hearing.

See, Dollface? I'm going mad.

No, you're not, Charlie. You're only taking on Death.

Come again?

Remembering everything. Replaying it all so that you can record it. All the good times. All the times you were close. This way he'll live on in your head. You should try and remember more, not less.

You're talking as if I'd forget him if I didn't try to remember.

No, you'll never forget him.

Dollface, my head's flooding so full with the past, it's nearly bursting. And I can't stand it because soon he'll disappear into a black void.

He won't disappear, Charlie. Nobody does completely, although some are harder to get in touch with than others. But they're always in your head somewhere if you let them be. Long after they're gone, they're there.

I don't understand what you're telling me.

You will. Let yourself remember.

How come you know so much about this remembering?

I've lost people. I know what helps. Memories are slippery things unless you pin them down with words. Give your memories words.

Dollface, I never heard so much garbage in all my life.

You'll see.

Sorry I said that.

No, you think you're right.

Yes. But I'm sorry if I offended.

You didn't. How could you?

Why are you so patient?

A troubled spirit with no one to talk to.

Are you, Dollface?

No, you are.

Who do you talk to, Dollface?

You.

Is there no one else?

No.

You don't take your own advice then?

About what?

Partner, family.

I was married once. I had a child.

Had?

The marriage ended. I lost my boy.

Then I really did feel guilty. All this time chatting and she'd never mentioned that.

What happened?

Death did. The how doesn't matter. Death is always the same: a temporary separation.

And you spend your time remembering him?

What else? I like to think of him being safe, being all right.

What was I supposed to say to that? 'Dollface, he's dead. He doesn't need safe or all right any more – he's beyond that.' From far away, I heard Dad's voice, teasing in that faintly malicious way he had *'See these intellectual spiritual types you go for, son? The whole pack of them rolled together wouldn't make one decent lay.'*

Charlie? You there? I suppose you think I'm mad.

No, not at all.

Being polite doesn't suit you, Charlie.

OK, Dollface. You're just this side of mad, in the nicest possible way. To paraphrase, you're taking on Death in your own way. If it works – fine.

When you have a child, it's for life. For beyond life.

I must have been delivered without the instruction manual. I got dumped like the pup bought for Christmas.

She must have been a very strange woman.

Well, she wasn't like you, Dollface.

'Challie…Challie'

Dad's coming round. Better go.

OK, Charlie. See you next week.

Dad was restless again. His hands felt cold. The sun was streaming in the window in a big golden shaft right across his bed, but his hands were like ice. I turned the central heating on full, afraid suddenly that the cold meant a change coming, an ending.

"Dad?"

His head moved from side to side, a feeble 'no, no' gesture that tore at my guts. His fingers plucked feebly at the bedclothes.

"Tray-sa. *NO!*"

Theresa. My mother's name. I felt a spurt of rage. I had no idea what filled my Dad's mind in his coma, but if she was part of it, it was no good. I thought of him lying there helpless while memories crowded into his skull the way they did into mine, making him miserable, even on his deathbed, and I couldn't bear it. I sat on the edge of the bed and cradled his head gently – "Dad, Dad, remember the good things…only the good things…me and you and the football season and the summers in Scarborough…that homemade chocolate shop. Remember the violet creams? We ate them by the kilo...."

I don't know if he heard, but he relaxed suddenly, and when I held his hands, they were warm again and the fingers curled snugly into mine like a baby's. We sat like that for a long time, till I got cramped and moved back into my chair. I took my sweatshirt off, the room was so hot…

Charlie rows and rows. There's no light and no way to tell direction. Dad is silent in the stern, his head turned away, peering behind the boat as if there were some difference between the blackness behind and the blackness ahead. Charlie keeps on rowing. Then with a clenching fear, he hears the hissing again, long and steady and closing in…he rows frantically. Outrun them, he must outrun the snakey swans. He looks wildly round but he can't see where they are in the darkness. The hissing is a sibilant clamour, smotheringly close to his ear, fierce jets of steam spitting out of soft black feathers. Dad is looking at Charlie now, right at him. He lifts his arm and points ahead. Charlie turns and in the distance sees a thin pale blue line leap across the sky. Suddenly the water is below and the sky above, where they should be. The blue deepens and spreads higher up, trailing a rosy veil behind it and forcing the blackness out of the way. The sun is rising. Charlie glances round. The swans are there, hissing, jostling to get near the boat, grey outlines tinged with pink, then grey-white touched with rose. They are too close, too clamorous. He doesn't like the big snakey swans spitting at him. He closes his eyes and screams till the echoes hurt his ears…then he is scooped up into the air, high

76

above the hissing. An arm holds him close, a hand rubs gently at his back. He buries his face in hair soft as feathers and huddles in close. She smells like flowers. When he looks down, the boat is a hundred miles below, tiny, empty, drifting, and a voice is lilting in his ear:
    "Challie is my darlin', my darlin', my darlin'
    Challie is my darlin', the Young Chevalier"

When I woke up, the room smelled sweet. It was a light clean scent, lily-of-the-valley, gardenia, something like that.

No, Charlie, you didn't make it up. That's a Scottish song. About Bonnie Prince Charlie.

I've never heard it before.

You must have, or you wouldn't know the words. Maybe when you were small.

It's a right rumpty-tumpty tune anyway.

Yes, it is. They used to play it on TV along with the test card. A Highland mountain scene. Just before the children's programmes. All the children used to sing it.

Maybe I heard it then. I'm surprised you admit to remembering it, you being so much younger than me.

Oops! But, then, I am ageless.

Lol. OK, Doll. You're ageless. I can't get that tune out of my head.

Why worry about it? It was a nicer dream than usual, apart from rumpty-tumpty music. You were rescued.

I didn't tell her about the perfume, how it cooled the room and stilled the air, and that somehow it upset me more than the rancid rot I usually woke to.

77

So what does the rescue mean, Madame Dream Diviner?

That there's light on the horizon. That things will work out all right in the end. Blue is the colour of hope.

You made that up to make me feel better.

No. Blue comes with dawn and drives away the night. It's spring and summer and it's water that makes things grow. It's the chink of light through the curtains after a bad night.

OK, I feel better. If you make me feel any better, I'll combust spontaneously right here in front of you.

Very funny.

How'd you get over the loss of your boy, Dollface?

I didn't. I never lost him because he's in my mind all the time. I have valuable memories. I see him and hear him whenever I want.

You're madder than I am.

One day you'll understand.

When we're in adjoining padded cells?

Challie, you're such a darlin' sometimes…

That rumpty-tumpty tune rollicked round my head hour after hour. When I sat with Dad and the memories activated, it got in the way. He and I would be talking, or I was imagining we were talking, or remembering him talking in the past – I don't know, whatever it was that kept happening in that room – and that daft song would erupt in my mind, drowning out what he was saying. It shrieked away the pictures, too, of me and Dad and the places we went and the things we did. And the more I tried to hear him and see him, the louder it got and the faster it got, till my head spun with a jangling discord and ached from a sweet drifting scent.

78

One time, I was remembering *Witchfinder General*. I could hear Dad laughing at the plunging necklines and heaving bosoms belonging to all the daft trollops who went prowling round creepy places in their nighties in the dark, holding candlesticks aloft to light the way. We knew, just knew, they were going to run into the vampire or the ghost or the gang of drunken troopers. There was always one, with an awesome bosom but not so pretty as the heroine, who came to a bad end through night-wanderings in her bare feet. Dad and I used to try and spot her before it happened – *Look for the one with the biggest boobs and the slight cast in her eye because she's the one who's not going to be rescued* – and if I spotted her first he gave me a Mars Bar...

OH, CHALLIE IS MY DARLIN'...

'Women were women in those days, eh, son?' He said it every Friday night at some point. Once I remember chirping, *'Daddy, why does ladies have different chests from men's?'* and he said, *'To please the men, son'.* I tried to remember his chuckling laugh, but I couldn't hear for the explosion of song in my mind – *Challie is my darlin', my darlin', my darlin'* – raucous and bold and thumpingly loud. I was furious. *'Daddy, why does ladies have...'*

MY DARLIN', MY DARLIN', CHALLIE IS MY DARLIN'...

"SHUT UP!"

It was Dad, in the voice that meant he was rowing with the current woman of the house. I actually jumped. And then there was blissful silence in my head. Dad looked peaceful, pale as his pillowcase, and I wondered dreamily which woman he was remembering. You'd think they'd leave him in peace on his deathbed...

Mummy is in the kitchen making soup. She shuts the door behind her, but Charlie can still hear the big soup pot clattering on the cooker. He is sitting under the table in the living room, playing with his boat. The sails are bright blue. 'Like your eyes' she said in the shop, when he couldn't decide between the blue sails and the red. He hears the key in the lock. 'Daddy! Daddy!'

'Where's my wee man?'

Peekaboo from under the tablecloth.

'Come out, come out, wherever you are!' Big laughing voice. Big laughing man. 'I'm coming to get you!'

Cupboards opened, sideboard drawers, the hearthrug lifted. Peekaboo.

'Oh, where's my wee Charlie? Is he lost?'

Daddy cries into his big white hankie. Charlie crawls out.

'No, I'm here, Daddy. Here.'

Up in the air. Toss. Catch. Toss. Catch. Toss – falling, falling – Catch!

'God, I nearly dropped you there, son!'

Huge sighs of relief. Big hugs. Giggle. Giggle. Daddy never drops him. Up in the air Charlie goes, round he swings, slaps the lightshade twice, sends the shadows darting round the walls. Daddy slumps into his armchair, sits Charlie on his knee.

'And what did my wee man do today? I phoned and there was no one home'

'We went to the park.'

'On an icy day like today?'

'Yes.'

Charlie waits expectantly. Daddy jangles coins in his pocket: the memory game. He puts pennies in a row on the arm of his chair. And a whole sixpence. Charlie wriggles with excitement.

'Let's see if your memory is growing as big as the rest of you. The beginning?'

'Breakfast. I ate up all my cornflakes and toast. Mummy burnt two slices.'

Pause. A penny from the chair to Charlie's hand.

'Mummy washed the dishes. I dried them. She says I'm a clever boy.'

Another penny.

'And Mummy dusted and hoovered. I helped.'

Another penny.

'Then we went to the shops for the messages.'

No penny. Charlie frowns, remembering. 'We got a loaf. And eggs. And strawberry jam.'

A penny.

'And how did you come to be in the park, Charlie? That's a funny

place to go on a snowy day.'

'The butcher didn't have any ham bones for the soup. So we went to Gispie's.'

'Gispies? Where's that?'

'Beside the park. The big butcher shop with the board with the picture of the cows on it.'

'Oh, Gillespie's.'

Daddy takes a penny back. 'Tsk! Tsk! You didn't remember that one right, Charlie.'

'And I saw a boat in the paper shop. And Mummy let me have it.'

'To sail in the park?'

'No! Silly Daddy! The pond is frozed. It's for my bath.'

'So what made you go into the park?'

'Mrs. Cameron. She was in Gillespie's as well. She said the pond was frozed and the birds were starving.'

Two pennies surprise Charlie. Mrs. Cameron isn't a two penny memory. Even he knows that. Daddy laughs. 'You said Gillespie right this time, son.'

Charlie whoops. Two pennies.

'Was it Mummy's idea to go to the park?'

Charlie shakes his head. 'No, I wanted to feed the birds. They was hungry. We had a big loaf.'

'And did she talk to anyone in the park?'

'Just me.' The sixpence on the arm of the chair is bright and shiny. A new one. Charlie wants that sixpence and remembers hard. 'She said afternoon to a man with a doggie.'

'Did they talk long?'

'No. He said afternoon, then she said it, and he throwed a stick for the doggie and went away.'

A long silence. Then Charlie smiles. 'But she was talking a long time to the man in the paper shop. They was laughing and smiling, Daddy. Lots.'

A sixpenny memory.

Charlie scrambles off Daddy's knee – 'Remember, Charlie, don't tell Mum about all your pennies. She wouldn't like you having all that money – and runs to his room. His piggy bank is nearly full. He has to cram his sixpence and his pennies in.

Something's hissing in the background. The soup boiling.

I had to get the doctor in that week. Dad's breathing was heavier. He checked him over, and said it was only to be expected: he was weakening, but wasn't in any pain. He kept looking at me. "You don't look so good yourself," he said. "Mustn't get ill." He mentioned the hospice again, not very hopefully because he knew my feelings on the subject. Later I looked at myself in the dressing table mirror – black shadows hooped my eyes and my skin had a greyish tinge: too much time in the bedroom, too many hours in the site offices, too many bad dreams.

You have to take better care of yourself, Charlie. It won't help your father if you get ill too.

Dollface had lots of suggestions: fewer takeaway meals (she was forever banging on about healthy food); early to bed and not so many nightcaps; walks in the fresh air; maybe a night out and some company, just now and again, to liven me up. In the beginning, her fussing had irritated me, but lately I had encouraged it, hinting at feeling seedy, being tired, all that. Childish. But it's a need, isn't it? To be cared for? To have someone bother about you? And no matter how vividly I relived Dad, he couldn't help me there.

How about nightmares, Charlie?

None this week. Just an odd dream.

I told her about the memory game.

Your fault, Doll, talking about valuable memories. I dreamed mine were worth a penny a go.

They're worth much more than that. This is a piece of your nightmare, Charlie. Your blue boat is in it. The one the swan attacked. You told me about it weeks ago.

I remember.

It must have been your mother who rescued you that day.

Dunno.

And maybe it's your mother who rescued you in the nightmare. The one who lifted you away from the swans.

Which mother? I had a fair few. Remember?

What did she look like? Your own mother? Like the woman in the dream?

I don't remember.

Try.

I didn't actually SEE her. I only talked about her.

Memories are breaking through, Charlie.

I didn't answer. She was always on about dreams and memories and my mother. Thought it was therapeutic for me. And it was mostly, except for my mother. I had no more interest in her than she had in me.

Charlie?

Here.

I was remembering something my Mum taught me. When you close your eyes to sleep, if you think very hard about something, that's what you'll dream about. Maybe you could dream your mother.

Dollface!

Wouldn't you like to see her face? Just once?

I have enough nightmares.

She's something in your life that you avoid facing. For good or ill, you ought to. Maybe there are things you don't understand.

Dollface, will you drop it?

I was thinking about the memory game. Such an odd game for a little boy, don't you think?

There was no memory game. It's just a nightmare.

It sounded real too.

I logged off then, didn't even say goodbye. "This is what happens when you tell people things about yourself," I said to Dad as I sat down by the bed. "Think they know better than you about your own life. Think they have a right to comment."

He lay white as an effigy on a tomb, and as silent. But I knew he would understand my anger – he had never liked interference in his own life. The last of his ladies had tried to cut down on his nights out, the number of pints consumed, the hours spent unaccounted for. *'Bloody women. They can never let you be. You're all that's wonderful until she moves in, then you can never be fine as you are again. It's called Lurv…'*

CHALLIE IS MY DARLIN', MY DARLIN' MY DARLIN'

Will you SHUT THE FUCK UP!

Charlie crawls behind the sofa. He wishes Mummy was good, then Daddy wouldn't shout, but she's bad. She makes men look. Charlie knows that's bad, and he got a penny for telling about the man whistling. He peeps out. She's going to get a smack because she's answering back. That's naughty. She's got her back to him and he can't see her face, but her shoulders are scrunched up. She's rubbing at red marks on her arms.
'But Tommy, I was only going to the shops. It was just some daft boy passing on a bike…'
'SHUT UP! I KNOW YOU, TRAY-SA! CHRIST, I KNOW YOU!'
'Tommy…'
Slap!
Charlie closes his eyes. He doesn't want to see, but he can hear her crying. 'Tommy! Tommy!' She's on the floor, rolling about, trying to

get away. Daddy stamps hard. She mews like a cat.

I woke up sweating and shivering. The room was icy. I phoned the Gas Board to come out – *I've got an invalid here, a man's dying, and I don't care if it's Sunday get somebody out here to fix the heating* – and I went downstairs and waited. It was Gary the Gasman again. Gaz the Gas he called himself. His little joke. Third visit in six weeks.

"Afternoon, Mr. McCallum. Same old problem?"

I nodded. He went up to the room, tiptoed in out of respect for my father, fiddled about with the radiator.

"Seems all right now," he said. His tone was neutral, shading towards sympathetic. I couldn't stand it.

"It wasn't an hour ago. The room was freezing."

His turn to nod. "Want me to have a look at the boiler? Bleed the radiators? Maybe there's an air bubble."

We both knew there was no point, but I said yes, and he shambled off downstairs to the utility room. He banged about willingly enough. I made him coffee and put out the biscuits. He asked after my Dad very kindly. I answered. He typed out a report on his laptop which said there was nothing to report, and left. "Call us any time, Mr. McCallum. We'll get to the bottom of this one day."

I took my time washing up the cups and sweeping crumbs from the table and decided not to go upstairs for a while yet. I might fall asleep and dream. I might stay awake and remember. That was the trouble, you see. I didn't know whether I was dreaming or remembering.

The nurse had the afternoon off, and so I had downstairs to myself. I couldn't help thinking about the dream. The stamping. The crunching bone. It never happened, so why did it feel so real? The house. The house it happened in – that couldn't be real. I'd have remembered that wallpaper round the fireplace. Christ, no one *could* forget that wallpaper! Purple with big sweetie pink, white centred flowers. The stuff of nightmare. And that narrow coffee table with the out angled legs and the black plastic gold striped trim, and a glass top over a pink flower! Nightmare. Silly. Daft. I'd never been in a place like that. *So why did it feel familiar?*

I was beginning to see an answer, but I didn't have to think about it for long because the phone rang, shrill and shriller.

SHUT THE FUCK UP! SHUT UP! SHUT UP!

Dad's voice. Now what's he so angry about? Phones don't bother him, only bad Mummies. Rumpty-tumpty thought skidding about in my skull. Nothing to be mad about, Daddy. Only the phone ringing.

'Oh, quick, Challie. Daddy's on the phone.' Challie scampers up the stairs at the front of the house. One. Two. Three. Four. Mummy's hands are thick with bandages. She can't get the key in the lock. The phone is ringing, loud and angry. Challie can't reach the key. Too high, so she lifts him up and bangs his knee against the door. The key is stiff and he struggles to turn it. In his ear, her breathing's quick and fast. She smells like flowers. 'Quick, Challie. Quick.' It turns. She puts Challie down and runs for the phone, but Challie gets there first. 'Hello, Daddy.'
   'Yes, I've been a good boy today.'
   'We was at the shops. To buy some pills. Mummy's hands is sore'.
   'We heard the phone. We was outside. Mummy couldn't turn the key. I did it.'
   'Yes, I'm a very strong boy.'

CHALLIE IS MY DARLIN', MY DARLIN', MY DARLIN'

SHUT UP! SHUT THE FUCK UP!

Daddy closes the book and Challie settles back on his pillow. Dreamily he watches shadows drowsing in the corner. Daddy doesn't tuck him up and say goodnight. He sits looking sad.
   'Was Mummy complaining about her hands?'
   'She said they was sore. She says you don't mean it.'
   'That's right. She makes me angry. She's not good like you.'
   Daddy's voice is deep and gruff and Challie can't hear right. He looks at Daddy and his heart stops. Daddy's crying big fat tears. 'Ah, son, you don't know how she hurts me. You don't know how bad a woman can make you feel inside. I don't want to hurt her. I'm good to that woman. You know I am. But she doesn't know what love is. She makes me do things...'
   Dad sobs. Challie can't stand it. He scrambles out from under his blankets and hurls himself at Daddy, crying and kissing better. 'I love you, Daddy.'

'I know, wee man. I don't know what I'd do without you. Will I give Mummy a surprise?' Challie nods. *'See, son, she thinks the living room is old fashioned. How about we get her that stuff she thinks is groovy?'*

Challie nods. If Mummy is happy, maybe she'll be good.

Daddy dries his eyes. 'So, when you went to the shops today, did you meet anyone on the way?'

The phone rang louder, as if it was shouting my name. There was no one on the other end of the line. Just the engaged tone. I slammed the receiver down. My head was jangling with voices and songs.

Daddy's smiling. Mummy loves her new curtains. Sweetie pink to go with the wallpaper.

'Floor length, for the big bay windows. Just like in the magazine, Challie.. And that wallpaper – it's the very latest. Your Dad's going to paint the doors white. The heavy varnish makes these old houses seem dark.'

She bends down to kiss him, smelling like flowers. She has big white hoops in her ears, and she has eyelashes and little freckles on her cheeks. 'Like Twiggy, Challie. See?' she said when she was painting them on. She looks just like Twiggy in the magazine. Big, big eyes and hair like little bird feathers. But Twiggy's hands aren't all bandaged up.

'He's going to get started this weekend. The doors first. This time next week we'll be living in a new world.'

Charlie helps. He has a little brush in his paint box and Daddy lets him paint round the door handles. Thick shiny paint and a strong smell that makes his head ache and his nose run. Open the windows, Daddy. Charlie hangs out the window, watches grey clouds tumbling snow on to the rooftops, sniffs the sharp clean smell of cold.

The phone screamed at me. Engaged again. I didn't hang up. Better the engaged signal than those pink curtains. I couldn't stand thinking about them: they made me angry; they made me feel sick. I listened to the phone instead. Whistles and clicks and a shrill whine. And somewhere in the whistles, a rumpty-tumpty tune. Not the engaged signal, definitely not the engaged signal. How could it be? It was the static you get when someone in the house is on-line. DAD!

I took the stairs two at a time and burst into the bedroom. His eyelids were curved closed like shells and the room was cool and still and piercingly sweet: lily-of-the-valley, gardenia…like that. I could have cried. The computer was on, a bright eye, unblinking, staring at me from the corner. My name was at the top of the private room along with Dollface's.

How did you get in here, Dollface?

Sorry, Charlie?

I logged off.

No, you were here all the time…showing on-line. I thought you had gone to see to your father. Or that you'd fallen asleep and had a nightmare. Thought I'd better wait for you to come back.

It's been nearly two hours.

Has it? I didn't notice. I was worried about you.

Thanks. Sorry. I thought I'd shut down.

What else could I say? I knew I'd shut down, I knew I had, but I couldn't be sure.

It doesn't matter, Challie.

Sorry.

It's all right. I don't mind. Is your father OK?

He's fine. No change.

Two hours. Nobody waits two hours.

I've forgotten what we were talking about, Challie.

So have I. Probably me as usual.

88

I know what it was – I was saying you could dream up your mother.

No, Dollface. No more today. Talk about you. Tell me about you. Tell me anything.

What?

Your marriage. Did it break up after you lost your son? Or before?

They happened at the same moment. What an odd question.

Together? What an odd answer.

I really don't like to talk about it, Challie. It's very painful.

I tell you painful things.

Yes, but some things are too painful. Your mother. My son. You understand, Challie.

What went wrong with your marriage?

That's old, old history.

Too painful?

Not now.

Tell me about it then.

It was nothing unusual.

Tell me.

It was a mistake from the start, Challie. He was much older than me. 35.

How old were you?

Just turned sixteen.

That's young.

Too young.

I played her trick and left the screen blank for long minutes.

Challie? Are you there?

Yes. I was waiting for the rest.

What rest?

Why it was a mistake from the start.

Long minutes. An acre of screen to be filled, Dollface resisting. And then

He pushed me into it. He was so SURE. And I wasn't sure of anything. Young girls never are. I was supposed to be going to university, but he didn't want that. Said it would waste too many years that we could have together. 'Gather ye rosebuds while ye may' he said.

'Old Time is still a-flying'?

You know it? It's by Herrick.

It's a favourite of my father's. Only poem he knows.

It's a favourite with a lot of people. It makes sense. That's why I nag you. You mustn't leave it too late to live, the way I did.

You lived too soon by the sounds of it.

I didn't live at all. Not with him. He lived for both of us.

You left him, didn't you?

90

Long minutes. An acre of screen. What was I expecting? "Yes, Challie boy, I did. I went to Welsh Wales and then years later, you'll never believe it, I met up with my longlost son in a chatroom. Fate. Kismet. All that."

I don't know what I was expecting. Something. Some connection. I thought she wasn't going to answer at all but

No, I never got the chance.

?

He left me all alone.

From the corner of my eye, I saw Dad lift a hand: "Challie Challie" in that dry gasping voice, then a sudden sharp, "No, Tray-sa! NO!"

Dollface, Dad's waking up again. I have to go.

No, wait. I want

Later. OK? I'll come back soon.

I shut down and checked I had done it right this time.

Dad was motionless in the bed, apart from a fluttering side to side movement under paper thin eyelids. I could almost see the fierce gleam of grey eyes through those lids. His hand had flopped back on to the quilt.

"Don't think about her, Dad. Past is past and past fretting over."

Somehow I knew he was distressed. I rubbed his hands, warming them between mine. "Remember that time we were on the site in Manchester and I fell in the big crater? That was funny. I was floundering about in the water, screaming. 'Dad! Dad! I can't swim!' And I'm flailing my arms and legs and spouting water like a whale and you're stood laughing at the edge of the pit. 'Dad, I'm drowning! Help!'

And you shout, 'Well stand up, you silly bugger!' And I did. And the water didn't even cover the top of my wellies.

91

I rubbed his hands some more, chortling. I hadn't thought about that day in years.

Stale water tasting like iron filings in Charlie's mouth, running into his eyes and ears. And a tightness in his chest, a horrible clenching pain. Can't breathe. Can't. Gasping. Wheezing. Dad jumps in the water beside him. 'All right, son. It's all right' and he hands Charlie up to one of the navvies and comes scrambling out after him. Hospital. Can't breathe. 'Does your son suffer from asthma, Mr. McCallum?'

A panic attack. There'd been a few of those over the years. That was one of the more spectacular ones. Dad always blamed her for them. *See, son. There's nothing wrong with you. You're not going to die or stop breathing. This is emotional. Your mother leaving – you were too young. That's what's caused it. You have to forget her, forget...*

A long scream of pain that swings into tune

CHALLIE IS MY DARLIN', MY DARLIN', MY DARLIN'

thumpingly loud, discordant, then softer, softer, lilting soft

'Challie is my darlin', my darlin', my darlin'
Challie is my darlin', my young Chevalier.
'Twas on a Sunday mornin', quite early in the year,
That Challie came to our town, the young Chevalier...'

'Is that song about me, Mummy?'
'You're the only Challie I know, aren't you?' A forefinger unfolds stiffly from under the bandages and touches the tip of his nose. Charlie laughs into her baby blue eyes. They are in the café, but they have to hurry. Daddy comes home for lunch because he's working nearby in the park up the road. A new pond to be dug. A great big one. So he pops in and out of the house all day: for lunch, for a cuppa, to do a bit more painting and papering to help Mummy be happy. He doesn't like to come home to an empty house.

'Challie, you've not finished your ice cream. I have a wee message to go. Just across the road. If I leave you for a minute, will you sit here like a good boy?'

92

Charlie nods.

'What are you going for?'

'Oh, a comic if you're good.'

Charlie sits at the window table, a good wee boy, licking his spoon. He watches her carefully for his Daddy. He likes the way the winter sun shows the warm red in her hair. She goes into the big train station. She doesn't stay long. She comes running back over the road, her big earrings tossing, her black fun fur flapping behind her.

'Where's my comic, Mummy?'

'Oh, Challie. They didn't have any left.' He knows she's telling fibs. Her face is red. She's biting her lip. 'We'll get one tomorrow.' Challie is so angry, he doesn't speak to her all the way home.

I surfaced from that long walk home with my head pounding. I was still holding Dad's hands. I had that feeling you get when you know someone is staring at you. I knew who it was before I turned to look. Sure enough, the monitor was lit up, quietly waiting, quietly demanding.

There's no way to tell who's at the other end of these messages, son.

"You're so right, Dad."

I pulled the plug on the pc, right out of the socket, and the screen turned ashy grey. I half believed it wouldn't, but it did, and I was relieved. I didn't understand what was going on, but I knew I had to stop it. I don't know why I thought cutting off the electricity would. I could silence her, but the past still rolled in like high tide. It rolled in before I even got back to my chair.

Mummy's humming, putting things in suitcases. His pyjamas. And his blue and white sloppy joe. His sandals. He watches from the doorway.

'Hello, Challie.'

She straightens up with his vests in her hand. She stops humming and her face is red.

'Challie. Can you keep a secret?'

Charlie nods. 'It's a surprise for Daddy. A wee holiday.' She folds the vests into the case. 'Yes, a wee holiday. After all his hard work decorating.' His socks go in next, his favourite stripey ones. 'Now, you're not to say anything, It's a BIG secret.'

She's humming again – 'Challie is my darlin' – and she's smiling but her eyes are sad.

The scene vanished like morning mist, although her humming hung on the air for a moment. Dad's hand tightened on mine. *See when a woman gets hot pants for somebody, son? There's no stopping them. Nothing gets in their road – not even their own wee boy.*

But she was packing my things.

See, son, a kiddie just gets in the way. The new man doesn't like the reminder that she's used goods. You're better off with your Daddy.

She was going to take me with her.

And then I felt sick, churning sick. She started humming again and I turned that cold sweaty way you do before you throw up. I sat down and I spoke out loud, not to Dad, but to her. "I don't want to know. I really don't want to know." She hummed more loudly.

CHALLIE IS MY DARLIN', MY DARLIN', MY DARLIN'

The sky is black and the water is black. The air is thick with hissing and the soft ruffling of feathers. Charlie rows desperately to get away, to leave the swans behind. He's worried about Dad: his head is lolling on his chest; he is tiring. The hissing comes closer. Charlie feels rushes of foul sour air on the back of his neck. The boat begins to rock violently from side to side. On a tideless windless lake it rocks. Dad staggers to his feet and falls back on to the bench again. The boat tilts, and he's falling soundlessly over the side, twisting slowly round to get one last look at Charlie. The hood falls back. The face is small and white enough to glimmer through the dark, the eyes are big, the hair like birds' feathers. There are big white hoops at her ears and tears sliding down her cheeks.
   'Oh, Challie! Oh, Challie!
   Such terror. Such longing.
   And then she's slipping under the black water...

I wake up. The room is cold. The fire is out. I look round by the dim light from the hall. The big pink flowers are like faces laughing at me.

I am looking for Daddy because he isn't in the bedroom and Mummy is fast asleep all by herself. But Daddy isn't here either. Then I hear footsteps on the gravel outside. I trot to the window, stand on tiptoe. The paint is still sticky. Daddy is putting something in the back of the van. It's Mummy's big suitcase. Funny. She's not to go on holiday. He shouted at her after tea when he emptied her handbag on the table. He waved little papers at her. *Two tickets! To Perth! Running away to your auntie? And taking my boy with you? You're going nowhere, doll. Nowhere at all.*

Daddy crunches back up the path to the house. I hide behind the sofa. I'm not allowed to wander about the house at night. I might fall downstairs. He comes into the living room, a tall wide shadow in the moonlight. He lifts Mummy's curtains, the new pink ones, from the sideboard, and takes them away upstairs. He leaves the door open. I shiver behind the sofa. It's cold. It's more than cold. The house feels funny. Too quiet. Too hushed. Not right. I shiver and shiver. Then Daddy comes downstairs slowly, heavily. He passes the door. The curtains are rolled up over his shoulder, a big bundle dangling down his front and back. I see bright hair flopping out of the end down his back. Mummy. She's stopped mewing now. That's good. She's not sore any more. Daddy goes out to the van and I run upstairs and jump into bed.

My piggie bank is by my bed. It was too full for the new pennies and the half a crown I got, so they are lying beside it on the table. Daddy's going to buy me a new bank on Saturday.

I wake up early in the morning. It's still grey outside, dull and grey. "Daddy! Daddy!"

He comes right away. He's got his clothes on already.

"Challie! It's early. Go back to sleep."

"I waked up. Where are you going?"

"To the site. I've got some rubbish to dump. I'll sneak in early and shove it in a hole. We're laying the stone base for the pond today. That'll cover it up. Saves me going all the way to the dump." He puts a finger to his lips. He's smiling. I don't like that smile. "It's a secret." And he winks.

"I'm hungry."

He thumps away downstairs and brings me a biscuit and a mug of milk. "That'll tide you over till Mummy gets up. Now, you leave her in peace until I get back. No crawling in beside her. She was awful tired last night. And she has a headache." I'm puzzled, but already Mummy wrapped in curtains is becoming a dream. She's in her bed with a sore head and I'm not to wake her.

She ran away to Wales while he was out. He came back to find her gone away with the boyfriend he'd suspected all along.

I closed my eyes, too tired to take it in. I didn't want to stay there in that house, but I didn't know how to get back home. After a while, the room began to warm up, and then I smelled the rubbing alcohol the nurse used against bedsores. I opened my eyes. Dad was in bed and the Lucozade was on his table and the sun was shining in the window. It didn't feel like safe home, end of nightmare.

She was in the room with us, waiting. I knew what I would see when I looked over at the computer. The plug was out of the socket, but the monitor was glowing anyway. I went over and sat at the desk. I didn't want to, but I couldn't not go.

Challie! There you are. I've been so worried.

Hi, Dollface.

So what's been happening?

I think you know.

Long minutes. Acres of screen waiting to be filled. Both of us resisting.

Challie, how could you think I'd ever have left you?

Long minutes.

Challie, it wasn't your fault. You were only a wee boy.

Long minutes.

Challie, he was too clever for both of us.

96

Long minutes. I couldn't think of anything to say. Then I was angry.

Why'd you come back? After all this time? Why let me know all this now? Why spoil everything?

Challie, I was dying of being forgotten. You never kept me in your head. I couldn't get near you. He was too strong for me.

Until now. When he's dying.

Yes.

You should have let him die in peace.

Why? I have no peace. Never any peace. Not in life and not in death. I lost my little boy. I've missed you.

I didn't miss you.

Oh, but you did, Challie. All your life. You're a sour man because you missed me.

And knowing all this will make me sweet? You're mad. You're fucking mad.

Don't speak to me like that, Challie. You sound like your father.

I'd rather not speak to you at all.

That's cruel, Challie.

Sorry, Dollface. What shall we talk about? The night you died? Did he kick your head in or strangle you or what? Or maybe you'd rather tell about what it feels like being under a pond with the stone holding you down and the foul water lapping round you?

You already know what it's like, Challie. All your nightmares. That's what it's like.

97

Look, I don't see the point of this. You've only made things worse.

You need new memories. That's why I've come. And I have the right, Challie. After everything, I have the right to be in your memories. You're my son. And I didn't know you long enough.

Long minutes. My eyes were filled with tears. Her hair was red and it shone like fire. Her eyes were big and baby blue.

There were good times, Challie. One of the best, the one I remember best, was that day we fed the swans. Oh, Challie, it was lovely. Try and remember. For me. Try.

What? Black hissing swans are a good memory? They haunt my dreams.

My fault, Challie. It wasn't meant to be like that. It's not easy to get through. Let me show you now.

Long minutes.

Challie, there was a time when memories were worth money to you.

I thought of pennies and sixpences and a whole half crown, and closed my eyes.

Charlie skips along and kicks flurries of snow into the air. He holds his boat under one arm. He thinks about the one with the red sails, but Mummy likes the blue because they are like his eyes. He takes her hand and grins up at her. She peeps out from under the black fur hood of her coat, smiling down.
    'Maybe you can slide on the ice, Challie, if it's thick enough.'
    'Slide on the ice?'
    'Oh, yes. You can run on it – CAREFULLY – and then stick one foot out in front of the other and WHEEE-EEE you're sliding.'
    She lets go his hand and shows him on the frozen path. He tries but slithers out of control and tumbles right into the big bank of snow

piled shoulder high alongside the path. Snow scatters down on him from the bushes, but he keeps tight hold of his boat. She laughs and brushes the snow off his balaclava and anorak.

He can't see the pond because the snow is piled so high, but when they turn the corner, there it is. He gasps at the huge shining sheet spread out before him in the quiet cold. The sun is low in the sky and deep red rays shoot out from it, like the drawings of the sun in his comics. The day is ending early and the red beams stain the ice a deep pink. The snow round the edges is pink too, and the ice on the path. Everything is pink. 'Mummy, can we slide? Can we?'

'Let me see how thick it is first.' Her breath comes out in little white puffs. Charlie hisses like a steam engine and the white clouds hang around his head.

'Look, Challie. Look! Swans!'

There are lots of them waddling across the ice, their long white necks hooked and their heads hanging down. Mummy waddles like a swan, rolling from side to side with her head hanging down. Charlie does it too and makes her laugh.

'Aren't they clumsy on land, Challie? They're beautiful when they're swimming. But look at the poor things. Two left webbed feet. What's that they're doing?'

It takes a minute to work it out. The swans are sliding. Charlie and Mummy, hand in hand, stand amazed. A swan takes some lumbering steps, gathers pace, spreads its big wide wings and flaps till they make a snapping noise, then WHEEEE it's sliding right across the pond. When it gets to the other side it waddles back and joins a line of swans all taking their turn, one after the other. Waddle, waddle, snap of pink wings, WHEEEE!

It's funny. Charlie giggles and giggles. He wants to go on the ice with them but Mummy says he'll scare them away.

'Let's feed them,' she says. She opens the loaf and tears off bread. Charlie throws it on the ice. A swan comes sliding across and gobbles it up, swallowing all the way down its long pink neck. It stands waiting, sharp black eyes watchful, fiery beak ready to snatch. Charlie throws more bread and the swans come skidding across the ice, crowding round, a seething mass of pink and white feathers, nipping at one another, hissing, crowding closer and closer round Charlie and Mummy.

'Mummy, they're like snakes!' screams Charlie, mesmerised by the

undulating flexible necks. 'Snakes!' he screams.

Mummy throws the rest of the bread far out on the ice. The swans head off after it. She lifts Charlie high and hugs him. He drops his boat. One swan is startled and hisses at it. Charlie clings to Mummy, who's laughing still.

'It's all right, Challie. All right. The swan was frightened. See? They're all gone now.'

And so they were, skidding and slithering after the bread. One slides so far it crashes into the snow banks round the edge and stands shaking its head, dazed. Charlie laughs, but he won't let Mummy put him down. She stoops to get his boat and then he rides balanced on her hip all the way to the park gates...

I opened my eyes. It was warm and cosy snuggled into her coat. And safe. And the swans – I had forgotten how it really was. What a sight they were...

Challie?

I'm here.

Wasn't that a good day?

I nodded, forgetting she couldn't see me. *Yes.*

There were lots of good days, Challie, and you've lost them. I want you to remember me. Let me live in your head.

Don't have much choice, do I? You'll never be out of my mind now.

Only the good times, Challie. The rest doesn't matter.

Long minutes. I couldn't think of anything to say.

She let me go then. Dad drew me to him with muttering and mumbling, but he fell silent when I sat by the bed. What was there for him to say? What were the memories worth now? The odour of death and staleness clung to him. But behind me, on the warm breeze coming in the window, was the scent of sun warmed grass and something sweet and light, lily-of-the-valley, gardenia, something like that. She's there. Always has been, somewhere and nowhere. She really has. It's good to know.

Sleepwalkers

She's running alone. No feet thud a together song with hers. She looks sideways at empty space, but memory gets there fast and fills it up with him. She takes the memory eyes front — his face a pale blaze in the dark, cut out of moonlight and all lit up, his eyes a wide-open glitter, mouth wide-open hungry. 'You run,' she said once, 'like you're swallowing the world.'

'I'm spitting it out,' he said.

So she's running eyes-front with his blazing face beside her and she's not alone. She's running and running and she's all lit up...

Anne-Marie is seven and on to Daddy Number Five. Her Granny says your mother never learns, but you're smarter, you know how to keep out of the way. And Anne-Marie is and she does and she tries, but quiet isn't enough and invisible isn't enough. Number Five comes looking.

"Cheeky wee bitch!" he roars. SMACK.

Her face burns, but she doesn't cry. They don't like that. She waits for worse or over for now, holding her breath. It's worse. SMACK. "Cheeky wee bitch. Don't you give me dirty looks."

He's breathing funny, growing bigger, filling the room. SMACK. Her ear bleeds from his sovereign ring. Her eyes stretch wide to hold in tears, and through a deep puddle she sees him lunge, hears him shout, "What are you looking at?"

She stands amazed when he trips and crashes down at her feet.

Run, a voice says, and she does. Neat as a cat she's over his head and down the hall, out into the close, her bare feet slapping on gritty stone. She keeps her eyes stretched wide, Supergirl eyes which brought him crashing down. Supergirl shoots magic beams of blue X-ray and cleaves the darkness; she spreads her arms and runs faster. She has lift off and is up, up and away. Her pink nightie balloons and her ear drips blood on the little world below. Cold winds blow her from star to star, blow her to nowhere, a pink wisp, until she catches her foot on the point of a star and tumbles screaming down, down, down...

Anne-Marie huddles on the pavement. She doesn't know how she got there. A broken bottle is jammed in her foot like a dark glistening star.

"Sleepwalking," her mother tells the police.

"I don't remember," Anne-Marie says.

"You always spoil it when things are going well for me," her mother cries.

Daddy Five says, "You're out of control but I'll teach you."

And he does. Anne-Marie has to stay in bed for three days after. She sleeps and dreams of flying.

Anne-Marie is fourteen. She is quiet and invisible and gives no trouble. Supergirl lives deep down inside and only comes out on special occasions. When Daddies come into Anne-Marie's room, Supergirl zaps them with her magical blue stare. Some of them get zapped right out of the room, but some of them shout, "What are you looking at?" SMACK. These ones stay, but Anne-Marie doesn't. She shrinks and slips out through a crack in the window pane. She spreads her arms and she's up, up and away and only comes back when it's safe. Supergirl never tells what happened when Anne-Marie was out; she takes it deep inside and hides it there.

Anne-Marie sleepwalks through the day, full of dread, she doesn't know why, but she's quiet and invisible and careful where she puts her feet. She gets by. Except when the dread boils up. Then she asks out of class, feeling sick, she says, and trots along corridors, faster and faster, until she's running across the playground with a strong wind at her back, going nowhere, but very fast.

"Why?" they ask her.

"I don't know," she says. How can she tell them she's afraid of this

104

man's green shirt or that one's hair, that she's sick to her stomach when she looks at them? They'd think she was mad and lock her up.

"I don't know," she says and cries a lot.

She meets Ricki at the truants' centre. They are all runners there, but Ricki's the best, no kidding, right out of the window when the teacher's writing on the blackboard. No kidding, Anne-Marie sees him. Once he jumps out of the taxi bringing him to school and he's gone for three weeks, all the way to London. She dreams of him running, long legs gobbling up the miles and circling the world; she runs beside him and they jump daisies, rivers, fences, walls.

She never speaks to Ricki. She is afraid of everyone, but Ricki most of all. He has a Stanley knife and he likes to cut. Everyone's afraid of Ricki because he is never afraid. Feared and not afraid. Cool.

Anne-Marie is back at school, cured of running. It doesn't matter. She writes her own sick notes now. And anyway, she is invisible: no one ever notices whether she's there or not. She goes to the mall and watches all the people. It's like being at the cinema and she wonders where the people learned to act. She walks about and wonders and never remembers where she's been. The day ends and it never happened.

Anne-Marie is sixteen when memory begins. She sees Ricki at the shopping centre. He and his friends spread out and skip-walk through the crowds, pushing and shoving and jabbing with their elbows. They are loud and twitchy, except for Ricki flowing cool as moonlight. They gather round a barrow stall, pick up scarves and shining ribbons, drop them on the floor, laugh 'sorry' like a challenge. They dart around like speeded up film too fast to follow. Security comes and they scatter. Except Ricki. He nods Anne-Marie over and pays the woman for a hair-tie shiny with sequins. He gives it to Anne-Marie and they stroll outside. She tries to give it back, but he pulls more from his pocket. They glitter in the sunshine, all for her. No one has ever given her anything before. Then he shows her a roll of notes he lifted from the barrow and they laugh out loud together. She has seen girls laughing with boys and wondered how they managed it, but it's easy. He tells her to come to the mall again next day.

That night she lies awake, eyes open in the dark, and replays the day scene by scene; she relives every detail of glitter and notes and cool flowing moonlight.

Meet me tomorrow...tomorrow...tomorrow.

Anne-Marie likes having a reason for her days. She likes being liked. Ricki says she's a cut above the others, like him. His mates' girls are slags, jumps, anybody's for the asking, and they chatter on like budgies and laugh too loudly. He likes Anne-Marie's quiet, the way she listens, the way she doesn't have a foul mouth or a face covered in warpaint.

Anne-Marie likes being a cut above, and she likes the memories Ricki makes for her. He is always in charge of the gang. They steam shops or rip off cars or phone boxes when he says so. He learned to be a leader from his Dad, a sergeant in the army. Ricki teaches Anne-Marie the rules:

> never take any crap from anybody
> get respect
> always go one better to even the score
> leave the drink and drugs to losers
> stand by your own no matter what

The rules work. No one ever crosses Ricki, not even Spaz who laughs at Ricki when he goes to the gym, but stops when he comes out. Nothing bad can happen when Ricki's there and Anne-Marie's dread goes away. She and Ricki watch the others getting drunk and stoned and laugh at the sight of them spewing, quarrelling, falling down, pissing themselves. They know they are a cut above all that.

Anne-Marie gathers up memories: the way the others make room for her at the table in the café, the way she has a special place beside Ricki, the way the other girls are jealous. Their painted eyes ask: what's she got? Once Spaz guesses out loud what she's got and Ricki cuts his face right there at the table, not deep, just a warning. Nobody looks at Spaz except Ricki and Anne-Marie. Ricki smiles, daring Spaz, and Anne-Marie can't take her eyes off the thin red line of blood bubbling across Spaz's cheek. She knows she'll remember it always.

The best memory is of the first time they run. Car windows shatter and then there are sirens and blue flashing lights. They pound pavement, get away, and she's not afraid, she's out of herself, whooping and yelling and running, running, running.

"You're a surprise," Ricki says. His pale face lights up the way it does when she does something right.

106

"It's like flying," she says. "Up, up, and away!"

He understands. The others run because they're scared, but it's different for Ricki and Anne-Marie.

At night she dreams of flying with Ricki, looking down on all the little people below.

Ricki is a surprise too. He always sees her home safe, which gives her little dreads because she knows what Spaz and the others are like. But Ricki only sits on the stairs and talks from the shadows about his Dad. His Dad didn't stand by his own the way he said he would. He left Mum for a slag, left Ricki to learn to be a leader by himself. The time Ricki ran away to London, he was looking for Dad and the slag. He was going to cut the pair of them, but couldn't find them. But some day he'll find them. Some day.

Anne-Marie reads his signs. There's more to tell, she knows there is, but his face is hard as thin ice, so she says nothing and leans against him. He likes that. The surprise happens when he kisses her. His mouth is soft and asking and he tastes of cool night air. His mouth tells her she's not a slag, she's special, a cut above. He makes her strong.

Another good memory is when Ricki stands by his own. The teacher chews her out for no homework. She doesn't squirm and cry and let Ricki down. She zaps the man with blue stare.

"Dumb insolence!" he shouts, and puts her out in the corridor. She doesn't stay there. She walks very fast out of school, faster and faster, going somewhere this time.

"Who's he calling dumb?" Ricki says.

That night they smash windows at the school, one after another. Smash. Smash. Smash. Breaking glass sounds like ice cracking. Anne-Marie is out of herself, beside herself, forgets herself. She jumps on glass and grinds it to powder. She tramples powder and makes a glittering path to slide on. The alarm is ringing, the others are running, but she can't stop.

"Anne-Marie!" Ricki shouts, and they run and run and they're all lit up.

"You got away quick enough," he tells the others.

Ricki and Anne-Marie laugh, but Anne-Marie reads his signs. Ricki only stayed behind for her and now he has to go one better. She smiles him on. They sit in the shelter in the park for a long time and his cheek and mouth are clean as night. She sucks him in.

"We'll burn it down," he says at last and smiles at Anne-Marie.

They burn it down. It's easy. The janitor hasn't put the alarm back on and they don't have to hit and run. They take their time and do it right, pile books and papers Guy Fawkes high and laugh when flame spurts. They scramble outside and watch red and orange fire roaring tall inside.

"It wants out!" Anne-Marie screams. "It wants out!"

She jumps at the moon and Ricki never takes his eyes off her. Then sirens shriek and they're on the run again, hands linked, through the park and into the town. She looks back and sees orange glow smeared across the dark sky; she looks sideways and sees the pale blaze of Ricki's face.

"Now everyone knows we've been there," she pants.

Ricki laughs all the way home. They sit on the stairs with their backs to the wall. Ricki studies his trainers, all scuffed and studded with twinkling glass. She reads his signs. He's going to tell her what he didn't tell before. Everything is coming out now. He coughs. "My Dad," he says. "My Dad knew I'd been there that time I went to London. I found his house and the freak in the woman's wig he was living with, a really pretty boy till he got all cut up. The stubble was coming through his make-up but the blood covered it up."

He looks at Anne-Marie, his eyes asking if it matters. Dread fills her up when she sees him so unsure, because it means he can be broken down and that mustn't happen because where would she be then? She reaches for him. She knows what he needs, somehow she knows. She holds him to her and it's easy. She stares wide-eyed and powerful over his shoulder and shows him things she didn't know she knew, and it's easy. She moves to the sound of his moans and whispers to him, breathing in night and smoke from his hair.

All that summer, everything is for her. He fights more often and cuts deeper. He fights other boys; he fights men straying drunk on his patch. He never loses. Anne-Marie likes it best when he lets her choose. She always picks grown men.

"That one with the greasy hair."

"That one with the chunky gold rings."

"That one with the big ugly fists."

And Ricki flows at them, smiling seriously, blade in hand, and the men come crashing down, clutching at ripped faces. All that summer, Ricki lays them at her feet like flowers. Sometimes, before they start running, she steps neat as a cat on a head. Ricki likes her style.

One night, Spaz gets drunk. He's mean when he's drunk and gets broody about the time Ricki cut him. He laughs because Ricki's in the gym again. "Only fags go in for all that body-building," he says. "They shave their chests to be like women. They rub baby oil on each other. Haw! Haw! It wouldn't surprise me about Ricki, considering his Dad…"

Anne-Marie's blue stare ought to cut him like a knife, but he won't shut up.

"…big tough sergeant kicked out of the army for sniffing after privates. Haw! Haw! Haw!…"

Then Spaz is on the ground. Ricki circles, kicking and kicking. Spaz spews and gurgles, choking. The boys pull Ricki off and Spaz staggers off into the darkness. A big mistake. Anne-Marie knows it's a mistake. Ricki's all lit up and electric tense. They should have let him settle with Spaz because he'll burn up if he doesn't get it out. His eyes pass over her, unseeing. She panics, but then she knows what he needs. Somehow she knows.

"The fags hang out at that club in the precinct," she says, and Ricki listens and sees her again. "You're worth ten of one of them. Come on. Cut one for me."

They all laugh and Ricki smiles right into her eyes.

They wait in an alley while the crowd thins. Anne-Marie stands close to Ricki, not touching, not speaking, only letting him feel her near. His face is like thin ice, hard and pure. Everything is going to be fine.

"That one," she says and points. "Look at it, for God's sake."

That one is walking alone, twitching and snapping his fingers, out of it. His clothes are too tight. His eyelids glitter with something he's stuck on. Someone makes a puking noise and everyone laughs except Ricki. He glides like a shadow into the street. He stands right in front of the man, smiling seriously. The man sways and grins, looking him over.

"Hello, darling. Lonesome?"

Ricki's arm sweeps up and slashes. Blood spurts and the man falls to his knees. It's time to run, but Ricki doesn't. He stoops and slashes again and again. The man curls up screaming and Ricki slashes and kicks, slashes and kicks, and the body jumps with every thud and scatters petals of blood all around. Anne-Marie runs forward.

"Ricki! Come away! Come away!"

He shakes his head. His teeth are clenched and his arm swings up and down, over and over. The screaming makes the others nervous and they scatter into the alleys and streets around them. But Anne-Marie stands her ground, stands by her own, and watches. Ricki's arm rises and falls, rises and falls. She knows he needs this. Everything is coming out now.

She watches, and suddenly she's watching from a long way off, looking down on the little world below. She sees Ricki and Supergirl letting it all out. Anne-Marie is shivering up among the stars, but Supergirl looks fine, her smile wide enough to swallow the world and bold enough to spit it back out. She steps neat as a cat on a head and grins when bone crunches. Ricki steps delicately too, and grinds, and he and Supergirl laugh when the screaming stops. Sirens split the air and Ricki shouts, "Run!"

Supergirl reaches for his hand, but he slithers in wet blood and falls hard on the pavement. CRACK! From a long way off, Anne-Marie hears the sound of bone breaking. She hears and fears and then licketty split she's tumbling down and down to be with Ricki. He's covered in blood and glistening darkly. She can't think how that happened; she can't think how she came here. She tries to help Ricki up, but he can't stand. They clutch at one another, slipping and sliding on sticky dark wetness, and fall over. The sirens come nearer. Nearer. Ricki pushes her and shouts, "Anne-Marie! Run for it! Run!"

So she runs, but she's running alone. No feet thud a together song with hers. She's running, leaving his pale face behind her. She's running and running, nowhere, very fast.

Princess

Whistling cheerfully, Raymond slapped on aftershave. He favoured Old Spice because it reminded him of his father and lent him a sense of daring. Life was full of daring these days: daring of risks, spice of secrets, daring of Raymond, sugar of Lorna, sugar and spice and all things nice. He flicked a comb through his hair and studied his reflection. Neat. Tidy. Clean. Like his father, although he didn't much resemble him otherwise. Except for the eyes. They were green, flecked with brown, and few people knew how like his father's they could be: he could will the potency of those long dead eyes into his own and make the green glow cold and the brown burn like sulphur. It was like summoning up the devil, a bit frightening really, but these hell lights were proof that he was a chip off the old block, no matter what his father had said.

There had been no need for hell lights for some time now. Since Lorna's arrival in his life, his face had changed its style: it dreamed at him from mirrors and smiled at him without permission. Studying his face was like exploring the gentle terrain of a foreign country. And Lorna was his passport there.

Still whistling, he took the stairs down to the hall three at a time. His mother was lying in wait, alibied by a yellow duster.

"Going out, Raymond?"

The duster flicked over already shining surfaces. Irritation flared in him like a struck match. Why didn't she come right out and ask what she really wanted to know? Raymond sighed over the answer to his own question: she didn't ask because she didn't know exactly what it was she feared. Like an animal, she lived on instincts and could sense the approaching storm, but hadn't the wit to get out of the way of the lightning.

Her careful unconcern as she dusted her prints of ballet dancers provoked him to a small viciousness. He stood directly behind her and stared at the back of her head until her nerve broke and her arm began to tremble. He grinned at her efforts not to cry out or move away. Once upon a time, she had found it easy to live with the pressure of his gaze and the great weight of silence between them. Changed days.

"Bye, Mum. Expect me when you see me."

He drove slowly to the park, a small indulgence he allowed himself from time to time. It touched him deeply to see Lorna waiting for him, restless, fidgeting, afraid that he would not turn up. And then the best part – the guileless flush of pleasure and excitement when she saw him coming along the path.

She was standing under their tree. Her head lifted at his approach and she skimmed like a bird out of the shade and into his arms. He tossed her high in the air.

"Princess! What have I got in my pockets today?"

"Smarties, Raymond."

"Maybe."

"Jellytots?"

"Might be."

Her fingers fastened on the tube in his short pocket.

"Raymond! Sherbet dabs!"

"Special treat for my little girl. I know Mummy doesn't like you to have them, but it can be our secret."

Solemnly, they touched fingers, their sign for promising never ever to tell.

They passed the afternoon in a mood of affectionate conspiracy. Lorna played and chatted and ran about free as a spring breeze. Raymond indulged her every whim while he struggled with his decision. Never before had he felt such protectiveness towards another human being, but then Lorna could call up kindness from a stone. His heart swelled painfully as he studied her. That openness, that trustfulness, that innocence – they were an unholy trinity bound to bring her sorrow and trouble. Raymond was wise about such things.

112

The certainty of her future pain clenched like a fist in his chest and filled him with a desperate need to stand between her and all the lies, betrayal, and corruption ahead.

Afternoon was dimming into evening by the time he had decided.

"Time to go home, Princess."

He took her hand in his. The intensity of his emotion made him want to crush those small birdlike bones; he could have wept, so powerful was the wave of tenderness which swept over him. Suddenly awkward, he dropped her hand, promising himself that he would love and cherish her always.

"Lorna, you should see your face." He smiled down at her. "You've got a sherbet beard and a liquorice moustache. And look at the mess down the front of your tee-shirt."

Comically, she squinted down her nose to see.

"Your Mummy is going to be very cross about that."

The child's mouth, flexible as plastic, dropped into the tragic downturn of a theatre mask. Raymond hated to give her a moment's anxiety, he really did, but in the long run it was in her own best interests.

"It's really worrying, Lorna. I've just thought – when she sees that, she'll know you've had sherbet and she'll want to know where you got it. She'll be furious when she finds out you took sweets from a stranger."

"But you're not a stranger, Raymond. You're my friend. I know your name and everything."

Her loyalty, so sweetly fluted in the violet light of evening, brought a lump to his throat.

"But I'm a stranger to your Mummy, Princess. You know what she's like about that. Oh, this is a terrible mess. You should have been more careful with all that sherbet. Do you know, she could get the police to come and take me away? And you would have to go to the home for bad girls for a while. They come and take you in the middle of the night and don't even let you take your own toys with you."

"But it's only sherbet. Mummy can wash it out."

They discussed the matter for some time, until tears sprang into Lorna's eyes, but Raymond hardened his heart. Sometimes the finer feelings had to be suppressed.

"Oh, well, it's too late now. The damage is done. We'll just have to face the music. Maybe she won't call the police. Maybe she'll just stop us meeting. She might just keep you in the house for weeks and weeks."

"But it's the Teddy Bears' picnic on Saturday!"

She wept all the way to the park gates. Much as it hurt to see her so distressed, Raymond offered her no comfort because he wanted her to appreciate the danger he was going to rescue her from. But her sobbing grew so loud that he was afraid she would attract attention. He dropped to one knee in front of her.

"Don't cry, Princess. I've had an idea. Suppose you come home with me and I get you cleaned up? Then Mummy need never know. There will be no trouble and you can take Teddy to the picnic on Saturday and meet me next week and tell me all about it. What do you think? Is that a good plan?"

With a gulp, she threw her arms around his neck. Raymond was so moved that he could hardly speak. He nuzzled his cheek against hers and breathed in the warmth of her sun-flushed skin and the smell of aniseed.

On the drive home, Lorna chattered incessantly. She was a typical female, Raymond thought fondly. Now that someone else had taken charge of her problems, she had forgotten all about them. With a savage tenderness, he studied her out of the corner of his eye. It was small wonder that women were always getting themselves into trouble – they were so pathetically easy to manipulate. If it wasn't for the fact that he loved her so much, he could very easily despise her.

Some knock-knock jokes kept her giggling all the way up the drive to the garage. Still giggling himself, he switched off the engine.

"Now, Princess. You stay in here while I go and wash your tee-shirt. And be very careful that no one sees you or Mummy might get to hear about this."

She pulled her tee-shirt over her head and burst into peals of laughter. The note of self-consciousness irritated Raymond.

"Stop that!" he hissed. "Someone will hear!"

"You're being rude, Raymond. You're looking at me."

"I certainly am not!"

"You are so. It isn't nice to look at people without their clothes on."

She blushed and his own face burned. Was she mocking him? Was she trying to flirt? He saw her fragile ribcage jerk with the force of her laughter. He beat a hasty retreat from the garage to the house.

It was the work of minutes to rinse through the tee-shirt, but he did

114

not return to Lorna. That cheap laughter, that knowing look, had unsettled him. Things thronged to the surface of his mind, things he didn't want to think about. He must not go back to Lorna until they had sunk back into the blackness where they belonged. And anyway, he had plans to make.

Lorna must be persuaded to stay with him. With patience and cleverness, that shouldn't be too hard to manage. After all, she didn't have much of a home life. He had seen her once or twice in the shopping centre with her mother. Mummy was one of that army of ill-tempered young women who spent her days ramming a baby buggy through crowds of innocent bystanders. She bawled at Lorna for the slightest fault, the tiniest mischief, which he found deeply distressing. He had guessed what sort she was anyway, from the mere fact that she allowed a six year old to play in the park alone, in spite of the dangers. It was that indifference to the child's welfare which had made it necessary for him to intervene in Lorna's life.

And it was necessary. He had only to recall that immodest laughter in the garage to be certain of that. He pushed away the memory of laughter and bare skin and stick like arms wrapped round herself as if she had something to hide. He pressed his hands to his temples. What had possessed the child to taunt him like that?

Raymond soon collected himself. He smoothed the tee-shirt flat on the draining board, was amused by its smallness and the pattern of silly smiling giraffes round its hem. Lorna had given each of them a name. The pretty childishness pleased him. She was still a baby, still young enough to be taught how to behave.

Behind him, his mother entered the kitchen. He sensed her hesitation and turned in time to see her eyes flicker over him. He made no attempt to hide the tee-shirt.

"Raymond, I thought I heard you come in."

Raymond noticed that she averted her eyes from the draining board. Naturally. Seeing and hearing had always been a matter of choice for her. Always. An old despair rose up in him like darkness. He bundled the tee-shirt into the tumble drier.

"Out of sight, out of mind, eh, Mum?"

She began to back out of the doorway.

"Stand still!"

Her closed face tormented him almost as much as her air of resignation. If he swung his fist, she would not duck; if he felt like it,

115

he could make her scream and cry. But he could never end the silence that lay between them like a grave. Black winds beat upon his brain and carried a voice up from the bottom of the pit in his mind. Ask me what's going on, it cried. Just this once, ask me. The voice pitched higher, his own voice, a child's voice, pleading and crying, but she did not hear, not then, not now, and she never had and she never would ask and it was a foolishness to expect anything different. There were only two voices in his life: his own endlessly screaming and his father's thick and hoarse in the night. Mummy was only a silence on the other side of the bedroom wall.

He struggled to breathe and began slowly to count her kindnesses to him. There had been kindnesses. Mummies could be kind. There had been visits to the park, sweets hidden in his schoolbag, even bedtime stories. But then again, nothing ever brought her to his side when he screamed for her. And sometimes he hated her kindnesses more than his father's cruelties, because they had taught him the bitterness of false hope and the worthlessness of love.

Raymond closed his eyes. He mustn't think about that any more – it was water under the bridge. Best forgotten. He had Lorna and her clean sunny love now, and Mum had no one. He opened his eyes. She was frozen with fright in the doorway.

"Go and have a lie down, Mum. You don't look well."

She flinched at the touch of his hand on her arm, but he let her go unscathed, a payment for occasional mothering.

He ironed the tee-shirt and made a cup of coffee. He needed time to calm himself. He wouldn't like Lorna to see him in this state. He didn't want to spoil the welcome she would give him when he returned. She had been shut up in there for some time now, along with the spiders which overran the place. She hated spiders. Oh, she was going to be so pleased to see him!

When he entered the garage, he found her huddled under an old blanket on the front seat of the car, red-eyed with crying.

"Raymond!" she wailed. "I'm cold. I want my tea." Her silvery voice was cracked with weeping.

"Whatever's the matter, Princess? Did you miss me?"

"I want to go home! Mummy will be angry if I'm late. I'll get sent to bed with no tea." The whine rose to a crescendo of harsh sobs. "I want my Mummy!"

"Poor baby. Did you think I wasn't coming back?"

116

He slid into the seat beside her and put his arm round her shoulders. He clucked and fussed, but to his disappointment, she only grew more peevish.

"Before you go home, we must make you all happy again. You can't go with your eyes all red like a little bunny rabbit's, can you? Cuddle up and I'll tell you a story. Then, when you're feeling better, I'll take you home."

His patience was rewarded. Lorna was soon absorbed in the story and snuggling close. Raymond, warmed by their togetherness, dropped a kiss on the top of her head when he reached happily ever after.

"Would you like to give me a little thank you kiss, Lorna?"

She grinned her gap-toothed grin at him and shook her head. "Mummy says kissing the boys makes your teeth fall out." She giggled. "And you can get germs."

The giggle spoiled the mood of the moment. It had a cheap, teasing quality. Why was she here if she wasn't fond of him? Sullenly, he pushed her away. "Oh, if you think I'm the kind of person to give you germs, I'd better go away and not come back."

"But you said you'd take me home!"

"That was when you said you were my friend. No, I'll just go away with my germs and you can stay by yourself in the car and go home in the morning."

"But it's dark in here!"

Raymond shrugged. He didn't want to quarrel, really he didn't, but it was definitely up to her to make friends again.

"I'll tell my Dad on you! I want my Mum!"

In the close confines of the car, her shrillness was deafening. Raymond's head began to throb painfully. "Why do you keep asking for that woman? She won't come. Do you really think she cares about you? You can scream till the world ends, but she won't come."

Lorna screamed even more loudly. He could see her terror. It was twin to his own, a togetherness of fear. Her wails were piercing. It seemed to Raymond that they were screaming together into a strong back wind. He could hardly think straight.

"What Mummy would love a naughty girl like you? You take sweeties from strangers when you know it's wrong, you KNOW it is, and you pretend to like people when you don't."

"Raymond, I'm frightened!"

Her fear made the darkness in him swell, made it strong and

117

powerful; feeding on fear, his and hers, it gathered strength and filled his skull and pressed against the back of his eyes. Helplessly, he pleaded with her.

"Lorna, don't scream like that. You're making me angry. You must stop now."

She pulled away, deliberately provoking him. Was this all the thanks he got for all his kindness? Whatever happened next, she had brought it on herself.

Anguish lit up his darkness with sulphurous streaks. He knew what she was seeing in his eyes, the cold green, the burning brown, and he could have wept for her. He caught at her flailing arms, maddened by their frailty. He wanted to hear them snap like twigs; he wanted them to twine lovingly round his neck. A voice not his own roared into the darkness.

"Don't you cringe away from me!"

Later, when he looked down at Lorna, Raymond was filled with the sadness of might-have-beens, but he supposed that some things were inevitable from the beginning, whenever that was. She was a grotesque creature, her face covered in blood and sherbet and snot. To think that he had once thought her pretty! He shook his head in disbelief. All water under the bridge. Best forgotten. He had plans to make. He must drive to the seaside. It would be dark by the time he arrived. There was a place he knew where the tide was strong and carried everything far out to sea.

With a twinge of regret, he covered her face with the corner of the blanket. In the long run, she was better off like this. After what had happened, she would have spent her life running before a strong black wind. Raymond was wise about these things.

Angel

Davy was quiet behind his newspaper. He never said much at the breakfast table. Not a morning person, he said, not civilised until after the third coffee and the first call on the mobile phone. Angel didn't mind; at least he had the good manners to explain himself, which was more than could be said for some. She slid his eggs, bacon and tomato on to a plate and held it out to him; when he didn't look up, she laid it on the table and brushed a kiss on the back of his neck. He nodded and turned a page.

Angel sat down opposite him. He read intently, ignoring his food. She had never known a man who could get so lost in a newspaper, not just the sports pages, but all of it. She nibbled at a Ryvita and enjoyed looking at him. He was quiet and still, but full of a shut-in energy which filled her tiny kitchen. It was a month since he'd moved in and she still had that pinch-me-I'm-dreaming feeling.

She sipped at black coffee, gleefully hugging the dark thrill of him to herself. Mornings were brilliant until he shrugged into his jacket, 'Must rush', and left her twice as alone as she had ever been before he came to stay. She froze inside when the front door slammed and the flat emptied of him, but warmed again when, like sunlight sparkling through glass, the thought came that he would be back tonight, every night, and always.

She had told Janine about her sunshine feeling. 'Christ,' Janine said. 'You look like the kid who's just found out that there is a Santa after all.' She had pinched Angel's cheek hard. 'That's to remind you,

119

pet lamb – there's no Santa, no free lunches, no such thing as a man for always. And if you don't believe me, ask his wife.' Angel had laughed. 'Ask her what? Davy says you can only learn anything from winners. Maybe it's her should be asking me.'

Angel smiled into her coffee mug. Ghostly steam prickled her skin. She could always rely on Janine to put a damper on things, but she could never be angry with her for long. Janine was like a big sister and it was only natural that she should be jealous because face it, and no harm to her, Janine was getting past it: twenty-seven and she'd missed the boat. You only had to see her with the customers at the club to know that. She was OK looking, but her smile never made it to her eyes, and everything about her screamed, 'Been there, done it, got the tee-shirt and I wonder why I ever bothered.'

Davy still wasn't eating. He might not say much of a morning, but he usually ate. Nerves, she decided; his wife played on them like a violin. She was never off the mobile: Bleep, bleep, Madame calling: 'Little David's had another attack.' 'Little David's on the nebuliser. He wants his Daddy.' 'Little David's been taken into hospital.' It was pathetic to use the boy to keep the man, but Davy fell for it every time. Christ, half the kids on the estate had asthma and nobody made all this fuss.

"Davy, your breakfast is getting cold. You should eat something." A hand appeared from behind the newspaper, fumbled for a fork, and speared a crispy curl of bacon.

"Have you worked out what you're going to say to her yet?"

The hand put down the fork and turned another page.

"Davy."

He lowered the paper and gave her his ask-me-no-questions stare, all blue and cold. He didn't like being pushed about his wife; he always said he could handle her without any help, but he had been tense all week and Angel knew that he needed some support. She smiled into his eyes and nibbled at a corner of her Ryvita.

"The thing is, Davy, the longer you let her drag things out, the harder it is for all of us. She has to face reality. The finances…"

He folded his paper shut with a snap. "I'm working on it." He glanced at his watch and in one smooth movement was up on his feet and into his jacket. "Must rush."

Angel followed him along the lobby. At the door, she leaned into him and teased her fingers across his chest. "Luck, Davy. Give little

120

Davy a kiss from me." She nuzzled her cheek against his. "And here's one for Daddy David." But he was already half way out the door. She listened to his feet clattering down the stairs, but before the emptiness of the flat could chill her, his voice floated up from the landing below. "See you, Angel."

Her sunshine feeling came flooding back and she almost skipped along to the living room. The curtain across the recess was still drawn.

"Benny!" she cried sharply. " It's time to get up!"

She pulled the curtain aside. Benny lay curled like a hedgehog in the corner of the set-in bed. The stench of stale urine caught at her throat and made her eyes water. Benny's blue eyes were hot with shame.

"I woke up needing, but he was still here, and I waited and waited and then I couldn't help it." His fluting voice threatened tears. "Why do I have to keep out of the way until he's gone?"

She tousled his hair. "It's just until he gets used to you, Benny. He's upset because he misses his own little boy, but he likes you really."

She stripped his bed and tossed his sheets on the floor. "Right. Up you get."

"I'm cold."

"No wonder, lying in that. For God's sake, you're big enough to change your own bed."

"I can't reach the shelf with the sheets!"

Small hands swiped at her in sudden rage. She gripped his wrists in one hand and fended him off with the other. "Don't you start on me this morning, Benny. I'm in a hurry. Now run through to the kitchen. The oven's on to give us a heat."

She gathered up his school uniform from the bottom of the bed and bustled along the hall. Benny, teeth chattering, was already warming the backs of his legs at the oven door. He smelled sour.

"Right. Jammies off."

She held a washcloth under the hot tap until it steamed. Benny tried to escape but she held him steady while she flicked the cloth over his face and bottom. "Just a lick and a promise, son. Now get dressed."

She hurried to her bedroom. It was warm and frowsty with the smells of the night before; Angel's eyelids drooped and her mouth dried as she breathed in the memory. That wife of Davy's should have taken better care of him; you didn't come across too many like him in a lifetime. Her sunshine feeling blazed and she pirhouetted the few steps to her wardrobe. "Winner-takes-all," she hummed, "and Madame Davy loses. How does it feel, Ma'am?"

Angel raked through her wardrobe for her sweatshirt and jeans. Her hand brushed against her waitress uniform, a short black satin skirt and a white scoop neck blouse with drawstrings. The customers were always trying to loosen those strings for a laugh. It drove Janine crazy and she kept hers tied in a double knot. Angel grinned. That was no way to earn tips. She drew her finger down the satin skirt with a sigh of pleasure. That skirt always made her feel good about herself.

Once she had seen an actress on TV explaining how she managed to play sex scenes convincingly. The actress said she wore something which put her in the mood – just like me and my wee black skirt, Angel thought – and let sensual thoughts flow into every part of her body. Then she pictured the Esso tiger, all sex and fur in slow motion and totally irresistible. The actress said that tiger walking was what gave her a sex aura.

Angel had practised tiger walking and found that it worked. When she was clearing tables at the club, the other waitresses might as well disappear into thin air as far as the customers were concerned. She had even improved the technique. Whenever she caught the eye of someone she liked, she sent the tiger packing and filled her head with other pictures – tangled sheets and arched backs and skin all sheeny with sweat. It never failed to draw men close.

Angel pulled her sweatshirt over her head. She hadn't needed that trick with Davy. The pictures had come by themselves, and she could tell that the same film was running in his mind. She hadn't believed in love at first sight until then.

She dragged a comb through her hair, remembering. 'See you outside,' was all he'd said. He was waiting in the car park at closing time. 'Get in,' he said, his voice all tight, and pointed to his car. He was so keen that he didn't even ask her name before he jumped on her bones. 'Night, sweet angel,' he said when he drove off. She'd been Angel ever since. Smiling, she went back to the kitchen.

"Benny!" The boy was kneeling on the kitchen chair with his shirt flapping open, cramming Davy's leftovers into his mouth. Yellow egg yolk dripped off his chin on to his vest. "Benny! I told you to get dressed!" She swung him off the chair and snatched a cold bacon rasher from his hand.

122

"Mum, I'm starving!"

"Don't start! Janine'll give you something to eat. She's taking you to school today."

She scrubbed so hard at his face that he headbutted her in protest. She sighed, wishing that he were old enough to understand that she had his best interests at heart.

She had him ready and across the landing to Janine's flat in minutes. Janine, tousled and bleary-eyed, answered her knock and smiled crookedly down at Benny. "Come in, wee man. Donna's by the fire." Benny slipped past her and she turned to Angel.

"So what's the big mystery, Lizzie?"

Angel hesitated. She had stopped telling Janine about Davy since he'd moved in. Janine could arch her eyebrows right up into her shaggy perm and let you know everything that was on her mind without saying a word. She had taken against Davy from the start. 'Another Thursday night stud, Lizzie, having a night off from the wife. Christ, you've been through this before. They're all the same. False names, false smiles, false teeth half of them, all singing the same song: 'She doesn't understand me.' A bunch of clapped out stallions prancing for the fillies, all talk and no action and home to the missus by midnight. And if by some miracle they should score, it's home to the missus full of guilt and offering to paper the living room for her. So don't waste your time waiting for him to reappear.'

But he had come back, week after week, and still Janine wouldn't believe he was different.

Angel studied Janine's mood. She could be vicious when she liked. It was one of the reasons she wasn't as well liked as Angel. As if Davy could be called clapped out! He was years younger than the workmen who came into the club! As for false smiles, he never smiled unless he meant it. And he didn't lie either. He had even been honest about being married. Which had made Janine laugh. 'Aye, right. Everything's hunky-dory then. It's just his wife he lies to.'

The trouble with Janine was that she didn't believe that Angel could win because she herself never had. She had been married less than a year when her husband walked out. Janine said it was because he wasn't happy about the baby coming. Angel, watching her friend fish her cigarettes out of her pocket, reckoned the rattiness of her dressing gown had more to do with it. Still, a thing like that was bound to make a person bitter.

Janine lit up and Angel's irritation died. She was too full of sunshine to be sour this morning.

"No big mystery, Janine. I'm off to the hairdresser. Davy's going to tell his wife that he's getting a legal separation. I've told him he's got to get his finances sorted out. And I'm planning a wee celebration when he gets home."

"Oh, aye. I thought you said he was going to Yorkhill Hospital to collect his wee boy and take him home?"

"He is. But she'll be there too. He'll tell her then."

"At Yorkhill? That's nice. I can just see them on either side of the wee man's bed talking it over. Never mind, Davy boy'll be in the right place if the missus decides to stick a knife in him. And the kid'll love it."

"Janine, he'd never say anything in front of the boy. He's too sensitive for that."

"Is he? I hadn't noticed. So what's the deal, Lizzie? She swaps her big house in Rouken Glen for your wee flat with the damp patches artistically arranged and the underfloor heating system that's too dear to run? Or will he be sensitive and give her and the boy the house and move in here permanently?"

"I've asked you a dozen times to call me Angel, Janine. And in case you haven't noticed, he has moved in here."

"Aye, right. And loving every minute of it."

"We'll get something better when his house is divided up. Half to her and half to him. I've said that's ok with me – "

Janine swallowed smoke and choked. "Oh, that's decent of you. She'll be falling all over herself to be fair with you as well, I expect."

Angel hid her anger and wondered why Janine couldn't just wish her luck. Did she know how cheeky her eyebrows were? But she couldn't afford to quarrel with her right now.

"Janine, will you mind Benny after school for me?"

Janine flicked ash on the stairs. "Sure, Lizzie."

"Right, I'm away then."

She arrived at the hairdresser panting but on time. The place was expensive, but she had the gas bill money in an envelope and the £20 she'd lifted from Davy's wallet the night before. She'd earned it.

"Blonde highlights, is it? What shade would you like?"

Angel studied the tufts of hair on the shade chart. Davy's wife was fair brown with sun streaks. Not exactly earthshaking. Angel reckoned she could do better than that. "Platinum Dream," she said and lay back to have her hair washed.

She would have died rather than admit it, but sometimes Janine shook her confidence: she never had a good word to say for Davy, and sometimes she sided with his wife. It was ridiculous because she didn't even know the woman. All the same, she harped on about her: 'Tell me this, Lizzie. If she's such a dreary dowdy cow, how come Davy, who could have his pick, married her? And if he's so wonderful, how come she's always nagging and driving him out of the house?'

Angel always had the same answer ready: 'Tell me this, Janine. If she's so great, what's he doing sniffing round me?' But secretly, she worried. She'd invented the nagging and the dowdy since wives were all much of a piece, but in fact she had no idea what the trouble was between Davy and his wife because Davy was too loyal to moan about her. 'Look,' he said when she pressed him for the full story, 'I don't talk to her about you, and I don't talk to you about her. Fair enough?'

Angel caught herself glaring in the mirror. "Are you all right?" the stylist asked. Angel managed a smile before sinking back into her thoughts. Davy's wife had come close to souring her whole relationship with Davy. Those first Thursday nights with him had been a nightmare, what with Janine banging on about his wife and Davy refusing to discuss her at all. The woman had haunted her. Sometimes, out there in the car park, she imagined Madame's ghostly presence in the back seat, giving her and Davy the cold eye. The thought had made her go at Davy like a wild thing, as if Madame could actually see what her man was like when he had a real woman to play with. But when Davy dropped her at the corner of her street and she was once again alone with Benny, she fretted over what he did with his wife the other six nights of the week. Sometimes she thought she would go mad.

Worst of all were the nights when Davy didn't show up. The excuse was always his son: 'I had to drive David to a birthday party' or 'David had an attack and wanted me with him.' She hadn't believed him. What man gives up the best sex he ever had in his life for a kid? Why couldn't Madame look after him? She had complained more than once to Davy, but all he did was stay away for weeks until she was terrified that she would never see him again. Every time it happened, Janine's eyebrows went soaring and Angel, dying inside, would say, 'He'll be back.'

And he always was. Angel sat rigid while the hairdresser cut and snipped. And when he did, it was always like that first Thursday. Sometimes she didn't see him come in, but she would feel his eyes on her back, his heat across the room, and when she turned, the same shock of pleasure as the first time. Exactly the same, every time. She would suffer endless hours of restless longing for the end of her shift when she could go outside and find him in his car with the door open and himself all unzipped and ready. 'Get busy, sweet Angel.' She had never known anyone as passionate as Davy. 'Thursdays are the only days I'm alive,' she told Janine. 'I'm dead Friday to Wednesday. Him and me, we're two of a kind. I wish every night was Thursday.' Janine hadn't been impressed, and neither had Davy when she said something like it to him. His face had gone very still. 'I will never leave my son,' he said. Later, alone in her flat, she had lain awake in bed, chewing the corner of her pillow, trying to believe that it was only his son who kept him at home.

He had stayed away for three Thurdays after that. 'He's not getting away with this,' she swore. 'Not again.' And when he did show up at last, she ignored him. He didn't try to talk her round; he just finished his drink and walked out. He didn't look back once. She had run after him, slipping and slithering across wet gravel. He had pulled her into the shadow of a hedge at the back of the car park and made her go down on her knees to him right there and then. After, she had clung to his thighs. 'Did you miss me, Davy?' and then, 'Would she do this for you, Davy? Would she?' He had flicked raindrops off the hedge on to her upturned face and laughed. 'Not her style, sweet Angel. Not her style at all.' It was the first time he had ever said a word against Madame. She hadn't been able to keep that one from Janine.

'See what I mean, Janine? We're two of a kind. We belong together.'

'Oh, aye, right. Two of a kind,' Janine had said when she fetched Angel a spare pair of tights from her locker. 'I suppose his knees are all grazed as well.'

Angel smirked at the mirror. Poor Janine: telling her about love and passion was like describing colours to a blind man.

The hairdresser touched her shoulder. "I said, 'Would you like to move under the heat lamps now?'" Angel rose and was startled by a tiny clicking in her ears. She glanced at her reflection and saw that strands of her hair had been threaded through dozens of little white

126

plastic rectangles. She hadn't even noticed it being done. The stylist lowered the red lamps and left her to stew.

Angel admired her platinum streaks. They were drying to a lovely colour, a lot splashier than Madame's from what she'd seen of her. She had gone out to Rouken Glen once, just to see the competition, and stood opposite Davy's house. Her luck had been in. Madame had appeared on the long sweep of the driveway and Angel's sunshine feeling had exploded into super nova. The woman was no competition at all: small, no bust to speak of, a pale face like a china doll's, and an awful plain dresser. No wonder Davy had strayed. It was only the boy keeping him at home after all.

She had hardly given Madame a thought after that, but she remembered the house with its row of diamond leaded windows and its stone steps leading down to a garden as big as a playing field. Benny would think he'd died and gone to heaven in a place like that. Increasingly, the house made Angel angry. The skinny wee bitch in the pink frock couldn't even be bothered to keep her man happy, but she was sitting pretty with her gold bracelets and earrings and a lawn like velvet while Angel had to rough it. The anger grew until her days were dark with it. Madame might have the fittings which went with Davy, but she shouldn't be allowed to sleep easy, not when Angel couldn't. Barry had come to mind. He was a bouncer at the club and was daft about Angel and had been only too happy to help out. One phone call and Madame knew in glorious technicolour what her darling Davy was up to in the car park.

Angel grinned at the memory. The truth was always better out than in, and in the long run, it was best that they all knew where they stood. It had all worked out better than she had hoped. Davy had turned up at her door at three in the morning. 'I've left her,' was all he said. Madame must have made him choose, Angel reckoned, and Davy wouldn't give Angel up. And from that moment on, every night had been Thursday night.

Angel noticed that the heat lamps were bringing her face out in blotches. They had better be gone by the time Davy got home. She would have to be at her best for him. He always needed to be perked up after a session with Madame. He never said much, but you didn't have to be a rocket scientist to imagine how mother and son ganged up on him: 'Daddy come home. Daddy come home.'

Angel had boxed clever. She was always calm and wise and

reassuring, making sure he kept things in perspective. 'They get over it, Davy. Divorce upsets kids at first, but once they catch on that Dad's left Mum, not them, they settle down to it. Half the kids on the estate have no dads and they get by. Some of them even like having two homes to go to. And wee Davy will always be welcome here. Benny and him could be friends. They'd have a great time and I'd look after him as if he was my own.'

He never did bring Davy for a visit and Angel knew who was to blame for that. 'You know, you can make her let you have him here. You're his Dad. You've got rights. She's using that boy – '

He looked hard at her, warning her off. 'She's not like that. I can see David whenever I want.'

Angel had to bite her tongue then. Sure, he could see his kid whenever he wanted, so long as it was at Rouken Glen. Daddy come home. Daddy come home. Surely he could see her game?

Angel paid for her hair and stepped into the coolness of the street. She let the breeze fan at her cheeks for a moment and then headed for the off-license. She needed something fizzy for the celebration. A couple of bottles of spumante would have to do until the finances were sorted and the champagne days arrived. On impulse, she stopped at a florist's and bought a dried flower arrangement. She'd seen big copper bowls of them on Madame's windowsills. They were a nice touch.

At home, she tidied up for Davy. She put the flowers in a milk jug on the kitchen table, and two wine glasses polished diamond bright beside it. Then she dressed up in Davy's favourite, her black shift with the Chinese collar and the red piping, and her black stilettos. She made up her face with two coats of everything for staying power, and began working on her mood: Esso tiger, sex and fur in slow, slow motion. She squirmed with anticipation as she tiger walked to the kitchen and wondered how Madame was taking the news. Probably having a hissy fit, and the brat too.

She sat at the table all afternoon and fiddled with the flowers and the wine glasses to keep her mind off the scene at Rouken Glen. Parched petals crumbled off the stems with a dry rustle. Davy was taking his time. Madame must be making a grandstand play. Or maybe the boy had had another attack. She wouldn't put it past him.

At teatime, Janine knocked at the door. "Benny wants to know if he can come home now." Her eye fell on the litter of petals on the table. "Oh, Lizzie. Has he not come back then?"

"He'll be here. Just keep Benny out of the way, will you?" Janine said nothing. For once, even her eyebrows were quiet.

It was late evening before he showed up. Angel bit her lip with relief when she heard his feet on the stairs. She had been afraid that the brat had won after all. She leapt to her feet and smoothed the creases out of her dress, careful not too look too happy. Davy was bound to be upset. She mustn't seem too pleased with herself. She stepped into his arms as soon as he came in the door. As always, her heart turned over at the feel and smell of him. He staggered and almost fell. Angel smiled. He was as drunk as a lord. Poor sod. It must have been a very hard session with Madame.

"How's wee Davy?" she said softly. "Is he all right?"

Davy nodded. "He's safe home." He lurched to the table and clutched at it for support.

"Oh, that's great, Davy. I've been worrying about him all day."

He swayed back on his heels and stared at the flowers and glasses. She rubbed his back gently. "You're all tensed up. Would you like a wee drink?"

She raked through the kitchen drawer for a corkscrew and picked at the foil on the bottle. He slumped into a chair and leaned over the table with his head in his hands. Angel popped the cork and smiled sympathetically. She could imagine how he felt – head bursting and Madame tapping like Riverdance on his brain.

"Did Jenny take it hard then?"

She watched him struggle to focus on her. "What?"

"Jenny. Did she take it awful hard? The separation?"

His face froze into ask-me-no-questions, but he wasn't getting away with it this time.

"Jenny. Did she give you a hard time?"

He grinned unpleasantly. "Oh, yes, she did." He nodded once, and again, and then he couldn't seem to stop talking. "She certainly did." He frowned and the grin thinned to a hard line. "Doesn't matter what I say, she won't take me back. I've practically gone down on my knees to her, but she won't change her mind." His eye travelled up and down Angel's black satin as though he'd never seen it before. "She says that you and I deserve one another." He shrugged helplessly. "Makes no sense, me and Jen splitting up over a slag like you. No sense – " He tailed off into baffled silence.

Angel's temper erupted. "Did Jenny call me that? Who does she – "

Davy pushed his hair out of his eyes and glared. "What's this 'Jenny'?" he said slowly. He seized a corner of the table and heaved. Flowers and fizz splattered on the floor.

"You keep my wife's name out of your dirty mouth. OK?" He heaved again and the table crashed against a wall. "OK?"

Yes

Mick watched the boys watching the blonde. Boys will be boys, he thought with a good-natured grin, and kept the milk float standing while they had their fill.

No.32 stooped to lift the milk from the doorstep. A mane of hair, wheat-coloured and tousled, swung over its face; it tossed it back with a jerk of its head. Wicked, thought Mick, pure wicked the way it stood there, early morning rumpled and fresh from its bed, on display for all the world to see. He noted the new dressing gown – a silky kimono thing with nothing holding the edges together but a narrow satin belt, all hide-a-bit-show-a-bit-and-wouldn't-you-like-to-see-more. There ought to be a law against kimonos. It yawned and went back inside, kicking the door behind it with a slim bare foot. Mick had to admit one thing about posh areas like Newton Mearns: you got a better class of tart here. He wondered if it had opened its envelope yet.

He became aware that he was being stared at. Flynn again. The boy's dark blue eyes held his with a question. Mick depressed the pedal; the float hummed smoothly to life. He drove a hundred yards or so in silence, letting the question hang between them. He knew what it was: Flynn wanted to know if they'd be playing the game again, but would not admit it. That kind of prissiness irritated Mick. As usual, it was the younger one, Fergus, with a sly sideways glance at his brother and then at Mick, who came right out with it.

"Come on, Mick. What's she saying?"

"Who?"

"No.32."

"Oh, her! What do you think?"

"Looks like yes to me." Fergus shot his eyebrows up and down and made a loud kissing noise.

Flynn stared straight ahead, but Mick wasn't fooled and had no intention of letting the boy off the hook.

"How do you read her, Flynn?"

The boy shrugged and turned his head away, but not before Mick had seen the dull flush creeping up from the base of his throat.

Mick nudged Flynn. "Sensitive type, your brother. Your Mammy keeps him nice. When he grows up, he wants to be a New Man."

Fergus sniggered, and Mick winked broadly at the back of Flynn's head. "Flynn is above our kind of thing, Fergus. Kept his eyes shut the whole time he was looking. A real wee scholar and a gentleman."

The blue eyes met his again, darker still with questions about things any boy worth his salt wanted to know, but which Flynn would not lower himself to ask. Superior little sod. Mick had him sussed, knew all about what he got up to on Saturday nights, and wasn't fooled by the butter-wouldn't melt act.

"Flynn's trouble," he continued, "is that when he goes to that university in the autumn, he thinks all he has to do is flash his A levels, and the world and all the girls in it will spread leg for him. But in real life you need to get your F levels. Right, wee man?"

Fergus licked his lips and punched Mick lightly on the arm.

"Come on, Mick. What's 32 saying?"

Mick brought the float to a halt at the top of the next street. He ran his hand through an imaginary mane of tousled hair and spoke in a breathless falsetto.

"My name is Miss Olivia Fuckin' Newton Mearns, and I don't talk to the likes of you. Not unless you can keep me in the gold chains I like to drape around my neck. My satin kimonos get you going, but all I'm saying is 'maybe.' I'll let you spend a fortune on flowers and dinner for two, and I'll make you sit through hours of talk about how compatible our star signs are, and the fascinating gossip about everyone I know. I'll give you the story of my life in glorious technicolour, including the books I like and the music I don't, and I'll show off by talking about intellectual stuff like 'When Harry Met Sally', and I'll prove how broadminded I am by saying that the bit in the cafeteria where Sally fakes it is the funniest thing I've ever seen, and just when you think I've got to the point at last, I'll change the subject and ask if you think men and women really can be friends or does sex always get in the way? And at the end of the night, I'll slam the door in your face, and if you're daft enough, you'll go home floating on air, dreaming about how close we're getting instead of thinking about all that time and money down the drain."

Mick dropped his voice to its own pitch. "Got it? 100% prick tease, hand embroidered in pink and blue like her kimono. And there's plenty daft enough to put up with her. They sit there with their balls turning blue, kidding on they're interested in every word that falls from those luscious lips, while she avoids the only word of any interest a woman can say...which is?"

"YES!" Fergus yelled and punched Mick's arm again.

"That's the one, son. I wish someone had put me wise when I was your age."

Flynn and Fergus jumped down from the float and rounded up the smaller boys and the crates from the back. Mick leaned over the side of the float and called after them. "Heard a good one the other day. Why do women have cunts?"

He waved the boys over and whispered uproariously, "So that men'll talk to them!"

The boys' laughter clinked like the bottles in the crates as they scattered down the street. Mick laughed too: that one wouldn't be long going round the school playground.

Mick sat back, wondering again if No.32 had opened its envelope. It must have by now, although it had shown no sign. Then again, 32 had no shame in her. Six envelopes so far, and still it turned out for morning parade on the front doorstep, letting on that it didn't know someone was watching. Not like Nos. 42 and 67. They were edgy, looking all round before they took their pintas in, or else sending the kids out for them. Sometimes when he strolled past their houses later in the morning, he saw them scuttling to their big fancy cars, jumping at shadows and trying to be invisible, which was hysterical in 47's case: since it had got pregnant, it looked like a rolled up duvet buttoned into a coat. Mick wrinkled his nose – they ought not be allowed to come out in public looking like that – and thought of No.32 instead.

A while back he had seen it in a pub with its mates, all dressed up in a short black dress with wee narrow straps and its hair rippling right down its back. The pals were dogs, both of them, so it had been the centre of attention, perched on a pink velvet chair under a potted palm, surrounded by a pack of flash looking guys. Their ties alone had been worth a month's pay. They were all gathered round the Queen of Newton Mearns, laughing like drains every time it opened its mouth, like a pack of performing dogs begging for favours. He had watched them dancing attendance for more than an hour and hadn't seen a real man amongst them, which went a long way towards explaining why her ladyship was so full of itself.

He had intercepted it on its way to the Ladies'. 'Hello,' he'd said, real civil. Its face had gone like a mask. 'Nearly didn't recognise you with your clothes on,' he'd added, sure it would make the connection then. Instead it had looked right through him, swept by as if he wasn't there, and left him feeling like a prat.

He had made up its first envelope that very night: a luscious centrefold he'd been keeping for a special occasion. There was a baby blonde with a gleaming hot pink pout, sprawled across satin sheets with its legs wide open, scarlet taloned fingers spread across its slit, its parted lips screaming an ecstatic yes! yes! yes! right at him. All the way down the arm, he had printed in big block capitals:

NOW YOU'RE TALKING, BABE!

He still laughed at the cleverness of that one, although his best was the one he'd sent to No.62. Ms. Filofax couldn't make up its mind whether it was a man or a woman in its man's suit jacket and its woman's skirt. It carried a briefcase stuffed full of papers – so important looking – and drove a top of the range BMW, much too powerful for a woman. It might not have been born with the right equipment to be a man, but it had all the right accessories. And the attitude.

No.62 liked to put a man in his place. Whenever he came for the milk money on Friday nights, it was sitting in its front window at a big desk covered with sheets of paper the size of centrefolds. Busy with its computer. Always busy and much too important to notice the milkman at the door. It always kept him waiting while it tapped a few more keys, and there was never an apology, just a cool, 'How much do I owe this week?'

He had sent 62 a photo story: 'Working Late.' Starchy lady executive in pin stripe suit and big specs, just like 62's, makes its big

134

handsome male secretary jump through hoops all day. But come the night, when everyone else has gone home, he gets his own back. Instead of taking dictation, he's in the big swivel chair, and Ms. Pinstripe is a lot less starchy wearing nothing but white collar and cuffs, on its knees and going to work on him. Mick laughed aloud. He'd had a hard time thinking up a slogan for that one, but his sense of humour hadn't let him down:

BE ALL YOU CAN BE

Right across its round white backside.

His chuckling reminiscence was interrupted by the thud of boys hurtling themselves on to the back of the float. Fergus climbed into the front with him. There was no sign of Flynn.

"Where's your brother got to?"

Fergus blew a kiss down the street. "Lovestruck."

Mick snorted. "Floral pyjamas and big fluffy slippers. Boys have funny tastes these days. You'd think she'd put on a bit of a show for him since most of their courting gets done on the doorstep.

Fergus's eyes brightened with malice. "What kind of show, Mick?"

Mick remembered just in time that the boys were brothers, even if they were chalk and cheese. "Only joking, Fergus. Your big brother's got himself a decent wee lassie there."

Decent wasn't the word for it. He saw them together, Flynn and his girl, every Thursday night when he was having his dinner in the café. They were a scream, the pair of them, strolling hand in hand, staring into one another's eyes. Flynn met it outside the Girl Guides' hall (where it was an officer and a Duke of Edinburgh Award winner as Flynn informed him frostily when teased about cradlesnatching) and took it to MacDonald's. One Coke, two straws, that kind of wild night. They never did anything much but talk. You'd think they'd run out of books and films sometime, but the closest old Flynn ever got to excitement was when his wee sergeant major let him toy with the ends of its hair, or twined its fingers through his. Mick had often followed them home, sure they must be up to something more once they were out of the public eye.

They were hardly worth the walk. They sat on the wall outside the sergeant major's house, swinging their legs and prattling away. Sometimes a bit of a kiss and a cuddle and some heavy duty eye contact, but when the midnight hour tolled, it was off to a maiden's bed, and Flynn went swinging down the street, whistling like he'd won the lottery.

What that wee lady needed was a red-blooded man who wouldn't put up with all that nonsense. He had brooded on that thought for days before inspiration struck. A booklet, tailor made, with a hilarious title: A GIRL'S GUIDE TO MEN. Underneath, carefully copied from his niece's Girl Guide handbook, he had drawn the trefoil badge, complete with the BE PREPARED motto. Inside, neatly cut out and pasted on to black cardboard, were dozens of studs going through their paces: standing, kneeling, lying, flying, face north, face south, and hanging from the wardrobe door – with and without accessories. Miss Butter-Wouldn't-Melt was on the way to getting F levels! Mick had hoped that it could tear its eyes away from the studs long enough to study how real women behaved. That was something they were never too young to learn, although the price was going up all the time. But the working girls were worth it – money on the table, straight down to body language, and no need to talk about it after.

Mick's thoughts were interrupted by the reappearance of Flynn, breathless with running.

"Mrs. MacLean wants to see you, Mick. She's not had her milk two days in a row. I told her I'd delivered it, but – "

Mick sighed and jumped down from the float, pushing his flat cap to the back of his head. "And here was me and Fergus thinking you and the sergeant major were having it away on the doorstep with all the neighbours tuned out to watch. Don't look so grim, son. Just a wee joke."

Mick set off down the street with Flynn and Fergus following close behind. He wondered if Mrs. MacLean knew that these days Flynn was getting a bit more than a kiss and a cuddle from her curly-headed daughter. On Saturday nights, when the parents were out, Flynn always came round to keep his girl company. Mick often took a detour past the house on his way to visit Shazz, who only worked from home. The light was always on downstairs. He had peeped through a gap in the curtains a couple of times to see what was going on, which was nothing very much. A prim and proper cuddle on the sofa in front of the TV. Then last Saturday, things had got a bit more interesting.

The lights were on upstairs when he came by, and so he decided to give Shazz a miss while he checked things out. The pair of them were upstairs for three hours, and then just before Mummy and Daddy came home, the upstairs light went off, the downstairs one went on, and the two of them were neat and tidy on the sofa in jig time.

Caught out at last! And Missy a Duke of Edinburgh Award winner too! Was nothing sacred? After that, Flynn's prissiness had really got on his nerves. The kid kept up the pretence that he was better than everybody else: never laughed at Mick's wee jokes and impersonations, never wanted to play the game, never dropped a hint about the hanky-panky going on between him and the sergeant major. The pair of them needed a lesson, he'd decided, and he had made up an envelope: 'Hanky Spanky For Naughty Little Girls' The schoolgirl in the picture had bunches and ribbons, a St. Trinian's boater at a jaunty angle, and a striped school tie dangling down between the biggest tits he'd ever seen on woman or cow. It was bent over a desk, frozen in mid-quiver, ecstatically awaiting the next swish of the cane.

WHO'S BEEN A VERY NAUGHTY GIRL THEN?
I SAW <u>EVERYTHING</u> YOU DID!!!

That put paid to any more Saturday nights for Flynn. From then on, Mummy and Daddy stayed home with Romeo and Juliet. And the girl was never let out alone. Flynn and Daddy escorted it everywhere – to and from school, to and from church, to and from Guides. As if he, Mick, was the one who was up to mischief! Flynn was the man they should be keeping an eye on!

Mick fidgeted on the Macleans' doorstep. "She's taking her time answering."

The sergeant major appeared at the side of the house. "Mum's in the garage. She won't be able to hear you. You'd better come round."

Flynn and Fergus led the way. One half of the garage door was shut. Mick called out, but no one answered. He peeped inside, then was pushed sharply from behind. He fell in. Flynn, Fergus, and the girl followed, pulling the door shut behind them.

It was crowded inside. 32 was there with what looked like three scrum halves. 47 and 62 had their husband's with them. 47's was even bigger than her, pregnant as she was, but with muscle. Mr. And Mrs. MacLean were frozen-faced, standing on either side of Flynn and the girl. There was some rough pushing and shoving, and Mick found himself in the centre of a circle. He could not take his eyes off Flynn. His blue eyes were a black blaze in the gloom. There was no question in them, only anger. Mick shivered.

"Time for Hanky Spanky," Mrs. MacLean said.

A voice came at him from behind. " Mick loves that."

32 cliqued arms with two of the scrum halves. The third was rolling up his sleeves. "He has to take his clothes off first. It's more fun that way, isn't it, Mick? You can keep your bunnet on, though. It's cute."

Mick stood paralysed. The scrum halves edged forward. "Needing a hand there?" One of them tugged at Mick's tie and slid the knot slowly up to his Adam's apple. "Come on, Mick. We know you're into this. No false modesty." Someone punched Mick right in the kidneys. He staggered and almost fell, but they held him up. It took him a while to catch his breath. They all waited patiently.

The scrum tapped Mick's chest and balled a fist. "Shirt first," he said lightly.

The guy was itching for him to refuse. Mick reached for the buttons. His fingers were swollen and nerveless, the buttons small as grains of sand. He managed somehow. The sergeant major emptied a large brown envelope at his feet. Glossy hot pink pouts and yesses yearned up at him.

"I had trouble with the diagrams," she said. "I need a demonstration."

Mick glanced round the circle, searching for a glimmer of fellow feeling. "Fergus! Tell them! I've always been a joker! It was just a wee joke."

Fergus grinned. Mick wondered what it was that had made him think he had an ally there. "Two hours with you, Mick, and I'm gasping for fresh air," Fergus said and pulled a camera from his pocket. He wound on the spool.

"Come on, Fergus – " Even to his own ears, Mick's voice sounded squeaky.

"Lost your sense of humour, Mick?" Fergus grinned. "You needing any help with those buttons?"

No one said anything after that. Mick struggled with the buttons. A cold sickness gripped at his belly as he wondered how far these lunatics were prepared to go. He stripped off his clothes, his eyes flickering from the door to the window. There was no way out.

Everywhere he looked, he saw clenched fists. He saw more sleeves being rolled up.

At last he stood shivering, his hands folded protectively in front of him.

"Come on, Mick. Strike a pose." Fergus blew a loud smacking kiss, then swooped and retrieved a pin-up from the floor.

"Try this one. It's a cracker." He held it before Mick's terrified eyes. "Exactly like this."

Mick shook his head. She was on her hands and knees like an animal. He would rather take a kicking! The air moved suddenly behind him in a loud swishing noise. He yelped loudly as a stinging pain slashed across the backs of his legs. The pain was agonising, and made him dance forward a few steps, his eyes watering, a sick nausea rising in his throat. No. 47 prodded him back into position with a garden cane. Another swish leapt like a lightning flash across his thigh. He dropped to his knees. Fergus's camera clicked.

"He's not doing it right," 62 complained. "Make him look over his shoulder and smile. Longingly."

47 swished at him again. Mick yelped and whimpered. His flesh was burning! He looked over his shoulder, his mouth twitching uncontrollably. 47's husband scowled. "Not much of a smile, is it. He isn't trying, doesn't look as if he's having a good time. And suck in that sagging gut, will you? It's revolting."

For half an hour, Mick rolled on the floor in the centre of the circle. Flynn made him smile and yell, 'Yes' to every instruction called to him. He posed cutely, submissively, seductively, erotically, lustfully, and as ecstatically joyfully as he could manage. The camera clicked frantically. In the end, Fergus yawned at Mick on all fours with one leg in the air, pouting a yes! yes! yes! at the camera.

"This gets boring after a while, doesn't it?"

"It isn't very thrilling," Mr. MacLean agreed sadly.

"Or funny," snarled 47.

Flynn raised his eyebrows in despair. "They just don't understand, do they, Mick?"

Mick was unsure whether to shout yes or no. Flynn nudged him with his foot.

"This is sexy and erotic and a total turn on, isn't it?"

"YES!"

"Clever and witty too, isn't it?"

"YES!"

"And you've enjoyed acting out all your fantasies, haven't you?"

Mick nodded wearily. "Yes."

"And if we see you back in this street, or even in this area, we'll know you want to relive it all again, right?"

"Yes."

Fergus unloaded the camera. "I'll send you a set of these for your collection. Maybe we could send some to those contact mags. Would you like that, Mick?" Mick couldn't answer. "No? Yes? No? You could meet lots of really interesting people that way. Well, perhaps not. We could just circulate them in the town instead. A memento of you now that you're moving away."

"Please – "

Fergus pushed him over with his foot. "Get up and get out of here."

The circle broke up and Mick's tormentors drifted off, leaving him scrabbling desperately for his clothes.

Marbles

15th March

Cold and overcast. My records show that this is the thirty third consecutive day without sunshine. But overnight the daffodils opened in the bed by the gate and in the afternoon the wind shredded the clouds and I saw patches of blue sky. When we went for walkies, Lukey and Razz snuffed the air and barked. Spring is on the way and the little sillies feel the excitement. My new neighbour has moved into the house across the street. I saw the removal van and heard a dog bark. I hope it's not a bitch to disturb the peace of Lukey and Razz.

Eight serious in the office today. No. 6 was especially difficult: an Irish whisper, fast, low, and hard to make out. Her silences grew longer and longer and I heard an old story in them. I am filled with foreboding.

Miss Buchan's pursuit of Ken was the talk of the street. She had lived there for years, keeping her dogs in luxury and herself to herself, and if it wasn't true that she never spoke to anyone, it was true that she was careful to whom she spoke. Or she was until Ken moved into the house opposite.

Mr. Ross saw the beginning. "Would you look at Miss Buchan?" he said, and nudged his neighbour, Mrs. McCabe, who was beside him at the bus stop. "She's blushing."

Mrs. McCabe looked, and sure enough, Miss Buchan was, though

Mrs. McCabe thought that the crimson was more like slap marks than blushes, which was more fitting somehow than that a sallow middle-aged woman should colour up like a girl. "What brought that on?" she asked.

Mr. Ross smirked. "Our new neighbour. See him going past her house?"

Mrs. McCabe turned and was in time to see Miss Buchan raise her hand as if to tap someone on the shoulder, but the burly white haired man she was staring after had already swept beyond her reach. Mr. Ross called cheerily, "Good morning, Miss Buchan!" The woman looked round, but made no answer. Mr. Ross shook his head. "Looked right through me. That woman goes about in a trance."

Mrs. McCabe knew that there was nothing unusual about that woman looking through people, although she was more inclined to blame standoffishness than trance states; less usual was Miss Buchan's present motionlessness: she was still standing with her hand frozen in a half wave.

Mr. Ross suggested that she go and ask if Miss Buchan was all right, but Mrs. McCabe refused. She didn't like talking to Miss Buchan because the effort made her queasy. "It's those fishy eyes," she explained, "big and grey and empty, always wandering, looking past you, beside you, through you, anywhere but at you. Makes me seasick. Anyway, it would be a waste of time to ask. All she ever says is 'Hello' and 'Lovely weather, isn't it?' and after that you're on your own." Mr. Ross knew exactly what she meant.

The pair were saved from further worry when Miss Buchan exploded into her customary frenetic gawkiness and dashed across the road in pursuit of her dogs.

"Daft biddy!" Mrs. McCabe snorted. "Didn't even notice she'd dropped their leashes."

"Still blushing like a kid," Mr. Ross laughed.

He fancied himself a student of human nature and entertained his neighbour all the way into town by insisting they'd just witnessed love at first sight. He called it Last Chance Syndrome, the old maid's complaint, brought on by the arrival of an eligible widower of clean habits.

18th March

Cold and overcast with not a patch of clear blue anywhere. My new neighbour has a golden retriever, a bitch called Cara. He called her to him and I turned. I don't know when I last turned at the sound of a human voice, but I was compelled. Such a voice he has, such a smile, such a face – unforgettable. 'Cara!' he called. 'Carissima mia!' – It struck a chord in me. Italian is such a romantic language. All day I could hear his pleasant golden voice: ' Cara mia, cara mia, carissima', as if he were calling me to him.

No. 6 hasn't rung again – that's three days now. She is absent, yet with me, detached, yet joined. Perhaps she won't call again and I'll never know why. My phone mate says he doesn't understand my calm. Calm! Strange how little of oneself appears on the surface, but when I consider my phone mate, I can see that's for the best. He specialises in screechingly audible compassion. It can be very wearing.

19th March

Heavy sleet today, but K went twice to the park and so I did too. Cara has a tartan coat to keep her warm. He went through the swing park, along the beech walk, then round the pond. Pets' Corner was quiet with no children about. He stood for a long time at the fence. Cara barked when she caught the smell of the animals, which made Lukey and Razz bark too. I kept them on the leash, but they struggled frantically to get to Cara. I was exhausted by the time I got home, what with restraining the dogs and keeping up with K. He walks very fast.

The office was quiet today. No. 6 still absent although her whispery voice runs constantly through my head and, worse, her devastating silences. I took in my knitting to give myself something else to think about – Lukey and Razz shall have a woolly coat each – but a new voice filled my head. 'Cara Carissima' it said, and it was never silent.

It occurred to me that K might go to the park when I am not there to see; I have asked for a change from the afternoon to night shift. I asked quickly, before I had time to think about it. Night shift means going outside in the dark, which I have always feared, but it means I shall be available all day.

Mr. Ross was not the only one who noticed the effect Ken had on Miss Buchan. Whenever Ken took Cara to the park, which was often because for all his seventy years, he liked the exercise, she shot out of her front gate like a gawky rabbit from its hole, dragging her spaniels after her. At one time or another, everyone saw her following him along tree lined paths, stopping when he did, walking on when he did, occasionally glancing sidelong at him when she thought he wouldn't notice. Young Susan Hay in particular, from her vantage point in the smoking den behind the hydrangeas, enjoyed the show. "Sub-til, very sub-til,' she said to her friends every time Miss Buchan slipped furtively by; and every time she said it, they all ducked down and giggled.

Of course, Ken did notice, he couldn't help but notice, but if he nodded in his friendly way, she only flushed an ugly plum colour and, with a smile thin as a splinter, sidled away down the path as fast as she could go. "Now, that's what I call playing hard to get," Susan Hay drawled, and her friends laughed till they choked on their smoke rings.

28th March

Milder today. The first green buds are unfurling on the trees. There is such a stirring in the air; all round the park a stirring and a movement. Lukey and Razz love all the extra walkies. If I so much as look out of the window, they think we're off to the park again.

He went past the swings today and into the walled garden. He is very spry for his age and could pass for much younger. 'Age cannot wither him nor custom stale his infinite variety.' My father said that about my mother every year on her birthday, except of course he said her instead of him, but it describes K just as well.

The park was deserted − it was very chilly − and so there was no one for him to stand and chat to. That was a relief as I didn't feel like loitering today. He stood by the pond for a while, watching the swans, while I sat in the shelter watching him.

He's what my mother used to call a gentleman of the old school. His shoes are polished like mirrors, a sure sign. She thought you could tell a lot about a man from the condition of his shoes: dull leather signified lack of character. Mother read shoes the way other people read teacups, palms, minds. She would think well of K's shoes, although she would have advised against leaving off his coat so early in the year – 'ne'er cast a clout till May be out' – but I'm glad it's off.

Coat. I mentioned the coat. I can't believe I did that after more than a week of avoiding it, but there it is in black and white. It crept in; it made itself heard. Objects have their little ways, and it's foolish to pretend that they are powerless, like prayers and curses, unless they are put into words.

3.30 a.m.

I must give it words. A record is pointless if things are missed out. His voice was the first thing I noticed, then his face and smile, then just as I was adjusting to all that, as if that wasn't enough to cope with, on the nineteenth of March he appeared in the herringbone coat and I was overwhelmed by it and pitchforked into the past, to another time and another place.

I smelled Ovaltine, malty and hot, and in my mouth there was sweetness and crunchy bits – Mummy didn't always dissolve the granules properly. 'Mummy, Mummy, it's got bits in it' – I heard myself say it – and she came and fished them out and licked them off the spoon, laughing. I heard her, I saw her, clear as day and solid as Lukey and Razz beside me. Her hair gleamed in the yellow kitchen light and I thought my heart would burst. She laughed, popped the spoon into the pocket of her floral apron, and turned away. 'Mummy,' I said, but she had gone.

'Mummy,' I said. Perhaps I spoke aloud, perhaps I was only remembering – the distinction isn't always clear – but the longing for her to turn back was real. We might have talked; after all, if she could laugh, a few words shouldn't have been impossible. But she was gone, the street was empty, and I was alone.

My heart did burst then – a tidal wave of longing broke through its walls, swept me along, and deposited me on the hearth rug, the red and royal blue one she liked so much. I lay on the rug reading my comic and sipping Ovaltine. The heat from the fire burned my cheek. I heard the ash sigh and fall into the grate, and the clock on the mantelpiece ticking like a big brave heart.

It was cold outside, colder and snowier than it ever gets now.

145

Mummy stuffed my wellingtons with newspaper and set them to dry on the hearth. I was drowsy with heat and then Daddy swept into the house in a flurry of snowflakes. It was cold outside, but before he closed the door, I glimpsed the snow, white and ghostly, lying thick on the hedge. He spread his herringbone coat, zigzagged with black and grey, over a chair at the fireside.

I learned to count on that coat; all the bones slanting one way were even numbers and the opposite ones odd. 'I'll give you a shilling if you can count all the herringbones,' he used to say. He only wanted peace to read his paper. I never got the shilling, except once. I was only six. I missed rows and had to start over, or else I fell asleep and woke up with his coat spread over me. I loved its heavy weight and scratchy warmth. And then he'd give me a threepenny piece for counting so well.

Words cannot describe how it felt to see them again, to be on the rug counting bones while Daddy lit his Senior Service and Mummy smiled in the yellow light. I was happy and quiet inside and so very glad to be home again.

It was a shock when the rain came on and I found I wasn't home at all, but standing in the street. I looked up the road and K had got clean away.

I ran all the way to the park. I was breathless and staggerylegged before I found him trotting Cara up and down the walled garden. He nodded and said hello. I have noticed before his compulsion to talk to me – strange considering that I can be of no interest to him – but the compulsion is there. It connects us.

I didn't answer; what could I have said? For me, it was enough that we were alone together in the garden. I couldn't take my eyes off his herringbone coat. It drew my eye and I followed it all the way down the beech walk and back to the crescent.

I mustn't risk visiting Mummy and Daddy again, which is a shame because the best time of my life was when we were all together under the ticking clock with Mummy humming along to the radio. But it would be selfish to go back now. The connection with K has been made – he feels it, I feel it – and I mustn't be distracted again because that's how K got out of sight last week. What if I hadn't found him again? So I'm glad that he's left off his coat so early in the year.

Ken gave up making friendly overtures. With a laugh, he told Mrs. McCabe that he was losing his touch. Mrs. McCabe sniffed and said he should consider himself privileged because at least he wasn't entirely beneath her notice, but later, when she was chatting to Mrs. Ross, she said that the old man was hurt because he liked to get along with everybody.

And he usually did. Within weeks of moving in, he had progressed from nodding acquaintance to first names with all the park regulars who stopped to pat Cara, a friendly animal, and, as Ken was quick to reassure anxious mothers, good with children. He was a thoughtful man too. He creosoted young Mrs. Campbell's fence for her, just walked into her garden with the tin in his hand, claiming he had creosote going to waste. "Dirty job for a woman," he told Mrs. Hay and Mrs. Ross, "and she's got enough to do since her husband left."

He was always doing something for somebody. The hard thing about retirement, he said, was filling his time, and so he would happily sit in for plumbers and electricians to help out neighbours who were at work, or pop down to the shops for the elderly, which made everyone smile because some of the elderly were younger than he was. But then, Ken was very un-elderly, straightbacked and lively with thick strong hair, even if it was white. He showed none of the old man's sourness when children were noisy or kicked footballs into his hedge. It was more his style to join in the kickabout. "Keeps me young," he said, puffing only a little after an hour in goals for the Campbell children.

But his spry friendliness never won a word from Miss Buchan and, in the end, he gave up. Oddly, abandonment made her heart grow fonder, as Mr. Ross insisted on putting it. By the summer, she had stopped slipping and sliding away from his smile. When he stopped to chat with anyone, she hovered just within earshot, hanging on every word. She never spoke herself, but everyone could see she was listening patiently, waiting for Ken to walk on so that she could be alone with him in her own peculiar way.

Susan Hay thought the whole performance was a scream and one bright Saturday morning, she couldn't contain herself. "You're winning, Ken," she said sepulchrally from the depths of the smoking den. "She's getting keener." Ken parted the bushes and peered in. "Mesdames Anonymous all present and correct, I see," he said sternly. "OK, who's going to do an old man a favour and take Cara for a run round the park?"

The dog barked and thumped her tail on the path. The girls scrambled out of the bushes and ran away squealing with Cara at their heels. Ken took a seat on the bench next to Mrs. Ross and Mrs. McCabe. "Best way to exercise a dog," he said and settled comfortably on sun-warmed wood. The three chatted idly until Mrs. McCabe nudged Ken. "Your shadow's here," she said, then smiling boldly, called out, "Good morning, Miss Buchan."

Miss Buchan, visibly flustered, retreated down the path. Ken said, "Don't stare at her, Jean. It agitates her", but Jean McCabe, who prided herself on her sense of humour, amused herself by staring Miss Buchan right out of earshot. Miss Buchan kept a sidelong eye on the threesome, but they all pretended not to notice. "Never knew a woman so timid in all my life," Ken said.

"Bloody snooty, you mean," Mrs. McCabe said sharply.

"No, she's just lonely and doesn't know how not to be," Ken said. "It takes people different ways."

There was a respectful silence. Ken had told them more than once about the loss of his dear wife and how loneliness had driven him to leave their old home. She had haunted every corner of it, the top of the stairs, the little passageway leading from the kitchen, everywhere really, and he hadn't minded that, but he had minded the black sorrow when he realised she wasn't really there. It was like losing her all over again.

The silence was broken by Susan Hay's little sister, Ailie. She came trotting down the path, tearful and sniffing, and squeezed on to the bench between Mrs. Ross and Ken.

"Did they leave you behind again?" Ken said kindly.

She slipped her hand into his and nodded. "They said I have to wait with you 'cos my legs are too short and fat to keep up." She stretched pink corduroy legs out for inspection. Mrs. Ross clucked soothingly and admired the sparkles in her new blue jellies, but Ken only laughed and said long legs were more trouble than they were worth. His friend Skinny Lizzie had legs which wouldn't stop growing no matter how hard she tried to stunt them. When she was seven, she had to tie them in reef knots before she could fit in her bed, but by the time she was twelve, only a round turn and two half hitches would do the trick. And by the time she was sixteen, the driver wouldn't let her on the bus because when she sat down, her knees touched the roof and showed her knickers, which caused a public scandal.

When Mrs. Ross told her husband about it later, she was still bewildered by what happened next. She was laughing at Ken's daft story when she noticed Miss Buchan circling closer and closer to the bench, moving so fast that no matter where Mrs. Ross looked, she could see her out of the corner of her eye. Then Jean McCabe grabbed Ken's arm and said she was sore laughing. Miss Buchan saw and heard and straightened up then, glaring like a wild thing.

She stepped up to the bench, her mouth opening and closing soundlessly like a goldfish. Ken said, "Are you all right, Miss Buchan?" It was obvious that the woman wanted to slide out of sight, but she stood her ground, and just when it seemed that something was going to happen, Cara came bounding up, Ailie squealed for a ride on her back, and whatever it was that might have happened, didn't. Then Susan arrived and made some catty joke about Miss Buchan's old brown anorak and Miss Buchan exploded.

"Susan Hay," she said, and her voice came out all squeaky. "Susan Hay — " For once in her life Susan shut her cheeky mouth because Miss Buchan was heading right for her. Susan's friends stopped laughing — the woman looked deranged — and Susan was as close to nervous as that wee madam was ever likely to get. But all Miss Buchan did was squeak: "Susan Hay, I wore pink once," which made the girls giggle. "Susan Hay!" Miss Buchan yelled. "Susan Hay!" The woman was fish-eyed and floundering and absurdly falsetto, which reduced the girls to helpless hysterics. "You silly girl. You nasty silly girl!"

Susan shrieked with laughter. "Ooh, pretty in pink. Pink to make the boys wink. Pretty as this were you?" And she turned and waggled her backside at the woman, her skirt so short that everyone got an eyeful of shocking pink and scarlet love hearts. Ken told her to behave herself, really sharp he was, and she turned sulky. Miss Buchan turned and fled into the walled garden.

Mr. Ross was unimpressed by his wife's tale, because he had been expecting a major drama. All the story did was prove what he had always said: Susan Hay was long overdue a good skelping, and Miss Buchan was mad as a hatter.

But Mrs. Ross lay uneasy that night, remembering that Miss Buchan's fuse had been lit when Jean took Ken's arm. And then Susan's pink knickers. Jealousy. It wasn't right. It wasn't healthy.

3rd June

...and he patted Ailie's arm and said, 'And so, little Caracarissima, don't pine for long legs. Remember Skinny Lizzie', and they all laughed, and suddenly I was at the bench and I don't know how I got there or what I intended, but they stared at me, all of them at the same time. I cannot bear being looked at. As for Little Miss Lovehearts and Spite, I wanted to say, 'Fuckdoll! Do you think K is interested in your underwear? Stupid fuckdoll! That's what you are in your scarlet and pink, a stupid little fuckdoll!'

But I couldn't possibly say anything like that – Mummy would have been shocked rigid. I don't even like writing it down, but a record must be true or there's no point – so I said the first thing that came into my head. I said,' I wore pink once.' Such a meaningless, ineffectual thing to say!

They think I'm mad. Someone muttered something about my losing my marbles. Susan's and Mrs. McCabe's sneers don't matter, but Mrs. Ross looked frightened – as if there was anything to fear from me! – and K's pity was unbearable. It's not how things should be – our connection was tainted by it.

Apart from anything else, the incident made me lose track of him. By the time I came out of the garden, he was turning out of the park gates with Ailie riding on Cara; I could see her fat little legs thrust out on either side. In a second they were out of sight. They could have gone anywhere. It was selfish to indulge my temper and draw attention to myself after all these weeks of going unnoticed.

How odd it is that after years of wishing that I could be seen and not overlooked, of wanting someone to look me in the face and put out a hand and say, 'Everything's all right', it should happen today. Everyone noticed me, and K, metaphorically speaking, put out his hand to me. It was unbearable. Now I want only to be invisible, to be everywhere K is, near him and watching over him.

2.30a.m.

Not much going on at the office tonight. A few drunk pranksters wanting to talk filth. We don't get many of them in the daytime, but at night they come out like moths. There was nothing too upsetting, which was just as well, because K was running through my mind. How organised he is: Cara draws people to him and K charms them into staying. I have lived here for years and never made a friend, but K is sociable. Today, fifteen people stopped to pat the dog: six children and nine adults. Cara offers her paw to anyone who passes and then K performs the introductions: 'This is Cara, mia carissima.' This community socialising didn't happen in the spring – too cold to linger, I suppose, even for a lovely dog and a warm golden voice.

I have nightmares that as summer goes on, more and more people will flock round him and that everything will get out of control. How will I manage to stay close then?

4.45a.m.

Confession. I won't sleep while this is on my conscience. Something happened at the office tonight. I was thinking about Ailie's pink corduroy and Susan Hay's pink and scarlet. I was thinking about them, the innocent and the coarse, how innocent the shell pink, how coarse the pink and scarlet, and was remembering when I wore pink.

A drunk woman phoned in, wanting to know if we could send someone round to rescue her cat from the garage roof. Well, really! I know what the training manual says, and I'm always patient and polite, but this was too much. The woman demanded to know what the sodding Samaritans were for if it wasn't to help people and people's sodding cats too. 'Fuckdoll!' I hissed without thinking. She became aggressive, but I don't have to put up with that sort of thing and I hung up.

All the way home, I worried about it, because the words popped out all by themselves – I had no say in them. I think it happened because she interrupted my visit to the past. But would it have happened if No. 6 had called? Would I have hissed her whispers into silence? Surely not! But the words erupted before I knew it. How can I be sure?

I had to remind myself over and over that 6 hadn't in fact called and that I had not driven her away. The thought calmed me, the thought and the night, which was pretty with stars and warm moonlight. I am getting used to the night, am even beginning to like it.

151

The dogs are company and we roam cool and airy and free, three capering shadows in the shining dark.

K's windows were in darkness when we passed and the darkness in them was thicker and heavier than the night, as if it was more than an absence of light. The thought sent me running for home and I am very angry with myself.

Susan Hay was at her garden gate with a gang of rowdy boys. The sight of me scurrying up my garden path set them off laughing and jeering, but Mrs. Hay called Susan in and the boys ran up the road whooping like wild Indians. They left Coke cans lined up along Mrs. Hay's wall, and those cardboard boxes for pizza. They wouldn't dare do that in daylight, but night is an invitation to be bold – now that I'm a night traveller myself, I understand that. Even I could be daring in the shadows, and should be, to make up for the scurrying.

And why not? Why shouldn't I caper a little?

Every lover needs a little luck, as Mr. Ross said when he told the tale of how Ken and Miss Buchan eventually got together. Miss Buchan's share came in the form of a neighbour's squabble. Several neighbours mentioned in passing to Mrs. Hay that Susan and her friends had been rather noisy the night before. Mrs. Hay was apologetic and promised to speak to Susan, but she drew the line at apologising to Ken. Susan denied absolutely that she had scattered empty cans and pizza boxes around Ken's front garden, and although Mrs. Hay was the first to admit that Susan was no angel, she was no liar either. But in the end, Mrs. Hay had to eat humble pie.

It was the queerest thing, she told Mrs. Ross later. She was weeding her front garden when Miss Buchan sidled up to her gate and mumbled that she had seen Susan and her friends with cans and boxes the night before. When questioned, Susan had lied. "What Coke? What pizza?" she'd said. "Where would we get the money for that?" And that was something else she'd be looking into, Mrs. Hay told Mrs. Ross grimly. In the meantime, Susan was grounded for a month.

Mrs. Ross told Mrs. McCabe all about it, and they were jointly astonished, not by Susan who came as no surprise, but by Miss Buchan. That was the second time she'd volunteered to speak in two days. "The power of love," Mr. Ross said. "She couldn't let the desecrators of darling Ken's garden get away with it."

He was less amused by what happened next. Two days later, when he and Jean McCabe were on the way to the bus stop, they saw that Ken's garden had been trashed. Flower heads littered his lawn and the contents of the wheelie bin had been dumped on his doorstep. Worse, his front door had been spray-painted. 'GRASS', the uneven letters read. Miss Buchan's door had been similarly treated.

"That Susan Hay wants a good thrashing," he said, and they hurried on by since there was nothing they could do.

7th June

Action is good for me. Today was a beautiful sunny day and everything about it was fresher and brighter than usual — sunlight dazzled green and gold through the treetops and haloed the cool clean shade below. I was reminded of a poem Daddy used to like which ended 'annihilating all that's made to a green thought and a green shade.' Green thought and annihilation. Health and destruction. It's a strange combination which I never understood before.

K was stopped a dozen times in the park — much headshaking about headless roses, spray paint, and the young of today and their general horridness. When I came close, the little crowd around him parted like the Red Sea and our eyes met. 'Miss Buchan,' he said. 'How are you?' There was concern in his voice; I heard it, warm and real, and I froze like a rabbit caught in headlights. They were all looking at me, willing me to speak, but I only nodded and hurried on. His audience was disappointed: he and I are fellow victims, after all, and should share the experience.

I suppose you could say the experience was mutual. Is it ever possible for two people to share an experience in exactly the same way?

He went round the pond three times today. Mrs. Hay was there with Ailie. I did my best to avoid her, although I do feel some guilt that Susan is being blamed. I have to remind myself that she is not a very nice little girl. Then Mrs. Hay saw K. Ailie went running to him. Mrs. Hay pulled the child away from Cara and complained noisily about K sending the police to her door, insisting that Susan had nothing to do with the vandalism last night. K said that either Susan or her friends were the obvious suspects, but then Mrs. Hay spotted me. 'Miss

Buchan,' she screeched. 'Did you tell the police that Susan – '

She blocked my path and I couldn't get by. I hate confrontation – I could feel myself shrivelling inside. I blurted out that I had said nothing and squeezed past her.

K followed me, hauling on Cara's leash, calling after me. He jogged at my heels all the way home and caught up with me at my garden gate. 'Couldn't you have backed me up?' he said, without so much as a hello or a good morning. 'It stands to reason that Susan – '

He must have seen my agitation, because he spoke more gently. 'Were you afraid, Miss Buchan?'

I managed a nod – I could not speak for my heart throbbing in my throat. He patted my arm. 'There's nothing to worry about,' he said. He was smug. It made me angry and I found my voice.

'Do you really think so?' I said. 'I've read about this sort of thing. Gangs get it in for someone and run campaigns against them.'

He smiled reassuringly, pityingly. A flame of anger scorched me. There's no room for pity between K and me. That's not how things should be.

'Susan and her friends won't want any more police attention,' he went on. 'They've had their fun.'

He was certain, smug, secure. My thoughts were green and ready to annihilate.

'Are you sure it was Susan?' I said. 'I saw a crowd of boys in the street last night, not the same ones as before. These were older. They hang around here at night, sitting on people's walls, breaking twigs off hedges.'

He said I mustn't let my imagination run away with me.

'But I had a good view of them,' I said. The boys – young men really – were very tough looking.'

He seemed a little uneasy as I closed my gate, which was a small triumph.

1a.m.

A distressing night at the office. There was a report on an inquest in the newspaper: a middle-aged Irish woman dead of an overdose, a nonsense note in her hand. 'Just taking the pins out,' was all it said. The coroner could make no sense of it. 'While the balance of the mind was disturbed,' he decided, and wrote her off.

It was No.6. She often spoke to me about being pinned to life like cloth to a pattern. Pinned all round, she said, and cut to shape, someone else's shape, and she couldn't find her own.

Now she has taken out the pins and drifted shapeless into the dark, airy and free at last. Her name was Theresa. I cannot silence the whisperings in my mind. Sometimes the whispers are hers, sometimes mine. Women whisper to themselves or to strangers on the phone. And sometimes to dolls.

My doll was Louby Lou. 'Louby Lou, Louby Lou, what can we do?' It was when the pins were going in and the cloth cut to shape.

3a.m.

I've been trying to remember the Louby Lou song.

> *'Here we go Louby Lou,*
> *Here we go Louby Light,*
>> *Here we go Louby Lou,*
>> *All on a Saturday night.'*

I think that's right, but it doesn't matter. I have to stop singing now — it makes Lukey and Razz whine. Anyway, I'd rather hear Mummy singing. I can hear her in my head. I like to think that, since I haven't visited her for a while, she has come in search of me.

We sang the song through twice. Louby Lou couldn't sleep unless she had her song twice. She had been my doll forever. Her long floppy legs hung permanently from the crook of my arm, and like me, she wouldn't eat vegetables. I told her she would be able to see in the dark if she ate up her carrots, and that brussel sprouts would make her big and brave, but she wouldn't touch them. Mummy said there was nothing for it but to set a good example and eat them myself. And I did, especially the carrots, so that I could be sure the dark round my bed was empty, but it didn't work; I was never sure, have never been sure. I still have to have a light on at night. Still. And the sprouts didn't make me big and brave. I stayed as floppy and useless as Louby Lou. I

155

could tie her legs round the bedstead above her head and poke her with pencils and she just lay there, curled upwards, floppy and silly and ugly.

Once I pulled and Louby came away from the bedstead minus a leg. Mummy had to untie it because I couldn't get the knot out. Louby's sawdust spilled all over my quilt and I screamed because I thought it would turn red like blood. Mummy said not to be silly and made me scrape it up with a soupspoon. I didn't let the stuff touch my hands, sure it would feel slimy like people's insides. Mummy sewed her leg back on, but it was skinnier than the other one after that and hung crooked.

'Her legs will fall off if you're not more careful,' Mummy said, 'and she'll be spoiled forever.'

'The dolls' hospital could fix her,' I said. Mummy shook her head and showed me the seams at the top of Louby's leg. They were gappy and the pink cloth was shredding. I screamed because sawdust trickled on to my arm. Any minute it would turn red and slimy. I knew it would. I knew. Spoiled forever. Forever and ever. I screamed and screamed.

For months I dreamed of twisted ruined legs endlessly leaking crimson slime. No matter how kind I was to Louby, I still dreamed. Even when I kept her legs dangling straight, even when I dressed her in her favourite pink satin dress and red satin shoes, the dreams still came.

I pestered Mummy to make us more clothes. Louby would feel better then. Her clothes were identical to mine, made from left-over scraps. All that summer, Mummy's dressmaker's shears crunched through paper patterns and stiff starched material — yellow gingham or pink cotton or fine green twill — and the room filled with the warm smell of new cloth. I was always impatient to see the shape Mummy had given the material and used to tear the pattern pieces off quickly and let them drift to the floor, not understanding that the pattern was what mattered, that the cloth followed it, that it couldn't do anything else.

People are like cloth: nothing in themselves, and before they know what's happening, they're folded and sheared and snipped into shape. Theresa, poor Theresa, knew all about that.

But I won't think about Theresa, not now. K is more to the point. He has kept his lights on all night. He's not so smug and certain now; he's learning that lights won't help him know who's out there watching.

It's dawn now and his lights are feeble and thin, fading into the rising sun. I've always hated the loneliness of that sight, but hated darkness more. Not now though. Tonight's dark was friendly and intimate. His lights reached across the street to mine and made a shining rope which bound us together.

This afternoon he asked, 'Are you all right, Miss Buchan?'

Tonight I would answer, 'Cara carissima, I haven't felt so right in years.'

6.30a.m.

Mummy is shouting and wakes me up. Her face is too close. There's lipstick on her teeth. 'What are you doing? Elizabeth, stop it!'

I sit in a puddle of pink satin and the shears are in my hand and the cloth crunches into shimmering strips. She shouts stop it stop it but I crunch and crunch and when she snatches at the shears, I stab them into her hand. Mummy, I didn't mean it, I didn't mean it.

Blood drips on pink rags and down her floral apron and I scream and she slaps and swings me up by the arm and shouts, 'What are you doing. Wicked girl, what are you doing? Your party dress! And Louby —'

I kick her shin and shout that Louby is silly and floppy and ugly and now she's dead and better dead. My kicking foot catches Louby's head and sends it spinning across the floor. Sawdust leaks everywhere and gets on my shoes and socks. I try to shake it off – I have to get it off – and I scream and scream that nobody can fix her now, nobody, nobody, nobody.

I hide behind the sofa, but she comes after me and her face is screwed up tight and scary.

Mummy, I didn't mean it. I didn't mean it.

The neighbours were outraged by the vandalism suffered by Ken and Miss Buchan. Mrs. Ross suggested setting up a Neighbourhood Watch scheme, but the organisation required seemed out of all proportion once Ken had tidied his garden and Miss Buchan had repainted her door. The only legacy of that night was the bad blood between Ken and Mrs. Hay.

The neighbours blamed Mrs. Hay for that. She couldn't get over having the police on her doorstep. If she and Ken met in the street, she ignored him. If Ailie went running to pet Cara, Mrs. Hay called her back. It was sad to see the dog's excitement when she saw Ailie coming, and their mutual disappointment when she turned away. The old man's pretence at not minding was pitiful.

Mrs. Hay's stock fell to an all time low when Susan buried the hatchet. She stopped at the bench in the park and told Ken straight that she'd had nothing to do with the mess in his garden or the paint on Miss Buchan's door. "Honest," she said. Ken nodded, and the next thing Susan was away up the beech walk with Cara and soon things were back on their old footing. Ailie even got her rides on the dog's back, although she always got off before they came in sight of her house.

17th June 3a.m.

I saw Ailie in the park today, riding on Cara's back, laughing and giggling. I had thought that particular game was over for good. Mrs. Hay wouldn't like it, but youngsters today don't care what their mothers like, even children as young as Ailie. Their mothers are to blame — they don't supervise their children enough; they don't ask enough questions. Yesterday Ailie dawdled at K's gate and put little heaps of dog treats along the wall for Cara. Then she walked to the corner and watched till K let the dog out. Cara stood up on her hind legs and wolfed down the treats while K stood at his window gently smiling; when Ailie crossed the road, she wriggled her fingers at him behind her back. They are in a conspiracy, K and his little caracarissima. The affection between them is palpable.

My first impulse was to tell Mrs. Hay, but that would only drive Ailie underground and me out into the open. Besides, Mrs. Hay is an aggressive woman and would shout. I'm not sure I'm up to that.

K is feeling smug and secure again. Tonight his house was in darkness for the first time since June 7th. Our rope of light is severed and I am alone.

I was startled awake by a voice singing 'Here we go Louby Lou, what are we going to do?' It was a relief to wake and find no one there, then a shock to realise the voice singing was my own. It was shrill and crazy. Or was it? Isn't it rational to ask what's to be done when something must be?

Without thinking, I snatched up the phone and dialled his number. I let it ring and ring until the light went on in his bedroom. His shadow was huge on the blind. I rang off without answering, then when his light went out, I rang twice more, and the second time, when he shouted at me to piss off, I hissed at him: 'Ssss...Sssss' like a snake. I surprised myself because I hadn't meant to say anything, only let him know he had company, but his coarseness provoked me. 'Ssss...Ssss'. He swore a lot, but he was afraid. I could hear it. After that, he kept his bedroom light on and put Cara out into the garden, as a watchdog, I suppose. That makes me smile. Cara standing guard! Cara who offers the paw of friendship to all comers!

He isn't so safe and smug now. We shall keep company till daylight and that's some satisfaction. But it isn't going to be enough.

People noticed that Ken was tired looking and sometimes missed his morning walk in the park. He told everyone that he wasn't sleeping well, and left it at that, but Mrs. Ross, gently questioning, managed to draw out of him that he was being plagued by prank phone calls. The old man tried to laugh it off, said he wasn't worried, but the deep shadows under his eyes told a different story.

She decided to let Mrs. Hay know what was happening, without making any direct accusations against Susan. Sometimes a word in the right ear...Mrs. Hay flew off the handle immediately and demanded to know if Ken was insinuating that her Susan was involved in this. Mrs. Ross assured her that he had done no such thing and then went home, terribly afraid that she might have made things worse, and resolving to keep her mouth shut in future. For once, she agreed with Jean McCabe: the young today were getting out of hand and it was time something was done about it. She couldn't think what though.

It was Jack Ross who advised Ken just to leave his phone off the hook. "As long as they get a reaction, they'll keep it going," he said. Ken was staunchly indignant because he didn't want to be seen to be giving in to bullies, but in the end, he'd agreed there was no fun in an engaged signal and no shame in depriving young morons of their fun.

15th July

I am shut out. The phone sits on my table, helpless, useless, empty of me, empty of him. I remind myself that I am not powerless, that his lights burn through the night because of me, that he is deprived of Cara's company at night because of me, that he looks haggard because of me. But I cannot reach him. I can only see his lights and feel the rope that binds us together.

We were company for one another! It's not fair — he can shut me out and I can't shut him out; I cannot silence his pleasant golden voice!

But Caracarissima isn't so easily excluded.

Half the street was roused in the middle of the night — police cars are noisy — but had to wait till the next day to find out what had happened. Except for Mrs. Ross who had been a witness. She had been up with the baby, walking the floor, when she heard police radios crackling. She looked through the slats of her blind and saw a Panda car outside Ken's house. The surprising thing was that when Ken opened his door, Miss Buchan was there beside him.

Mrs. McCabe's eyebrows defied the law of gravity when she heard that. "So that's where she goes at night, is it?" And she roared with laughter. "Sly bitch! Oh, God, it's disgusting!"

"Don't be silly, Jean," Mrs. Ross said, wishing she'd never mentioned it. "She was passing by — "

"Must have been," Mrs. McCabe sniggered. " I don't suppose he asked her over, not when he can have his pick of the geriatric ward. That sly biddy has been hellbent on getting her foot in his door since he moved in. The thing is, does she know what to do now she's there?"

"It wasn't like that," Mrs. Ross said stiffly, remembering Miss Buchan's pale haunted face, "although if it was, that's their business. But she was only trying to help."

"Heard it," Mrs. McCabe chortled. Mrs. Ross, who was still upset by the night's events, and didn't much like Jean McCabe anyway, stalked off, and Mrs. McCabe had to wait to hear the full story from

Mr. Ross at the bus stop. Which was fine by her, because there was nothing prissy about Jack Ross.

It turned out that when Miss Buchan was out prowling with Lukey and Razz, she saw shadows moving in the dark alley beside Ken's garage. Her dogs had barked like mad things, and the shadows, which turned out to be flesh and blood and thug-sized, ran down the path and pushed her to the ground. Five or six of them, Miss Buchan had said. She had knocked up Ken and together they had found obscenities, real filth, scrawled all over his garage wall. And worse, sheets of loft insulation material soaked in paraffin pushed against the wooden door. The police had reckoned Miss Buchan had disturbed the thugs in the nick of time.

Mrs. Hay was incandescent with rage when the police turned up on her doorstep again: she was quick to tell everyone that no accusations had been made, as obviously Susan wasn't thug-sized, but everyone heard her yelling at her daughter – "If you know anything, if you or any of your friends…" and exchanged knowing looks.

Everyone except young Mrs. Ross, who wasn't sure what to think. She had been walking the floor with Baby Angela for an hour before the police arrived and had heard nothing: not Lukey and Razz barking; not half a dozen thugs pounding along the quiet street; not Miss Buchan's screams when she was pushed. She'd heard nothing at all until police radios cracked the darkness apart.

Of course, Baby Angela had been teething and whiney and perhaps she'd been too distracted to notice. But every time she closed her eyes that night, she thought of lit fuses burning sparky paths around Ken, and Miss Buchan's wandering grey eye refusing to meet hers.

16th July

I could not go to the office tonight. I am confused. I know I'd have been useless. I almost lit the fire last night, almost, and then realised it might carry to Mrs. Ross's house next door. Baby Angela sleeps in the side bedroom – the smoke might have gone into her tiny lungs. I was paralysed by the thought of the choking, the closing of the throat, the fighting for breath. I felt it all so vividly that I could not breathe myself and had to sit down on the path till I was calmer. Cara came nosing over and I had to give her more biscuits to keep her quiet. My only comfort was that although I appear to have lost half my marbles, I still retain my community spirit.

I had to adjust my plans to fit the circumstances – after all, my aim was not to watch K's garage burn. Or perhaps it was. I'm not sure what I planned. I was in a fit of night anger at the time, there was a burning in my head, that's all I can say. But when my sense of civic responsibility overcame me, I was still able to salvage something from my shadow capering. I rang K's doorbell. I knew I had done the right thing when from behind his front door, he quavered, QUAVERED, "Who's there?"

He sounded old and nervous which was very satisfying. I led him straight to the graffiti and saw his reaction first hand. The colour drained from his face – even in the moonlight I could see his pallor – when he saw it and smelled the paraffin. I exclaimed in terror, "Arson! Dear God, that could just as easily have been your front door, and if it had caught, and if I hadn't happened by – "

"Now, now, Miss Buchan, don't get carried away – ". But his face was bone white.

We waited for the police in his front room. He fussed over me, courteous and gallant, eager to soothe me after my encounter in the dark, desperate that I should not leave him alone. And so once again we were company for one another and found mutual comfort. His hand trembled as he poured the tea, whether from fear, or from emotion over the loss of his dear wife, which he insisted on telling me about when he saw me glance at the wedding photograph on the wall, I really couldn't say.

I was rescued from this mawkishness by two charming policemen who escorted me home once I had made my statement. They checked all my doors and windows – infuriatingly slowly – and so it was some time before I was alone with K again.

He had opened all his blinds, but soon went round and closed them again. I understood at once. If the blinds are closed, he can't see who's outside – anyone could be creeping closer, like a cat padding towards its prey; but if they are open, anyone outside could see in and know exactly where he is and how he looks when he's afraid.

He kept all his lights on all night and our old togetherness was renewed. We kept company until the sun came up, one at either end of a glittering rope.

My heart ticks brave and steady as a big loud clock.

17th July 9a.m.

Woke up choking on anger and fear. It was Lukey who roused me, whining for his breakfast. There was fog. I was lost in the fog and crying, 'Daddy! Daddy!' It is confusing to wake from sleep but not the dream. The fog was all around, cotton wool thick and smoky, filling my mouth and ears and nose; even when I slipped on my dressing gown to go downstairs, the November fog followed me, shredding and thickening and wrapping itself round me. Figures loomed in front of me and disappeared as suddenly, leaving muffled hacking coughs behind them to die in the fog. The yellow light from shop windows is blurred and dimmed and I'm choking and spluttering, there is something in my mouth, I put my hand to my mouth and it's my red woollen scarf. Everything is all right, it's only my scarf.

November. Daddy and I are going to buy fireworks. Mummy puts a handkerchief over my mouth and nose and ties it in place with my scarf. This is to stop the fog getting into my chest. The red woolly pixie hood is to protect my ears — my ears are a big worry in the winter. It has been dark with fog all day, and she's not keen on my going out in it; neither am I, it's spooky out there, but when Daddy says, 'Come on, Little Red Riding Hood, time for sparklers and Catherine wheels and rockets ', I'm not afraid any more. He takes my hand and tucks it in his pocket and everything is all right.

We wade through fog like heavy dry water and here's the shop. I can just see the orange masked guy in a barrow at the door of the shop, slumped to one side, grinning. We buy two boxes of fireworks, dark blue, the lids bright with red and yellow flames, huge boxes, and Daddy has to carry them in front of him when we head for home. He is right in front of me in the fog, tall and solid, and I hang on to the tail of his herring-bone coat and trot behind. But his steps are too long. I can't keep up, I stumble and let go. He doesn't notice and strides on. Daddy! Daddy! I stand still. That's what you do when you get lost, you stand still and Mummy and Daddy will come and find you. But no one comes. I hear harsh winter coughs but can't tell where they are coming from. I squawk, 'Daddy! Daddy!' but the sound is deadened by my hankie and scarf. I turn round and around and can't see anyone, and

*then suddenly he's there, a huge shadow looming ahead. He doesn't
see me and strides past, but I grab the tail of his coat and tug. He
stops and turns and bends down with his hands on his knees. 'Hello!'
he says. 'Who can this be?' His voice is warm and golden, but he isn't
my Daddy. 'Hello,' he says again. I step back and something cold
presses against my leg. I squeal. The warm voice says, 'Sit, Cara.'*

    *Cara sits, but she's still as tall as I am. The man laughs. 'It's all
right. She's good with children. Friendly.' He laughs again. 'My
goodness! What big eyes you have, Little Red Riding Hood!' I laugh
too because he knows my Daddy's joke and everything is going to be
all right.*

    *Cara was friendly. I wonder how many Caras there have been over
the years? Caras-good-with-children, come-into-my-garden-Caras,
come-and-play-with-me-Caras. The nice big man and his dear wife
never chase you away. 'I don't mind kids round the place,' he told
Mummy. 'We've never been blessed ourselves. It's nice to watch them
play.'*

    *Something cold presses against my leg. Cara? No. Lukey, the little
silly. He was getting impatient for his breakfast. I was in the kitchen
with the tin in my hand. I must have been there for half an hour. I don't
remember going into the kitchen, but I must have.*

18th July

*K and I met in the park today. He was sitting on a bench in the swing
park with Mrs. Thompson. I sat as close as I could get. Children were
queuing up for rides on Cara − Ailie, and the Campbell children, the
little girl who lives round the corner, others I didn't know. Too many
to keep track of. Mrs. Thompson was entranced. She likes to see
children at play, she said. K made the children come and say their
names. He gave them sweets if they would tell a joke or do a
handstand. They all showed off like mad, even Cara. She stood on her
back legs, balancing a sweet on her nose till K called, 'Snap, Cara!'*

    *It was like a circus round the bench with K as ringmaster and Cara
the focus of all eyes. He spoke to me several times, but I have no small
talk and he soon forgot I was there. I mentioned that the children were
tiring Mrs. Thompson, but she said that she didn't mind, and laughed
till the tears came when Ailie tried to balance a square of chocolate on*

her nose for as long as Cara could. Cara and Ailie: Two well trained little bitches sitting up pretty together, although Cara's the better performer – she's been doing it longer. Lukey and Razz were wild to join in, but on principle, I have never taught them tricks. I told Ailie to pat them and she did, but only out of politeness. She couldn't wait to go back to Cara and K.

I heard him tell the little Campbell girl that he would take her to nursery in the morning when her Mum was at the dentist. Good old K, ever helpful, ever obliging, ever there or thereabouts.

I can't be everywhere. I must be more constructive, more rational. What have phone calls and paraffin and graffiti achieved?

Cara is the big attraction.

Ailie's screaming brought everybody running. The poor mite could hardly speak for crying, Mrs. Ross told her husband later. And it was a terrible sight which had upset her. Cara was lying on the front lawn, writhing and twisting, and there was bloody froth at her mouth and nose. She whined and snapped at anyone who came near her. It was heart rending, and almost a relief when her eyes glazed over and she died. Some kind of fit, the Rosses concluded, and so did everyone else. Ken was a solitary and pathetic figure when he went walking in the park. He seemed to age overnight, Mrs. McCabe said, and predicted knowingly that he'd go downhill quickly now. Old people were like that.

Ken was the centre of attention for days. All his neighbours expressed their sympathy, even Mrs. Hay. Ailie and Susan were heartbroken, she said, and Ailie had had to be kept off school for two days. She described to Mrs. Ross how the old man's eyes had filled with tears when she told him that. "They're good girls," he had said. "Always kind to Cara."

The peace between Mrs. Hay and Ken lasted until the results of the autopsy came through. Cara had died of rat poison, ingested with dog treats. Unbidden to everyone's mind came the vision of Ailie heaping treats along Ken's wall. No one seriously suspected her, but the culprit wasn't a hundred miles away, and if it wasn't Susan herself who had poisoned the dog, then those friends of hers who'd been causing trouble – well, she ought to be made to name them. First vandalism and funny phone calls, then arson, and now a poisoning. Someone really twisted was on the loose.

20th July

Mrs. Ross is still looking at me strangely. She seems always on the verge of saying something, but I hurry on by. It's a pity, because she is the nicest of my neighbours. Not that we've ever talked much, but I've seen her on a bench in the park with Baby Angela. The baby bounces up and down on her lap, crowing and waving her fists, and Mrs. Ross laughs and blows kisses on her cheek. They are lost in their own private world.

That was my world once, mine and Mummy's. I have a photograph of her sitting on a sunny sea wall. I am standing on her lap, wearing a knitted hat with rabbit's ears. She has turned me to face the camera, but she is looking at me. Her cheek is pressed against my fat baby face and the wind is blowing strands of her hair around our heads. Any moment I am going to bounce and crow and she will laugh. That was our world when everything was all right. Left to ourselves, it would have been like that forever.

I remember the long narrow skirt she's wearing – it was cobalt blue with covered buttons at the vents – and the clatter of her tall spiked heels. I was only a year old, but I remember. Children suck up memories like sponges – the feel of things, the colours, the patterns, the rattle of high heels, the things they don't understand and save for later.

I cannot put Cara's agonies out of my mind. She took a long time to die. I had thought it would be unpleasant, but quick. The little girl Ailie cries herself to sleep at night. I can hear her through the wall. Susan too. The sound of little girls weeping is unbearable. It has made me cry for the first time since I was little.

I met K in the park and offered my condolences. To my horror, the tears sprang to my eyes. He reached out and patted my arm. 'You're a dog lover too,' he said. 'I know you understand.'

And I do. With a dog along, a walk in the park is a delight; without, it is a dull and pointless exercise. I would never set foot in the park if not for Lukey and Razz. I don't expect K will for much longer. I think he might be persuaded to move house; at the very least to stay out of the park.

He is concerned for my two little sillies, what with a mad poisoner at large in the area, and advised me not to let them out of my sight. He threw a stick or two for them, but his heart wasn't in it. We took the bench outside the walled garden. People stopped to enquire after him, but no one stayed long. It is easy to discourage people. I've been doing it all my life – a look, a silence, a hint of impatience, and they're gone. Children need a little more encouragement. 'Don't startle the dogs,' I said. 'They're not used to children. They might bite.'

We were soon left in peace together. He treated me to a long lecture on dog training and insisted that I had a responsibility to make Lukey and Razz safe for children, who can't help being attracted to dogs. I assured him my sense of responsibility to the community was alive and well, that I do my best to keep children away. Then he said he couldn't go on calling me Miss Buchan and asked my name.

'Theresa,' I told him. It seemed a fitting memorial somehow.

I can still feel the pressure of his fingers on my arm.

The neighbours shared many a joke about the geriatric Romeo and his scrawny Juliet. They courted on the hoof, strolled round the pond, accompanied by the sharp excited barking of Lukey and Razz. Mrs. Ross and Mrs. McCabe saw them often in the park and passed them smiling, Mrs. Ross indulgently, Mrs. McCabe with sly malice.

"What does he see in her?" Mrs. McCabe said once.

"Well, they're company for one another," Mrs. Ross said vaguely.

"Company? She walks him like she walks her dogs. Never talks to him, never smiles, just steers him three times round the rose beds, down the avenue, and home again."

Once on that subject, Mrs. McCabe was apt to go on and on. Mrs. Ross scarcely listened. The truth was, she too often wondered what the attraction between Ken and Miss Buchan was. Jean McCabe was wrong about one thing: Miss Buchan did in fact talk to Ken, but Mrs. Ross didn't much like what she talked about. Ken was still in a fret about a story Miss Buchan had read in the paper: a pensioner harassed for months by teen thugs, his windows smashed, his house broken into, and finally a murder. It was extraordinarily tactless of Miss Buchan to tell him about these things.

3rd August

I did not anticipate this. He has taken to calling round when it is time for the dogs' walkies. He is chatty and charming, as if there were only one interest in his life – getting to know me. It's Theresa this and Theresa that, and many helpful offers to walk the dogs for me if he thinks I look tired. He is pitiful sometimes. 'I miss Cara,' he says often, and asks to borrow my animals with tears in his eyes. I understand: a man alone in the park, chatting to children, draws attention; a man with dogs is unremarkable. But I won't lend him my dogs: a man with dogs and a middleaged spinster has his style cramped. And so I must put up with his company and he with mine. Another shared experience. He wants to train Lukey and Razz. It was Ailie started him off on that. She stopped to chat and asked him if he'd teach them to balance chocolate on their noses. He said that trick took time to learn and that they had to be trained every day. She promised to meet us in the park as often as she could. They ignored me entirely, made their plans without consulting me. I told Ailie I could see her mother coming and she shot off. But she'll be back. She's very determined little girl. I was sharp with K and said that training living creatures to behave in a way not natural to them degraded them. There was a burning in my head and I couldn't stop. 'Some people find fulfilment in exercising power over animals – even over other people,' I said. 'I disapprove.'

He laughed. 'Theresa, it's as much fun for the dogs as it is for their owners. They like it.'

My head burned and burned. 'Like it! How do you know that? How do you know what it feels like to be made to perform? To be made to do things, to curry favour, to fawn? To be laughed at and giggled over? You cannot possibly know how that feels!'

I took one of my spasms and had to clench my jaw to stop my head jerking. 'You will not train my animals,' I said through gritted teeth.

'There's no need to get so agitated, Theresa,' he said. 'If you're so dead set against it, then of course I won't.'

I wanted to walk away, to leave him standing and never speak to him again, but I was brought to my senses by Ailie, who came galloping up, gap-toothed and grinning, to say that the ice cream van was at the gates, and that it would be lovely to have an ice lolly. The Campbell children were lurking a few feet behind her, shy and hopeful. I had to stay then and apologise for being so sharp. I had to go to the van with them. He bought us all a treat, the children and me. I had to eat an ice cream. I had to watch Ailie putting out her tongue and licking her ice lolly. I wanted to be sick.

'Ailie, go and play with your friends now. You're making a nuisance of yourself.' She stared me out, pert and mutinous, and my voice rose. I couldn't help it. 'Will you do as you are told!'

She eyed K and licked raspberry slush from her lips. Their twinkling eyed silence bordered on insolence, but after a long moment, she turned and ran off, crying, 'I'll see you tomorrow!'

'You don't like children much, do you?' he said kindly.

'I don't dislike them. I don't know any,' I said.

'Their friendship is a privilege,' he said. 'You should make friends with Ailie. She's a lovely child.'

Cue for more mawkishness: his dear wife and the sorrow of her life – childlessness. And another rendition of how she haunts him in all the old familiar places. 'We were never blessed,' he said and my head spun. 'Theresa, you've gone quite pale. Would you like to go home? I could take Lukey and Razz for their run.'

'We'd best both leave,' I said, and with some inspired prevarication, got him out of the park.

Everything is getting out of control.

4a.m.

I've given up on sleep. I'll only dream. I'd rather be awake: remembering isn't as bad as reliving.

Never been blessed, he said. That was how they always put it, K and his dear wife, whenever they came to visit. The first time I heard it was in my mother's kitchen, in the yellow light, that time I got lost in the fog. 'We've never been blessed,' he said, with a casual smile and a glance in my direction. I was on the red and blue rug with Cara, running her silky ears through my fingers. It was good to be safe home with Mummy, good to see Daddy's relief when he arrived and found me there, good to see them all so friendly, fun to hear Daddy and K thrilling over the boxes of fireworks. 'You're like a couple of kids,' Mummy said. 'Even Elizabeth isn't so excited.'

I was more interested in Cara. I was afraid of dogs, but K said

Cara liked me, he could tell. And she did. She sat with her head up and her chest thrust out, panting, while I ruffled her fur and tugged her ears. It was a perfect night: I had had an adventure and been rescued; I had been comforted with Ovaltine and was swaddled in the warmth from the coal fire and the quiet laughter from the tea table. Cara gave her paw to everyone and was fed scraps; I counted bones on Daddy's and K's coats and K gave me a whole shilling. And when the evening was over, it didn't really end: K was to bring Cara and his wife to our bonfire and we were going to roast potatoes and melt marshmallows on sticks.

6a.m.

She haunts me too, K's wife, with her moth pale face and ruby lipstick. I visited their house often, to see Cara. They lived just round the corner from my school. Mummy hoped I wasn't making a nuisance of myself, but they liked having a child around the place, not having any of their own. Yes, K's dear wife haunts me in all the old familiar ways, in all the old familiar places, on the stairs, in the passage leading from the kitchen, at the bedroom door with the clothesline in her hand. 'Do you learn knots at the Brownies?' she said. 'Come on, I bet I can tie you up so tight that you can't escape.' She was hopeless at knots – they fell off when I giggled and tugged. She swore to learn harder ones for the next time I came. K, leaning on the doorpost, laughing. 'Time for tea,' he said. 'We've got trifle tonight. She's better at that than knots.'

Lots of knot games. Other games too: tiddlywinks, ludo, snap, nets of twinkling marbles.. Kids' games. I won sixpence every week. But knots were my favourite. Loops and whorls of rope, complicated arrangements, impossible bonds from a book about Houdini, but they always fell off. 'Tell Mummy you're learning knots for your Brownie badge'.

It was spring before she learned the knots to keep me tied. 'Come round in your party frock before the birthday tea. We have a present for you. And we'll take a photo.'

Me and Louby Lou in pink satin and red shoes. Photos. Flash. Flash. 'I've learned the knots,' she said with a giggle. Into the bedroom with the brass bedstead. 'But you don't want your pretty frock crushed.'

170

Pink silky slip and matching knickers with rosebud trim, a present from my Gran. This is a special knot, a round turn and two half hitches. Wrists. Ankles. Bedstead. A cry of protest. Too tight. K shaking his head, what a baby, what a big baby you are. Skinny Lizzie, she says, and prods. Slip pushed up. Do you know what Apache Indians do on their birthdays? They paint themselves. Ruby lipstick. Colouring in. Flash. Flash. Flash. Photos. K's funny smile. Slimy stuff on my tummy.

Mustn't tell. Mummy would die if she knew what a bad girl I was. I'd get taken away. Anyway, I have to be trained before I'm eight or it's too late, I'll never be a real woman.

There's a lot to learn: how to please, how to look pleased, how to sound pleased, how to guess his mood and not make him angry, how to sit up pretty, say I love it, love him, over and over, so I can be his carissima. Poke and prod. No tears, don't tell me you don't like it, stupid wee fuckdoll.

Flash. Flash. Flash. Photos.
Photos. Flash. Flash. Flash.

9a.m.

'I disapprove,' I said to K yesterday. The harshest words I've ever said to him. As always, I am futile, useless, powerless. I was patterned too young, pinned all round, I'll never be any other way now.

Is it possible to DECIDE to be braver?

Mrs. Ross had another uneasy night. She had overheard Ken and Miss Buchan talking at the ice cream van. Ken had given out goodies all round – those kids knew a soft mark when they saw one – and then he and Miss Buchan had drifted nearer to the bench where she and Angela were sitting. Miss Buchan said she'd heard noises from his garden a couple of times this week, but since nothing had happened, she hadn't wanted to worry him about it. But there were some tough looking young men with motor bikes by the park gates who seemed familiar, and they were staring at Ken. One of them was coming over. It might be an idea to leave the park…

Mrs. Ross had looked up from Angela then, and was shocked by

Miss Buchan's ghastly yellow colour. The next thing, Ken was escorting her to the side gate at a rapid trot. The biker had come towards Mrs. Ross and she had felt a chill of fear – all that leather and long greasy hair, Miss Buchan's sallow terror – but he only went to the van and asked for six cornettos. And when Angela threw her fluffy duck out of her pram, he stooped and picked it up for her. 'There you are, little pretty,' he said, and placed it carefully on her coverlet. He had quite a nice smile really.

Mrs. Ross lay awake thinking about Ken. He had developed an old man's stoop which hadn't been there in the spring, and he had a habit of continually looking behind him. It was no wonder he was nervy with Miss Buchan harping on about thugs and helpless old people; she didn't seem to realise she was actually making him more nervous. Jean McCabe had been right about Ken going downhill – but even she hadn't thought of Miss Buchan giving him a good hard push.

Mrs. Ross had asked Jack if she should drop a hint to Miss Buchan about being more careful about what she said. Jack had only laughed. 'Old people enjoy their miseries,' he said. 'It makes them feel close to each other.'

5th August

The same policeman turned out as last time. Had I seen anything? Heard anything? Only the breaking glass, I said, and then the police sirens. I told them I was impressed by how quickly they'd turned out. I could see they were pleased. I don't expect they get much appreciation. They said they'd been keeping an eye on the street in view of the recent problems.

That was unwelcome news – I hadn't noticed them about the place. I must be more careful. It would have been undignified to be caught tossing a brick through a neighbour's window.

I don't know why I did it. It was an impulse born of opportunity. I was sitting thinking things over, remembering, and then saw that K had gone for a bath in the middle of the night – the bathroom window had steamed up. He must have taken my advice about letting a bath soothe and relax him. It was easy to get at the rear kitchen window through the gap in the hedge.

The police said K was in a dreadful state. And so he was. Quite pale and trembly. I made him a cup of tea with a shot of brandy in it. He said it was good of me to come over. 'You've been right all along about this, Theresa,' he said.

'It's the times we live in,' I said and swept the broken glass off the sink unit. He tells me he's buying another dog on Saturday. Another Cara — he can't see past golden retrievers: reliable and safe around children. He thinks the new dog will be nearly as good as I am at alerting him to the presence of strangers. Then his eyes filled with tears. He's missing Cara, he says. And with apologies to my good self, he's going to teach the new one tricks. It will be fun for little Ailie.

I have sat here for hours, listening to the ticking of my heart, louder and louder, braver and braver. I must be braver.

Mr. Ross had a friend who worked for a home security firm. He managed to get Ken a good deal on an alarm system and a dusk-to-dawn light. He was amused to see that Miss Buchan was the first to be invited in to see the new fixtures and fittings.

"Maybe he's trying to tempt her to move in. Home security is all he has to offer," he laughed.

7th August

Fort K was in darkness. I called in on my way home from the office. 'I just wanted to check you were all right when I saw the lights were out,' I said.

I was inside in minutes. He said he didn't need lights now that he had an alarm system so sensitive that nothing could penetrate it.

'If you're sure,' I said, 'but there were three figures at your gate when I turned into the street. Oh, they weren't doing anything — only hanging around. They made off when the dogs barked.'

We went out and inspected the gardens. There was nothing amiss, of course, much to K's relief. 'You must have scared them off before they had the chance to — ' he broke off with a catch in his voice. 'Where do you work anyway? You keep such odd hours.'

'The Samaritans,' I said.

'I should have guessed. You're certainly my Good Samaritan.'

We had tea and brandy. After three, he confided that dusk is when the terror begins.

'I can imagine,' I said. 'Yes, when night falls. The dark always feels so full of things, doesn't it?'

He is very sorry for himself. I wanted to tell him about real terror, how it lives on in a series of flashlit scenes, Skinny Lizzie blanched and petrified in white edged photos. Terror began when I was seven and he was thirty and it has never stopped. I have no pity for him: I have spent my life with Hell at my heels. And now he has Hell at his. I think there is fairness in that.

He walked me to the door. I said I'd left my scarf on the sofa. He went to fetch it. I noticed that he has developed a shuffling walk. While he was gone, I scattered marbles all over the step. Little glass ones with coloured twists in the middle. Kids' game. It took him five minutes to find the scarf which I'd hidden under a cushion.

'Don't forget to switch on the alarms when I'm gone,' I said. 'Those men might be back −'

I listened to him lock up when he'd shut the door. Two deadlocks. Two bolts. As if terror can be kept out. Silly man − terror comes from within. Always.

By the time I went to bed, the lights were on in every room in his house. He's under house arrest, shut in by keys and bolts and locks and bells. And he still doesn't feel safe.

We were company for one another all night, as we have been since I was seven. His lights and mine joined together and made a long glittering rope which bound us together.

Mrs. McCabe and Jack Ross saw the ambulance on their way to the bus stop. Someone had booby trapped Ken's front steps with marbles and sent him crashing down on to the concrete path. He suffered a broken hip, wrist, and collar bone. And a fairly serious concussion. Jack Ross was furious − his friend had assured him that a field mouse couldn't slip past those alarms. He felt responsible somehow.

Mrs. Ross stopped worrying about Miss Buchan's treatment of Ken. While he was in hospital, she was a model neighbour, visiting him twice a week and minding his house and garden for him. As she said to Mrs. McCabe, it was surprising how alike the two of them actually were − always ready to help out a neighbour in trouble. She reckoned

Ken had brought out a hidden side in Miss Buchan. Mrs. McCabe only snorted.

1st September 3a.m.

They're keeping K in for another week. I never dreamed that finding my marbles would be so spectacularly successful. He has lost weight and his air of nattiness — doesn't shave, slouches like an old man. He doesn't talk about coming home any more either — he feels safer in hospital. I promised there was nothing to worry about, that I'd keep an eye on him and his house. 'I'll always be there for you,' I said. He could not speak for emotion.

I dreamed of Mummy last night. She was tight lipped the way she used to be when I did something horrible: that time with the scissors, the times with the matches, the tantrums. Doctors couldn't help. ECT couldn't help. She got resentful when I didn't respond to treatment. So did the doctors. Well, they didn't understand what they were treating me for. Nor did she. I never forgave her for not knowing, not understanding. We were not on speaking terms when she died.

She was tightlipped in my dream, but I spoke to her anyway. It's time we made up.

'Mummy,' I said. 'I've done something right.'

'Have you, Elizabeth?'

Her voice was cold the way it so often was, because of the things I said, the things I did. She came towards me, her high heels clicking. Then she frowned and turned away.

'Mummy!' I was shrill and desperate. 'Mummy!'

All of a sudden I was little again. She came back and bent and scooped me up in her arms. She took me to the window. It was snowing outside, more heavily than it ever does now.

'Watch for Daddy, Elizabeth. He'll be coming round the corner any moment.'

We peered through swirling white together. 'And what have you done that you're so pleased about?' she said.

'I helped my friends, Ailie and Theresa.'

'I haven't met them, have I?'

'No. We played marbles together.'

'That's nice. Oh, look. There's Daddy.'

And he came swinging round the corner and as usual his eyes went straight to our window and he smiled and waved. In a moment, we were all together again and it was so lovely to be home.

Underground

The river of people flowed off the Underground platform into the train, and she was carried along with it, frozen in a tight locked mass of elbows, knees, brollies, and brass-cornered briefcases. The sardine togetherness always made her claustrophobic, but today was worse than usual. She was trapped in the centre of the aisle, wedged upright by the press of bodies all around, one arm pinned across her chest and the other bent at an uncomfortable angle behind her back. Above ground, it was raining, and the smell of wet hair and clothing was overpowering.

She swallowed and tried to relax, but it was impossible. She felt as if a snake were twining slowly round her rib-cage, squeezing tighter and tighter; soon it would be difficult to breathe, and the snake would find its way up to her throat and squeeze again until sweat broke out on her brow and black stars danced before her eyes. The fear of fainting and not being able to fall down made her heart hammer in her chest.

She tried harder to relax. Claustrophobia could be controlled: she could force her mind to take her somewhere far away from the crisis. She concentrated and summoned up an image of high hilltops patched with snow. She could see blades of grass, green and cool, spiking through the whiteness; she saw herself climbing up the lower slopes. The turf underfoot was thick and springy and a keen wind slapped at her cheeks. The chilly freshness of open space refreshed her. The snake coiled round her loosened and fell away to the floor and her breathing evened. She continued up the slope. With a determined effort, she knew that she could make the climb last all the way to

Hillhead Station.

But in the end, imagination was not enough. The closeness of so many people was an assault on her senses which no amount of visionary moor and fantastical breeze could cancel out. She found herself blaming the man directly in front of her. Her face was pushed into his chest and was becoming damp as his sweat seeped into the pores of her skin. Her concentration was disturbed by the deep slow pounding of his heart in her ear, and totally destroyed by the smell of the expense account lunch which he was breathing down on her: a charmless concoction of too much garlic, too many spices, and a viciously sour red wine, a common impoliteness among the middle aged, middle class executives who travelled on the Buchanan Street − Hillhead stretch of line.

As if that weren't bad enough, his suit was damp from the rain and the pungent smell of wet wool caught at the back of her throat and threatened to choke her. Traces of him settled on her face, hair, and clothes. She felt invaded. A wild panic hissed and coiled snake-like round her. She fought for control and tried to ward off the notion that contact with the man had a quality of deliberate menace about it, but his solid bulk and pervasive smells were too much for her.

She took refuge in another mind-game. She concentrated hard and sent out her own presence to battle with his. Her scent was a piercing floral one and more than a match for his aftershave, but his lunch had the victory over her salad and orange juice. Her PVC raincoat could not at first compete with his stinking wet wool, but it was spattered with raindrops, and if she focused on them, something of their pure cleanness penetrated the hissing panic in her head. From the rainwater, she conjured up a soft and gentle mist of rain, the kind you get in Ireland, cool and full of the tang of the sea. Gradually, the man receded from her awareness, vanquished by image after image of towering cliffs and the green rolling waves of the Atlantic.

From that safe distance, she was able to be charitable and concede that it was hardly the man's fault that the train was overcrowded, or that she was oversensitive to the crush, or even that his hipbone was grinding into hers. She was firm with herself: it was all accidental, unintended and nothing to be concerned about. She even forgave him his lunch before she disappeared into a fine mist of Irish rain.

She didn't stay there long. Not even the sight of the sun going down over Galway Bay would have been enough to cancel the sensation of her wet mac riding up her leg. For a moment, she was mystified, and then turned cold from the bone marrow out as she registered the movement of a hand slithering up her thigh. With a furious jerk, she swung her hips sideways to dislodge it, but it clutched at her leg, seized a chunk of flesh and pinched hard. She bit back a yelp of pain and kicked at his shins, but there wasn't enough room to get up any momentum, and her foot slid harmlessly across his ankle. Like a gentleman, he returned the caress and rubbed his foot up and down her calf.

Her thoughts scattered like sparks from a bonfire and she could not think what to do next. A scream might help, but her throat seemed stuffed with cotton wool and she knew no sound would come out. She struggled to free her arms, in the hope of reaching down and pushing his hand away, but the effort proved to be a mistake. He liked it when she wriggled: the tempo of his heart went into double time and the increased agitation of his hand scorched her thigh. When he leaned heavily against her, she almost bit him, and would have done had she not suspected that he would take that as a sign of encouragement too.

The hand rapidly approached lacy edges. She was just about to bite when suddenly it was all over: the train lurched, the crowd swayed, and her arms fell loose. A surge of anger electrified her, and without thinking, she seized his hand and hauled it up above her head, like a referee proclaiming the world champion. "Who's a naughty boy, then?" she yelled.

She was appalled by the loudness of her voice in the silence which fell like a shadow over the compartment. Everyone was looking at her. Everyone was staring. Her heart quailed at the sudden publicity and all she could think was that she who lives by the sudden impulse shall surely die of shame. Her one consolation was that he was equally exposed.

He was frantically trying to edge away from her, as if his hand held high above her head was disembodied and nothing to do with him, but the crowd had closed in around them again and he was trapped in the spotlight beside her. There was nothing to do but put a bold face on it. She dug her nails into his palm and enquired with a hiss how he liked the feel of *that*. She enjoyed her small revenge until she realised that her hand was a prisoner up there with his and that she could no more release him than he could get away from her. Capturing him was all very well, but what was she going to do with him? She hadn't bargained for a minuet all the way to Hillhead.

She caught the eye of a woman sitting opposite. The woman was making no attempt to hide her amusement at the spectacle before her: her cushiony shoulders shook and her pillowy bosom heaved as her laughter bubbled up and foamed round the compartment. She eyed the man up and down and chortled. "I've always wondered what one of THOSE looked like," she called out.

There was an answering ripple of female laughter from every corner. The laughter fluted or trilled or flew sharp-edged as broken glass, but all of it beat upon the head of the captive. She felt him sag slightly, but the floor was too solid to let him sink through it. She was more than avenged for her pound of bruised flesh, and was warmed by the show of solidarity from her travelling companions. Of course they had all experienced THOSE in one form or another – gropers, kerb crawlers, phone pests, the everyday nuisance of the furtive and the sly. It didn't happen often that one was captured and put on display though. Pride in her achievement made her bold and she decided that it was time to see what one of THOSE looked like.

She gazed up at the steeple of their joined hands and saw a dark blue sleeve and a sparkling white cuff half concealing a flat Rolex: trash with class. She studied his face. It was disappointingly ordinary: round, beefy, a touch petulant, and at the moment, seriously tense. She peered into his eyes. They were the colour of whisky and glowing with sullen anger. It was a novel experience to look into the eyes of someone who seriously wished to murder her. She grinned cheekily, knowing that she was safe enough. Without his anonymity, he could never be anything but ludicrous. He must have read her thought, because he flushed and looked away.

She had a sudden urge to ask him why he had picked her, what it was about her that had made him think she belonged to the gropeable class; after all they'd been through, she surely had the right to know. But before she could speak, the train ground to a bone-jarring halt, doors hissed open, and there was room to move. The man wrenched his hand free and leapt back a couple of feet.

"Cunt!"

Which, she supposed, as he fought his way out of the carriage and on to the platform, was all the answer anybody ever got.

Madeleine

[In 1857, Madeleine Hamilton Smith stood trial at the High Court in Edinburgh. She faced two charges of attempted murder by poisoning, and one of murder. The alleged victim was her lover, Emile L'Angelier. She was found Not Guilty on one charge of attempted murder, and Not Proven on the other two charges. Extracts from her letters given here are authentic.]

Madeleine stepped into the dock. The court was not at all what she expected: it was dim, untidy, and very small, lit only by wedges of dusty sunlight which forced a fuzzy warmth through its tall windows. The roars of the crowds outside – 'Hoo-er! Hang the wee hoo-er!' – died down and she was startled by a new sound, a steady drone like the buzzing of wasps in a byke. It was a murmur of excitement from dozens of male throats. She glanced across at the public gallery and saw that gentlemen were lounging with their feet on the brass rails. They were peering at her through opera glasses. And they had kept their hats on in her presence. A warm flush of affront crept up her neck.

The friendly wardress whispered, as if Madeleine were some music hall performer pleased to draw a crowd, that the gentlemen had paid golden guineas to secure a seat in court, and double the amount for a place on the day when her love letters would be read. A high pitched gibber of fear filled Madeleine's head at the mention of her letters. She tried to catch Mr. Inglis's eye, needing his granite reassurance, but her advocate was riffling through his papers. She steadied herself with what he had told her: *'Evidence of immorality is not evidence of murder, Miss Smith; evidence of the convenience of a death does not prove that it was hastened; and suspicion is no evidence at all.'* She repeated his words silently, but his mellifluous confidence dried in her mouth and tasted of too much protesting. The crowd had roared 'Hang the whore', not hang the poisoner. Immorality could be proved, poisoning not, but would that matter?

It would be better not to think. As the clerk read out three separate charges of wicked and felonious administration of arsenic, she lowered her eyes to her lap, to her small hands gloved in lavender kid, and began to count the stitches in the seams. She counted all through the reading of the charges and the examination of the first witnesses and never looked up, not when the Lord Advocate, the clerk to the court, and the witnesses all in turn mispronounced Emile's name; nor when the pathologist explained that Emile L'Angelier had died of enough arsenic to kill six men; nor when he said that the medium for the poison was likely cocoa; and not even, especially not even, when witnesses described Emile's death throes: his vomitings and purgings, his writhings, his weepings, and his green arsenious bile.

But if Madeleine did not look up, she heard, and her face coloured pink and sweet as an angry rose. She had never heard the like of this evidence in all her life. She grimaced and tugged at the cuff of her glove. They were no true gentlemen who subjected her to such coarseness! And to think that Emile had considered suicide by poisoning a romantic end for a disappointed lover! He was fortunate indeed to have been spared this last disillusion.

Witnesses gave tedious evidence of arsenic mixed with soot, and arsenic mixed with indigo, and which kind it was she'd had in her possession and which kind it was that killed Emile; they produced tables to show that arsenic could not be suspended in cocoa, and charts to show that it could; they opined confidently that Emile's death was convenient to her, and with assurance that it was not. Their certainties brawled and knocked one another out of the witness box. And all the

182

while the opera glasses remained trained on her face.

Madeleine's heart lurched. They were looking for signs: gentlemen prided themselves on being judges of dogs, horseflesh and women: they knew what to look for and if they found her wanting, they would hang her. The opera glasses scanned her face, seeking out the flicker of an eyelash, the quickening of a pulse. Madeleine's heart lurched again. The Daniels were come to judgment: my learned friends, the gentlemen of the jury, the gentlemen of the Press, the gentlemen of society who had left their manners at home with their wives – all were come to sit in judgement. But that was the way of things – always the gentlemen must be pleased. Quiet rage bloomed prettily in Madeleine's cheeks.

That night the friendly wardress told Madeleine that she had made a good impression on the court. She had not been what they expected. Her modest demeanour and shy blushes had given all present pause for thought, and her purchases of arsenic were scarce spoken of at all.

Alone at last in her cell in the failing summer twilight, Madeleine studied the newspaper the wardress had smuggled to her. There was a lurid account of Emile's death throes and a sketch of him which she disliked on sight: something about his light waving hair and upturned eyes suggested a martyred saint. She scanned the densely printed columns: apart from an irritating excess of exclamation marks, the bulk of the reportage pleased her. It was concerned with her background, her upbringing, her education, her stylish new bonnet, her fine grey eyes. Poor Emile, so vilely mispronounced, so dramatically and excessively dead, had been quite upstaged – how piqued he would have been had he known!

Editorials agonised over her downfall, demanding to know how it had come to pass. Madeline stared sightlessly into the gathering dusk. She hardly knew herself how things had come about. The trouble was that she had changed so much that it was difficult to remember what she was like at the beginning; that Madeleine was a stranger to her now, a stiff and distant little figure seen through the wrong end of a telescope. She had not been what she seemed, that young girl, but then in the end, neither had Emile.

She took up the newspaper again, and studied the sketch which had been made of her. Her much admired bonnet was lovingly drawn and shadowed meekly downcast eyes. She recognised that posture at least.

It had been painfully acquired over many years. As Mrs. Gorton used to say, a young lady's posture must always show her breeding and education. The younger Madeleine, whom she could not think of as 'I', only 'she' or 'Madeleine', had tried very hard to be what everyone expected...

Madeleine is eighteen and just returned from Mrs. Gorton's finishing school, pruned and shaped into one of her white blooms of innocent womanhood. Papa studies her final report and is not displeased. Her wilfulness, which Mrs. Gorton complained of before, ('Miss Smith, no gentlemen will marry a woman of discordant character') has mellowed to a decent decorum; she can discourse charmingly about suitable novels and current affairs ('Miss Smith, you were vehement with the curate in conversation last evening; gentlemen discourse with ladies to be entertained, not to be disputed with'); she can net purses, paint a little, play the piano prettily, and recite screeds of romantic poetry.

Mrs. Gorton has only one complaint: Miss Smith's penmanship is impenetrable, sprawling spikily across the page, right into the margins and beyond. ('Miss Smith, how will your future beaux ever be able to decipher your billet doux if you cannot control your pen?').

Papa considers. Madeleine flutters helplessly, a sweet and rueful clown, and Mama's fan flaps wildly like a trapped bird; if Papa frowns, Mama will have a fit of the vapours and need the sal volatile again. But Papa does not frown. "Well, Madeleine, I never intended you to be a clerk. You show every promise of turning out as dear a little woman as your Mama." Mama's fan recovers its equilibrium and Papa gives Madeleine two golden guineas for a new bonnet.

Later, alone in her bedroom, Madeleine tries on the bonnet and considers her accomplishments. She can flirt discreetly without being in the least forward and has even managed to extract a compliment from that vapid little curate; from her reading of romantic novels, she has discovered that there is nothing a gentleman so admires – no, not even the netting of purses – as a pair of white shoulders rising snowy from the neck of a ballgown; also, by assiduous study of Chamber's Journal, she has discovered that an application of arsenic in solution is efficacious in whitening the complexion and said shoulders.

Madeleine poses at the mirror. She is ready for life to begin.

184

The morning went badly for Madeleine. The Lord Advocate, Mr. Moncrieff, appearing for the Crown, established beyond any doubt the fact of a criminal intimacy between Emile L'Angelier and the panel, Madeleine Smith. Madeleine was chilled by the greedy concentration of the court as deceit, furtive slyness, and a depravity beyond the ken of decent folk were all repeatedly proven via the evidence of self-righteous servants and stammering clerks. Her reputation was destroyed utterly. With dull despair she saw her own advocate rise to cross-examine on a painful subject that should have been passed over in decent silence, at least by her own side.

It was some time before she understood what was happening. Mr. Inglis had a persuasive voice and a wonderful way with a meaningful pause. Emile's reputation was shredded by the hail of deadly silences which Mr. Inglis discharged like grapeshot at the witnesses parading before him.

"Now, sir, this A-meel Long-jelly..."

Pause for the court to reflect that A-meel Long-jelly was a villainous name and cause for suspicion in itself. "This Long-jelly..." – a squint down his nose and a hitch at his gown – "was, you say, full twelve years older than the panel who was fresh from the schoolroom?

Pause.

"A wordly man, would you say?"

Very long pause.

"And he pursued the panel, Miss Smith? He besought you to make an introduction to her? In spite of the differences in age, rank, and education?"

He executed the quick sideways step which Madeleine soon learned was a sign of excited disapproval. You can see how it was, the step seemed to say, you can surely see how it was...

Madeleine is eighteen, exotic among the dumpy Bessies and Marys of Glasgow. Her world consists of Sunday to kirk, and weekday visits to aunts who chime the same notes of approval and disapproval as Mrs. Gorton. She blooms white and sweet behind her thicket of stern headmistresses and nothing ever happens. She is likely to die of suffocation if something doesn't happen soon...

"Now, sir, you did not introduce him. Why not? In what way not a respectable person? Come, sir, this is a court of law, not a valedictory service."

Pause.

"I see. He bragged of his sordid liaisons. A barmaid in Leith? A lady in Dundee who admired his 'pretty little feet'? Sundry females in Paris? A Lady in Fife whose position and inheritance he found appealing? And when he desired to pay his attentions to Miss Smith, he set out to cultivate the acquaintance of people who could perform an introduction?"

Madeleine stared down at her lavender gloves. She and Emile had often laughed together over the superhuman efforts he had made to meet her...

A grey February afternoon in Sauchiehall Street. Madeleine shivers and wishes for the interminable Glasgow winter to end, for winter to end and life to begin. And then it does. He looms out of the driving sleet, a smiling blurred shadow. He is elegant and wears his stove pipe at an angle, and is slim pretty, not Scotsman square and sturdy. He is so bold with his eyes that she blushes hotly in the raw air. The introduction is barely proper, the conversation not at all, but she is out of the schoolroom now and despises missishness. And besides, his accent is charming.

That night she lies awake and thinks of M. L'Angelier. She has never known a man so confiding, nor one who has led such an exciting and adventurous life! And when he speaks of it, his skin glows with a spirit which animates his every word and gesture. Madeleine lies awake and whispers his name to her pillow; she tries on his accent with its French precision and beguiling little slurs. 'Enchanté, Mees Smeeth,' she whispers, 'enchanté.' She turns restlessly in bed and the darkness is lit by his pale face and burning revolutionary eyes. 'In the Révolution of 1848,' she whispers, 'when I manned the barricades in Paris in the name of Liberté, Égalité, Fraternité; in '48, when I summered with mon ami the baron at his estates in Malmédy...'

She mimes and whispers and tries him on. 'Malmédy,' she whispers, sometimes with precision, sometimes with a slur, 'Liberté. Enchanté, Mees Smeeth, enchanté.'

She despairs that she will never see him again, that she will live forever behind her thicket and never again catch a whiff of revolutionary cordite.

But she does. When she walks in the Botanic Gardens, he is there

186

behind the hydrangeas; when she visits Mr. Ogilvy's bookshop, he emerges smiling from behind the bookstacks...

"And he pursued this young girl to the point of obsession, you say? He discovered all her regular haunts and followed her there?"

The bookshop is her favourite trysting place: Emile belongs among the romantic gilt-edged pages of Mr. Ogilvy's novels. He stands before her, wrapped in the cloak of his pride, and confesses that he is only a clerk with Huggins & Co., which would matter nothing in France where such things are of no account, but he fears that Glaswegians are flinthearted and that love means nothing to them, only wealth.

Madeleine is above such small mindedness. She tells him that like Mary, Queen of Scots, she would go to the world's end in her petticoats for love's sake. His eyes moisten. He has found his twin soul, he says, his rebel heart, and they will be together to the world's end and beyond...

"Now, sir, let us be clear. He bragged of eating arsenic? Did he say why he indulged in this practice?"

"For his complexion, you say? For the lustrousness of his hair?"

Pause to reflect on the oddities of foreigners. A ripple of amused disbelief in court. "And to enhance his...what? Speak up, sir."

An incredulous pause. "You did say his virility?" A full round turn and two half hitches of the black gown. "I see. His virility."

Long and deadly pause. Excited scuttling sideways step.

"Surely he was aware that arsenic is deadly? Ah, he was. In fact he bragged of it to show his devil-may-care courage. I see. He told the decent young men he worked with about this filthy habit?"

Twist of mouth, very like Mama's the evening she had twelve to dinner and found a cockroach in the pastry.

"This Long-Jelly, he had the temperament usually associated with gentlemen of continental extraction? He spoke freely of his passions? He threatened suicide when his affairs went not to his satisfaction? Because he liked to impress, you say?"

Another incredulous pause. "And it is your recollection that he threatened suicide for the Lady in Fife? And for the panel's, Miss Smith's, sake. On many occasions?"

The deadliest silence of all.

Emile explains that he is a man who grapples with passions stronger than those of ordinary men. For him, life is only worth living when fired with extremes of feeling. He tells Madeleine often of the boulevards of Paris and the women he knew there, women who lived only for love and thought nothing of dying for it. He himself, he says, has many times been suicidal over disappointments of the heart. He shrugs off her horror with Gallic nonchalance and a swish of his cane which decapitates a clump of daisies under a hedge. 'Little Mimi, you are such a child. You know nothing of a man's passion. But in time I will teach you.'

She shivers at this talk, hot and cold as if in a fever. But not so much as she does when Papa finds out that she has been seen walking with a gentleman not of his acquaintance. His rage scalds her. He will turn her from his door if she has further connection with that Frenchified little popinjay. Mama takes to her bed with the sal volatile. Madeleine weeps helplessly, her rebel heart broken.

She finishes with Emile, but his bitterness, and the justice of it, wounds her. Oh, but her love is a poor thing compared to his! Night after night she shivers and frets, hot and cold, afraid of Papa and missing Emile, humiliated by her failure to defy Papa, and by her failure to match Emile's revolutionary spirit.

Emile writes that he wishes he were dead and makes her shiver; Papa says he'd rather see her dead and makes her shiver. She must continue in the shadow of the thicket. Oh, God, she shivers, she would rather be dead.

She and Emile are reunited. Love cannot be denied. They cannot be blamed for deceit forced on them by Papa's intransigence. They meet when they can, and when they cannot meet, they write...

Every evening, the wardress brought Madeleine the speak of the court. "Oh, the bailiff says none of them like the cut of his lordship's jib one wee bit," she snorted. "Him and his glossy curls and his wee feet and his virility! A queer lot, the French – "

Madeleine forbore to point out that Emile was from the Channel Islands. To the good folk of Edinburgh, the one was as outlandish as the other. And besides, Emile had always been thrilled to be taken for a Frenchman. It was fitting somehow that he should be judged as one.

The day's newspapers were devoted to her case. Madeleine read until the candle guttered, throwing one last shadow up the wall before sputtering out. The dark blue gloaming softened the harshness of her cell while she mulled over what she had read. Much was being made of her practised deceitfulness; and Papa and Mama came in for a good deal of criticism for sending her to England for a newfangled education. Too many novels and nonsense, wrote irate readers from all over Scotland, not enough of household management and a daughter's duty to her father. The more chivalrous pointed to the ladylike humility she had displayed in court as evidence that there was very little wrong with her breeding, but that no system of education on earth could protect an innocent from the machinations of the lascivious French.

There was a good deal about hapless innocence, which comforted Madeleine until she remembered that soon she had to face the public reading of her letters. Mrs. Gorton had been quite wrong about her penmanship; no one was having the slightest difficulty in deciphering it, right into the margins of her letters and beyond, where there was nothing at all of helplessness or innocence. Why, oh why, had Mrs. Gorton never warned her girls against putting anything in writing…

Madeleine veiled herself on letters day and was glad of the concealment: the buzz in court was deafening, and the winking opera glasses dazzled her. The Lord Advocate prosecuted vigorously, fully armed with the dates, times and places of licentious behaviour. He made it clear that murder was the natural consequence of her moral collapse. From the sour faces in the gallery, Madeleine judged that many gentlemen were in accord with him.

Her hand closed around the silver topped bottle of sal volatile, sent by Mama who had taken to her bed with an attack of the vapours. As had Papa. It spoke volumes against her that neither parent had come into court. What would the jury make of it? Behind her veil, anger crimsoned her cheeks and she hoped that her parents' vapours might rise and choke them.

The Lord Advocate introduced a selection of her letters into evidence. Madeleine closed her eyes when the clerk to the court, drenched in sunlight and dust motes, rose to his feet, holding her letters at arms' length, and began to read aloud. Slowly the well of the court filled with the musky scent she had doused her writing paper with, and conjured up a new participant in the drama. Emile's naughty

Mimi slouched languorously into the dock beside her. Madeleine resisted the urge to draw her skirts aside and endeavoured to look as shocked as everyone else.

The clerk, a little bird-faced man with a high sing-song voice, recited Mimi's musky passions as if chanting the names of strange territories unvisited by civilised persons:

'O-my-beloved-why-did-you-not-come-to-me-a-kiss-a-fond-embrace-sweet-pet-Emile-it-was-a-punishment-to-me-to-be-deprived-of-your-loving-me-for-it-is-a-pleasure-no-one-can-deny-that-it-is-but-human-nature-o-my-beloved…'

The clerk's sinuses were affected by the musk perfume and he sneezed often into the deep silence in court.

ATT-ISḢ-OO! 'I-was-in-my-nightdress-when-you-saw-me-would-to-God-you-ATT_ISH_OO!-had-been-in-the-same-attire'

Papa has her watched and reads all her mail. No matter how often she assures him that she has forgotten a certain person and broken off all contact with him, Papa is ever vigilant. His lack of trust infuriates her, but she will not fail Emile. She writes and writes…

The clerk to the court had a special distaste for words like fondling and petting and spat them out like a boy spitting peas. Madeleine wondered if the words of passion when passion was spent always sounded so foolish. If the Daniels laughed, she would die. But they did not laugh. The explicit words written in heat and musk were punctuated by groans of horror and disgust from the public gallery, and slowly she realised that if they could not laugh at her, then she might really hang.

'Sweet-pet-Emile-I-love-you-truly-fondly-last-night-I-did-burn-with-love-Emile-I-dote-on-you-with-my-heart-and-soul-I-would-be-wishing-you-to-love-me-if-I-were-with-you-now…' ATT-ISH-OO!

She burns for him. Days pass when they cannot meet. Papa keeps her busy and out of mischief. She smiles meekly, but she burns. Every moment spent visiting her aunts, or taking the minister's sermons to heart, is time spent longing to be with Emile, to be his Mimi, to be kissed, embraced, to hear his yearning heart thudding under her cheek. But love finds a way. Emile leaves red roses on her doorstep; she sends him pressed flowers and letters, a snowstorm of letters...

The clerk read on. A gentleman leapt to his feet and fled the room, declaring he'd never heard anything like it in his life. Madeleine sniffed delicately at the smelling salts in an appeal to chivalry, but the hubbub in court reached a crescendo: a woman so lost to all notions of decency was entitled to no such appeal. Behind the veil, Madeleine flinched a step nearer the gallows. She struggled for composure, reminding herself that evidence of immorality was not evidence of murder. But the gentlemen were making more of a stramash over her letters than they had over the three wicked and felonious administrations of a noxious substance.

She risked a sideways peep at the gallery and a thought occurred. Could it be true that they had never heard anything like her letters? She pitied them fleetingly; but on reflection, pitied their wives even more.

Mr. Inglis introduced his own selection of letters. "May it please the court. An extract from the panel's first letter to Long-Jelly, written within a month of their acquaintance."

'I-am-trying-to-break-myself-of-all-my-very-bad-habits-it-is-you-I-have-to-thank-for-this-which-I-do-from-the-bottom-of-my-heart-I-shall-trust-to-your-telling-me-all-my-little-faults.'

Mr. Inglis was brisk with witnesses. "Now, sir. He boasted that he would forbid the panel, Miss Smith, to do such and such? To wear such and such? He bragged of his mastery over her?"

'I-shall-love-you-and-obey-you-I-shall-do-all-that-you-want-me-to-I-know-what-awaits-me-if-I-do-what-you-disapprove-of-Off-you-go...'

This was the acceptable language of love, fragrant with the sweetness of the white flower. The tension in court eased. Mimi the Mistress was nowhere to be seen; Madeleine the Maid, submissive and ladylike, was in every line. Mr. Inglis took many excited little sideways steps – you see, the steps seemed to say, you see how her very proper sentiments were twisted by a worthless man to his own vile purposes.

Madeleine understood her defence at last: the worse she behaved, the more Long-Jelly was to blame. Behind her veil, she was brick red with humiliation. She did not care to be reminded of her slavishness, which she found a thousand times more mortifying than her depravity. Her letters were a bitter reminder of that silly girl Madeleine's foolish notions...

Emile is masterful and hard to please and Madeleine's faults are many. He warns her that she must improve herself or else be a disappointment to him. He rebukes her for the things she does which cause him unhappiness and constantly seeks an opinion of her behaviour from his genteel spinster friend, Miss Perry. Miss Perry entirely agrees with him that she is not to go to balls or assemblies, no matter what her Papa says, and she is not to be at her flirting, nor is she to wear her fetching pink bonnet; a discreet fawn one is more suitable for a young lady who is spoken for. Madeleine smiles fondly at this. Emile fears that some other gentleman will carry her off. As if Papa would allow any such thing! Or even any flirting!

'I-shall-be-guided-by-you-entirely-I-shall-not-be-thoughtless-and-indifferent-to-you- dear-love-I-shall-be-more-affectionate-in-future'

She is to write to him telling him all her private thoughts and all that she does when he is not there to supervise her. He explains patiently that she has only herself to blame if he treats her coldly after she sends him letters which are brief and lacking in affection. Madeleine tries harder. She writes adoringly, effusively, apologetically, for page after page, because he is kinder when she tries to please. He teaches her the joy of making the one she loves happy. And she does love him. He has only to clasp her waist between his two hands for her to be sure of that; the swooning heat she feels is proof. If only he were not so hard to please, or if she herself were more adept, like his former loves of the boulevard...

'O-dear-love-why-am-I-not-always-what-you-want-me-to-be-but-I-cannot-help-my-carelessness-I-know-your-love-for-me-is-great-when-I-am-good-but-you-are-cool-to-me-when-I-am-bad.'

All is not well between them. For months, for a year of months, they snatch at meetings when they can, at one another when they can, in friendly dark corners, in empty rooms when the household sleeps, but their stolen moments leave them irritable and quarrelsome. Emile is disgusted by her refusal to confront Papa with the fact of their secret engagement. Always she must be sorry for her cowardice, for her failures in affection and obedience.

Things are difficult at home too. Papa is distant and suspicious. Always she must be sorry for her past failures in duty and obedience. She quails at the thought of facing him with her engagement and urges Emile to elope with her. She will not mind being poor so long as they are together. But Emile minds: recognition from her family is his right; her marriage portion is her right. And they must consider her reputation.

Their clutching in the dark, once so warm and vivid, is soured. 'Let me, Mimi, let me' he gasps at her ear, at her throat, at her bosom, and she is only too willing, but always he pulls back with a despairing reproof. As a man he is subject to his passions, he chides her; as a lady she must never be. Madeleine remembers that Mrs. Gorton used to say much the same thing, in much the same admonitory tone, but had never hinted at how difficult it was.

They quarrel endlessly. He threatens that if she does not confront her Papa, he will enlist in the French army, or emigrate to Lima and find work on a coffee plantation. This he will do for her sake; this is how much he loves her.

'Emile-for-pity's-sake-do-not-leave-me-I-will-do-all-that-you-ask-only-do-not-go'

She lies awake at night weeping for fear that he will leave her alone with her ragged nerves and restless burning.

'For-pity's-sake-Emile'

She cannot eat or sleep and suffers from mysterious glooms and spurts of temper. Papa tells her that a certain matter is now forgiven and forgotten and that they are friends again; Mama doses her with her own nerve tonic, but Madeleine cannot stomach it; the doctor prescribes strong wholesome cocoa to soothe girlish megrims. Nothing helps. Desperately, Papa decrees holidays at their country house at Rhu to restore the roses to her pale cheeks.

She weeps at Papa's kindness, which she does not deserve, and at the thought of being separated from Emile, which she cannot bear, and at Emile's anger that she is being taken away from him, because she knows that she will suffer for it. Sometimes Emile follows her to Rhu and they can snatch an hour together; sometimes he does not and spends his time in Glasgow studying the shipping schedules for Lima. She longs for peace of mind...

She tells Emile that they must elope; he insists that she must confront Papa. Sometimes he threatens that he will confront Papa himself, or else kill himself for her sake. The thought of either leaves her white, shaken, sleepless and nauseous. Mama makes her drink more cocoa.

She tries to break it off with Emile for the sake of her peace of mind – how she longs for peace of mind – but his throaty endearments lure her to him in the dark. She tells him that she is ill, but he only reproaches her that she has not enquired after his latest cold, caught and suffered in the hideous climate of Glasgow which he only endures for her sake. He is sure that his health would improve in Lima.

'Emile-for-pity's-sake'

Night after night when the household lies sleeping and she flounders in twin pools of despair and yearning, she rises from her bed to write to him. She takes care to write lovingly and with endless concern for his catarrhs and nervous stomach, both aggravated by her lack of true love for him. She writes by moonlight, a blanched flower in the silver beams which wash over her but do not cool her heat. She writes in heat and longing, and by the light of the bright spring moon, she slowly blooms scarlet and wise and understands at last what will bring them peace of mind and happiness.

There comes a May night at Rhu. In the violet twilight, Madeleine flickers like a flame across the lawns, out the back gate and into the arms of Emile. They clutch and hold, but this time she does not let go and they lie all night under the trees.

At dawn in her bedroom with the smell of crushed clover and grass still clinging, she scribbles a letter full of joy and fulfilment. She has the resolution now to face Papa's wrath, she writes, and come what may, they will be together at last.

His reply soon follows. The servant smuggles it to her, and she has to hide it in her long sleeve all day until she has privacy. That night in her bedroom, in the circle of yellow light around her lamp, she reads greedily, and as she reads, she pales and shrinks inside herself.

He got home safely, he writes, although the walk did his cold no good. He was happy with her last night, but...

'I-regret-it-very-much-Mimi-why-did-you-give-way-after-all-your-promises-you-had-no-resolution'

'Think-of-the-consequences-if-I-were-never-to-marry-you-Mimi-only-fancy-if-it-were-known-you-would-be-dishonoured-if-Miss-Perry-did-know-it-what-would-you-be-in-her-eyes'

'It-is-your-parents'-fault-if-shame-is-the-result-they-are-to-blame-for-it-all-You-will-have no-one-to-blame-but-yourself'

Oh, but it was a different tune he sang last night. 'Let me, Mimi, let me...' Her heart turns over at the memory of sighs and groans and cries of pleasure. Aloud, as if he were there, she snaps, 'Well, I don't regret it. Never shall!'

She reads again and hears the scandalised delight of respectable spinsters in 'only fancy'; she hears a perfect cacophony of stern headmistresses, disapproving fathers, and prim Church of Scotland ministers. At last he is teaching her something about a man's passions. And she hears the threat not to marry her. She must speak to Papa, he says, or for very shame he will leave the country.

In the yellow lamplight, she shrinks and pales, then flushes with anger. Threats, always threats, always she displeases, always she is to be abandoned. She has fallen from grace, not given it, and Emile has another stick to beat her with. Her mouth twists and she smells a whiff of revolutionary cordite; for a moment she sees him clearly, her shabbily respectable revolutionary, but her own anger frightens her, for there is no going back now that she has given herself to him. What if shame were indeed to be the outcome? They must marry. And soon.

She paces in and out of the circle of light. Emile is overwrought. He has no inner strength. But they can still be happy. She must believe that. But she does not speak to Papa.

The Lord Advocate thoroughly explored Madeleine's illicit connection with the deceased. The criminous intimacy was continued in the gardens at Rhu, in the laundry and drawing room of the panel's home at Number 7, Blythswood Square, in the park behind the rhododendrons at dusk, and – the Lord Advocate was heavily emphatic – at her basement bedroom window where it was her custom to pass Long-Jelly cups of cocoa through the iron stanchions.

The wardress was thoughtful that night. "Well, you're right, lass. They didn't like the letters much. Very surprising from a young lady. But the bailiff says it's clear you were under that puffed up wee Frenchie's influence. How else would you ken how to write all that stuff? Anyway, for all their protests, they're men of the world in that court. They know the ways of a man with a maid."

She lifted Madeleine's plates on to a tray, then looked at her with unexpected shrewdness. "And mind, while they're all taken up with fornication, they're not thinking overmuch about arsenic."

Madeline hid a smile. It was just as well, then, that she had never explained that after that one time at Rhu, there was never another criminous connection, not even clandestinely in the laundry.

Emile, shocked by the force of her passion, insists it must be curbed. He has quite forgot that they are revolutionaries. He bleats milk-and-water hymn sheet sentiments at her: her purity; her reputation; her marriage settlement. They return to their old game of pleading and resistance, by which he has some satisfaction and she has none, but which has this to be said for it, that Madeleine does not disgrace herself again. She grows cold to him and discovers the pleasures of making him suffer. She torments him with letters passionately explicit and brings him running to her, his new found virtue in shreds.

'Let me, Mimi, let me.'

Earnestly she declares that they must not sully the purity of their love.

'Let me, Mimi, let me. You did before.'

She reminds him how conscience stricken he was before.

He sulks and threatens Lima or enlistment. She is silent, but after some consideration, cautions against such rashness; he must realise surely that he is not suited to the rigours of the climate in Lima or the brutishness of military life.

He abandons Lima and enlistment and hints again at suicide. She perfects a half smile in response which goads him to tearful reproaches that she no longer loves him. She smiles again and he looks away. At last they are beginning to understand one another. It is an unpleasant experience, but she can't quite finish with him, not yet. She often wonders why.

She has not the slightest intention of speaking to Papa.

The Lord Advocate was in fine form the next morning. "From her letters, gentlemen, it is clear that she promised to marry the deceased in September and refers to him still as 'sweet-pet-Emile-o-my-beloved' while simultaneously she accepts a proposal of marriage from Mr. William Minnoch, to whom she writes in more decorous vein:

'My-aim-in-life-dear-William-shall-be-to-study-you-and-please-you'

Madeleine winced. It was just as well that Billy too had taken to his bed for the duration of the trial. What would he have made of all this? He would think her insincere. She knew perfectly well that, as the old song had it, it was best to be off with the old love before you were on with the new, but Emile had refused to be off. She would have liked to be honest, but his intransigence had forced deception on her.

Papa decides that Madeleine is ready for life to begin, and for marriage, which is the same thing. There are new tarlatan gowns and satin lined cloaks and little dancing shoes which are soon worn out; there are routs, assemblies, and balls; there are endless letters to Emile protesting that she only attends these functions at her father's insistence and that she has done nothing to warrant the title of Glasgow's leading belle. As for the gossip about Billy Minnoch and her, it is just that. Gossip.

He does not believe her. His suspicions are dark – he knows full well of what licentiousness she is capable. He warns her that he has a husband's rights, and she the obligations of a wife. That is the law, he says, because they are contracted to one another.

197

Wearily she agrees and protests her devotion. Wearily she recommends cocoa for his colds, catarrhs and nervous stomach. Wearily she agrees that she has much to learn about being a perfect lady.

Sometimes her patience snaps and she tells him that he can go to Lima or the dark side of the moon for all she cares. Sometimes she means it.

With Papa's approval, and to Mama's delight, handsome Billy Minnoch, rich and charming and the catch of the season, comes courting. He adores Madeleine and finds no fault in her. Papa says she could do worse than Billy Minnoch. She already knows this. She lives in dread of Emile's jealous interrogations and his hectoring sermons, but just when she thinks that she cannot stand one more carping letter, just when she thinks that one more bleating complaint will drive her mad, a look from him, or a touch, or the realisation of his utter misery softens her and she steps weeping into his arms and he is loving and kind. She often wonders why falling out of love has so few of the certainties of falling in. But she knows that a future with Emile is impossible, would be intolerable, and has known it since Rhu.

Life is complicated. She must assure Emile of her undying devotion but that the time is not right to speak to Papa; she must assure Billy of her undying devotion but ask that their engagement be postponed until the spring, her favourite time of year. And before that time comes, she must disentangle herself from Emile.

She picks quarrels, ignores his letters, and has no time to meet him. He suffers it all. The man has no pride. Finally, she writes in the coldest terms that their engagement is ended.

He laughs at her. She has given herself to him and he has her letters to prove it. He has only to show them to her Papa, has only to broadcast her looseness, and what man will marry her then? She is to fulfil her obligations to him or she knows what will happen. She is to be quite clear about that. Madeleine is clear and is devastated.

'Emile-on-my-bended-knee-do-not-denounce-me-it-will-kill-my-mother-I-humble-myself-before-you-I-crave-your-mercy-despise-me-hate-me-but-do-not-make-me-a-public-scandal'

She begs hard enough to please him. Graciously he forgives her. They are reconciled.

198

That night the wardress was especially kind. The Lord Advocate would sum up next day. Already the timetable of events had been laid before the jury: the proposed spring engagement to Billy Minnoch, Emile's two sudden and desperate illnesses just before it was announced, her last letter to him, inviting him to visit her, his death that very night. The wardress shrugged. "The whole business is the talk of the town. The betting's on Mr. Inglis, though. He's a canny lawyer and the bailiff heard him say they've proved nothing, only thrown a lot of mud."

Madeleine sat alone in the gathering gloom, aware that the tide of public sentiment had turned in her favour. The world loved a repentant fallen woman, it seemed. She had letters, dozens of letters, from gentlemen all over the country, offering their forgiveness for her erring ways, which they dwelt on in nauseating and lingering detail, along with their hearts and hearths and gentle guidance for the future. As if she hadn't had enough of men's hearts and guidance to last her a lifetime.

'O-my-beloved-come-to-me'

Her last letter to him. To hear the Lord Advocate, it was a declaration of intent to murder. "She invited him, and he came. The panel insists that he did not keep the appointment and that the arsenic she purchased had nothing to do with his death. She bought it, poured it in a basin, and washed in it. Gentlemen of the jury, do you believe that? He told his friend that more than once he had been taken ill after imbibing cocoa served to him by her. He said that if she were to poison him, he would forgive her. What was it that had aroused his suspicions? Should not we also be suspicious? It has been suggested that he killed himself for her sake. Is it conceivable that a man would attempt such a death, such an agony, three times?"

'O-my-beloved-come-to-me'

Mr. Inglis was succinct. "There is no proof that the letter refers to the night that he died; there is no proof that they met on any of the occasions when he was taken ill. If it is inconceivable that a man would attempt such an agonising suicide three times, is it remotely conceivable that a man who suspects he is being poisoned would continue to accept cocoa from her hands? Long-jelly was an hysteric: he threatened suicide many times; he told his friend that if he could not have Miss Smith, then no one would, that he would make sure of that; he declared that if she were to poison him, he would forgive her. Long-jelly had the overheated temperament of a parlourmaid. Have we a case of murder to try? Or a suicide? Or a Machiavellian conspiracy to punish Miss Smith for her audacity in rejecting him? Could his death in fact have been an accident? It is known that arsenic eaters often kill themselves by mistake. Any one of these explanations is as likely as any other. Gentlemen, the picture is murky and there is much reasonable doubt. Consider carefully."

It was time for the jury to decide. Madeleine watched the jurymen's thoughts march across their faces. The opera glasses were trained upon her again, magnifying her, as if by enlargement the secrets of her heart would be exposed and the events of that night at the window of her basement bedroom put on show for all to see.

There were two versions to be considered:

'O-my-beloved-come-to-me…'

He did not come. She waited. At length she put out her lamp and retired to bed. L'Angelier's movements that night were unaccounted for. He was missing for five hours. Maybe he got his death elsewhere. Maybe he killed himself in despair. Maybe he was careless with his poisonous medicine. Any one was as likely as the other. The picture was murky.

Or the other possibility:

'O-my-beloved-come-to-me'

He came. He tapped at her window. She opened it, standing in her nightdress with the yellow light behind her, her hair flowing darkly over flounces and ruffles of white lawn. And then – the picture was murky. There might have been an impropriety or a murder or both or neither.

Madeleine knew from the wardress that these were the scenarios being considered by the jurymen. All Edinburgh was considering them along with its tea and scones. Madeleine needed no opera glasses to see what happened that night. She thought of it occasionally, at unexpected moments…

'O-my-beloved-come-to-me'

He comes, stooping out of the darkness to tap at her window, blinking in the lamplight. She smiles a welcome, a well trained bitch brought to heel.

He is pale. His stomach, he says, has not settled since that last bad bout and his cough is worse. He has strange, frightening tinglings in his fingertips and toes.

Madeleine is all concern. He must see a doctor. She told him so last time, but he never listens.

His eyes, dark and watchful, lighten. She would not mind if he saw a doctor? An expert? It would not trouble her? Truly?

The more expert the better, she says smiling. Why on earth would she not want him to consult such a person? The illness continues too long and must be investigated. This is only common sense.

Yes, he says, common sense. He smiles and his pale face glows.

She clasps his hands through the bars at the window. Perhaps he should accept the invitation to visit his friends in the Isle of Wight. The mild air would benefit him. He should go next week. And consult a doctor there.

His eyes darken with suspicion. Why does she want him out of the way next week?

She says she only wants him to be well soon, so that they may marry.

Marry? he says. There are rumours of a marriage. Billy Minnoch's marriage. That it is to be announced soon.

She weeps. These endless suspicions. She has told him over and over that there is only friendship between her and Mr. Minnoch. She cannot be held responsible for gossip. Cannot he forgive past misunderstandings?

He forgives, he says, but cannot forget. She understands, doesn't she, that he will never let her marry another, that she will never be rid of him?

She presses his hands between hers. She does not want to be rid of him. Why must he torture her so?

He weeps and says she does not know the meaning of torture. She cannot know what it is like to be him and to be so tortured.

He tortures himself, she says, but soon he will never know another moment's unease on her account.

He raises her hand to his lips. Yes, he says, they will be happy when they are wed.

She says his lips are cold. It is a raw night. He must have something to keep out the chill. She has cocoa warming on her little stove. She brings it to the boil, stirring all the time to make it smooth. He complained of grittiness last time. Drink it down, she says, while it is hot. It is good for a nervous stomach.

He warms his hands around the cup. If he is harsh, he says, it is only because he loves her. In future his reproaches shall be more gently given.

Yes, she says, yes. For her part, she is only sorry that she has been such a trial to him.

He drinks deeply. Does she truly love him?

Yes, yes.

He presses his forehead to the bars and weeps. Sometimes he thinks she only says things for form's sake.

Emile, she protests gently, I have always loved you. Always.

He drains the cup and kisses her between the bars. Love will find a way, he says. He goes home happy.

She wipes her mouth carefully and rinses the cup and the saucepan several times. Oh, that dreary wee man! He should have taken his chances in Lima.

The verdict, when it came, provoked a storm of cheering the length of the Royal Mile. Madeleine was displeased by the wishy-washy Not Provens, and also by Mr. Inglis's pointed refusal to shake hands with her. But she shrugged off the insult, which was of no consequence. She was free and ready for life to begin at last.

Previously from Elastic Press

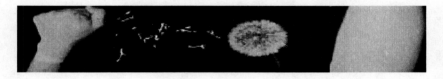

Second Contact by Gary Couzens

Exploring the twin themes of time and identity Gary Couzens manipulates our sensibilities in a major collection of nineteen powerful stories, drawing on the fascinations that dwell within the hearts of us all.

Forthcoming from Elastic Press

Milo & I by Antony Mann

The freshest purveyor of weird crime singularly redefines the genre with twelve entertainingly bizarre stories that stand charged with originality. Welcome to Mann's world.

Antony Mann is one of the most exciting of the new generation of crime writers – Mat Coward

For further information visit:

www.elasticpress.com